"Hang on, Mr. Mayor." Leah pushed out of her car. "Let me give you a hand."

Gil let out a breath he hadn't realized he'd been holding. Something about seeing her made the tension in his shoulders ease.

"Stop twisting around. Just...stop." She placed her hands on his shoulders and looked up at him. The surprise that jumped into her blue eyes vanished when she ducked her head and unclipped the straps to pull the baby carrier free.

"Okay." She turned him around and locked the carrier into place across his shoulders and underneath his arms. "Now all you need is the baby."

"I've got him." Eli gurgled and squealed as Gil brought him toward his chest.

"Ah, nope. Other way." Leah plucked Eli out of his hold and handed him back. "He's old enough to need a view. Not that your chest isn't a..." She trailed off, her cheeks turning an unfamiliar yet entertaining shade of pink.

Gil grinned. Who knew he could make Leah Ellis blush?

Dear Reader,

All good things eventually come to an end. Six years ago, my first Butterfly Harbor romance was released and my world, my life, changed. What better story to end the series with than Mayor Gil Hamilton's.

I always knew the final book would be Gil's, but it wasn't until Leah Ellis (unexpectedly) popped up in *A Dad for Charlie* that I knew who he'd end up with. Gil's been complicated and, in a lot of ways, misunderstood from the start; this makes him perfect hero material. I love a good redemption story and I hope that longtime readers of the series will fall as hard for him as I did by the end. As far as Leah is concerned, she has one objective as the story opens: to take Gil's job. But as the election draws near and Gil needs her help, she begins to see that there's more to Gil than most of the town has ever known.

For the last time, I welcome you back to Butterfly Harbor. I welcome new readers to Butterfly Harbor. And maybe one day, we'll revisit there again.

Best,

Anna J. Stewart

HEARTWARMING

The Mayor's Baby Surprise

Anna J. Stewart

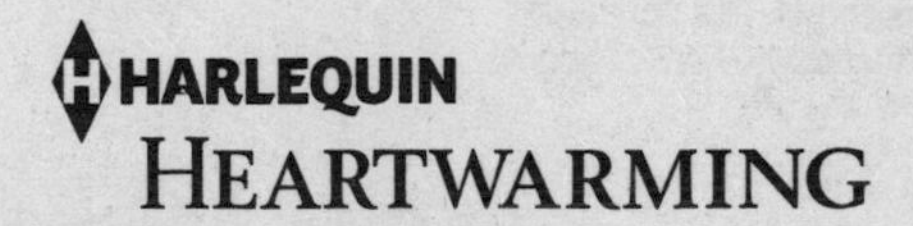

Recycling programs for this product may not exist in your area.

ISBN-13: 978-1-335-42672-7

The Mayor's Baby Surprise

For questions and comments about the quality of this book, please contact us at CustomerService@Harlequin.com.

Harlequin Enterprises ULC
22 Adelaide St. West, 41st Floor
Toronto, Ontario M5H 4E3, Canada
www.Harlequin.com

Printed in U.S.A.

Bestselling author **Anna J. Stewart** is living the dream as an author for Harlequin's Heartwarming and Romantic Suspense lines. Building family-found romances is where her heart lies—no matter the genre or story she's telling. When she's not writing, she's binge-watching her favorite shows (hello, *Great British Bake Off*), planning her next trip to her favorite place on earth, Disneyland, and corralling her two crazy cats, Rosie and Sherlock. You can read more about Anna and her books at authorannastewart.com.

Books by Anna J. Stewart

Harlequin Heartwarming

Butterfly Harbor Stories

The Bad Boy of Butterfly Harbor
Recipe for Redemption
A Dad for Charlie
Always the Hero
Holiday Kisses
Safe in His Arms
The Firefighter's Thanksgiving Wish
A Match Made Perfect
Bride on the Run
Building a Surprise Family
Worth the Risk

Visit the Author Profile page
at Harlequin.com for more titles.

For all the readers of Butterfly Harbor.

Thank you for making this little town of mine your between-the-pages home.

CHAPTER ONE

"I'M COMING, I'M COMING." Gil Hamilton muttered his way along the hall, resisting the urge to turn on the light as he tugged on a T-shirt and headed downstairs. It was barely five o'clock, and given someone's propensity to start his day off on the completely wrong foot, he could only hope this wasn't a sign of the hours to come.

He couldn't afford a bad week, let alone a bad day, not this close to the election. He was already catching flack for cutting the number of events at the town's annual Monarch Festival in an attempt to draw a larger crowd to the butterfly sanctuary opening next month. Butterfly Harbor was still celebrating of course, with local businesses offering up specials and sales, and the banners and town decor had been displayed as usual. You couldn't pass a window on Monarch Lane without seeing a flittering of wings or a flash of color. Next year, he told himself. Next year, he'd make sure the festival was bigger and better than it had ever been.

If he was still mayor, of course.

As if the universe thought he needed a reminder about remaining grounded, his foot caught on the bottom step and he nearly pitched forward but caught himself on the banister. Gil reached down and scrubbed the heel of his hand against his thigh. The leg he'd injured in the office fire last year still gave him problems, especially first thing in the morning. Karma, he supposed, for past actions. For the most part, he'd been able to ditch his grandfather's walking stick in the umbrella stand next to the front door, but mornings like this, he was tempted to grab it.

Irritation and frustration threaded through him as he headed for the door. Whoever had rung his doorbell at this unholy hour had better have a darn good—

Gil yanked open the door and was instantly slapped in the face by the cold ocean air whipping its way through town. But that shock was nothing compared to the absolute panic surging through him at the sight of an oversize basket sitting on the front porch.

With worn soft sides and piled high with a blanket the color of ripe peaches, the basket waited for him in eerie silence. This close to Halloween and given his dismal popularity right now, there could be anything inside, from a bushel of poison apples or a stink bomb set to detonate the second he picked it up.

He stepped out, looked up and down the street, but only the dim glow of the fall-decorated street lamps gleamed back at him as the early morning fog rolled in off the ocean.

"Mmmmfh!"

Gil watched in shock as the blanket shifted at the behest of a tiny clenched fist. The round wide-eyed face that appeared had him gaping.

"What the—" Gil bent down, not as easy a feat as it had been before the fire last Christmas that had destroyed his office. A baby? Someone had left a baby on his doorstep? "I thought this sort of thing only happens in books."

He reached out, half expecting the infant

to vanish before his eyes. But it didn't. Big blue eyes that seemed oddly familiar had him searching the memories of his social life. Like he needed to recall that he hadn't had an actual date in over a year. He spotted an envelope sticking out of the large green-and-lavender-striped diaper bag situated next to the front door.

Feeling the cold in his own body, Gil quickly grabbed the basket and brought it inside, then retrieved the bag and closed the door. A few minutes later, he was in his kitchen, coffee brewing and a basket full of baby sitting on the table.

The baby squirmed, grunted, frowned for a long second, then seemed to resettle and kick free of his blanket. The bright blue, cozy one-piece footie pajamas sagged around the baby's feet and tummy, but the infant looked healthy enough. Bright pink cheeks. Lively expression. Expert drooler, given the way the kid was sucking on a fist. The baby kicked again, squealed and tried to scoot up and out of the basket.

"Oh, hey now, don't do that." Gil quickly re-covered the baby and rested his large hand on the baby's stomach. The sigh that emanated from the infant had his heart twisting in an unfamiliar, unsettling way.

With his free hand, Gil slipped the envelope out of the bag and, after a bit of a struggle, pulled out the note inside.

> Gil. My baby's name is Elijah. He's almost six months old. I can't take care of him anymore and you're the only family he has. Please keep him healthy and safe and tell him I loved him.

"Someone must have gotten the address wrong." But that couldn't be true. They'd used his name. Gil struggled to recall some person he was connected to who had an infant of this age, but there was no one. "Elijah, is it? Or maybe Eli?" He felt his lips twitch as the baby gurgled. "We'll play that by ear. Let's say I call the sheriff and see what we should do from here." He pulled his brewed coffee free and took a swallow, welcoming the jolt of energy. Cell phone. He needed his cell phone. "You stay right there, little guy. I'll be right back."

The baby let out a wail of megaphone proportions the second Gil left the kitchen. He winced, returned to the kitchen. Elijah went silent the second he saw Gil.

Reassured he was settled now, Gil tried again.

Same result, only louder.

"Someone's used to being the center of attention. All right." Sighing, Gil picked up the basket and, making a slow go of it, brought the baby upstairs and into the bedroom with him. Leg throbbing, he swooped his comforter aside, set the basket on the bed and grabbed his cell.

Finger poised over Sheriff Luke Saxon's name, Gil hesitated. Butterfly Harbor was a safe haven city. Babies could be surrendered at the sheriff's station or the firehouse, no questions asked, at any time. And yet the baby's mother had purposely left Elijah with Gil and asked *him* to take care of the little guy.

Gil sank onto the edge of his bed, pulled the blanket back to look into Elijah's wide blue eyes. Protocol dictated he call the sheriff. It was what he should do. But was it the right thing?

He let out a long breath. The mother's letter had carried an element of desperation; he could hear it in the words she'd written, feel it in his blood. There must have been a reason she hadn't taken him to the authorities to keep him safe. For whatever reason, she'd trusted Gil. And that, surprisingly, even to Gil Hamilton, meant something.

Gil had the reputation for doing the necessary thing, not particularly the right thing. It was a reputation he'd earned with his focused actions over most of his life. No doubt that was why he was having second thoughts right now.

Maybe he should wait, just to see if the mother changed her mind and turned up. It could be she'd be back later today or even tomorrow after she realized what she'd done. What she'd given up.

Memories long buried surged to the surface, twisting his insides into knots so tight he could barely breathe. He knew what it was like to be left behind. To be forgotten. Gil had been significantly older than Eli when his own mother had left. It was a wound to his heart that had never come close to healing. He gazed at the baby as that same wounded heart skipped a beat even as resolve blossomed inside of him.

A child belonged with its parents, or at least, one of them. If he turned Elijah over to the authorities, chances were it would make it more difficult for the mother to ever regain custody of her son. If he could make things easier for Elijah and his mother…

He peeked over the edge of the basket again, found himself smiling back when Elijah blew him a champion-sized spit bubble. "You want to hang out here a couple of days, little guy? Give your mama a chance to come back?"

"Ba! Babababbba."

Gil took a deep breath. "Sounds like a yes to me."

The rest of the day, he told himself. Two, three days tops.

He stood and scooped the baby up and into his arms. The second he placed Elijah over his shoulder, an odd sense of peace settled within him. "That's okay, little guy. I've got you." Patting the baby's back, he headed into his office and sat at his computer. "I've got you."

A few days.

How hard could it be?

CHAPTER TWO

Ten days later...

THE FIRST THING she needed to do, Leah Ellis told herself as she parked in front of Mayor Gil Hamilton's pretentious showcase monstrosity of a house was get her temper under control.

It wouldn't be easy, considering the man inside had been elevating her blood pressure ever since she'd first moved to Butterfly Harbor a little more than two years ago. Just the mention of Gil Hamilton was enough to send an EKG machine into conniptions. Ineffective, short-sighted, self-centered...and those were the nicer adjectives she could use to describe the small town's legacy mayor who, as far as Leah could tell, had all but abdicated his responsibilities by completely disappearing off the grid for more than a week.

She shoved out of her car, the ocean blue of

her tailored pantsuit catching the midmorning sun peeking out between the clouds. With the cooler weather rolling in off the ocean, it was time for her annual wardrobe exchange. Not that she'd dress any less professionally. A projection of leadership began with the visual image presented, something she'd learned from her activist mother and grandmother. If Leah was going to be the next mayor of Butterfly Harbor, and her "staff's" internal polling certainly pointed in that direction, she needed to show residents precisely who and what they'd be voting for.

She grabbed her purse out of the back of her car and, out of habit, clicked her remote to lock down the Mercedes, the one remnant from her previous life as a high-powered defense attorney. Besides her wardrobe, the vehicle was the only thing she'd brought with her when she'd moved west. Butterfly Harbor was meant to be a new start, a clean start, and yet no matter where she went, she always seemed to end up having to deal with messy situations caused by ego-driven and self-serving men.

This morning was the last straw. After rescheduling the quarterly meeting of the town council for the third time, the council members along with Leah, who had been invited to attend as a representative of the local business relations committee, had had enough. Whatever was going on with Mayor Gil Hamilton and his virtual evaporation from his elected obligation, it was going to stop. Today.

Leah nipped up the stairs like a woman on a mission. If he was sick, of course she'd dig up some sympathy for that, but this lack of communication and existing through email wasn't productive by any means and had Leah wondering what the man was really up to.

The house, one of the oldest in town, had served as mayoral headquarters for some of Gil's progenitors. The Hamiltons had been at the top of the Butterfly Harbor pyramid for far longer than Leah had even been alive, and considering she was in her midthirties, that was saying something.

The house didn't show its age, however. Of course it didn't. As a protected historic landmark, city funds had no doubt been used for the upkeep of the three-story, Victorian-inspired home that stood, much like Liberty Lighthouse and the sunshine-kissed Flutterby Inn, as a spire of tribute to the town's longevity. With its glossy silver-gray paint and bright white trim, the wrap-around porch reminded Leah of a grand old idyllic home. With the changing of the seasons, Gil displayed homespun decorations, like the carved pumpkins perched along the porch railing and the hand-painted wooden barrel filled with shiny red and green apples at the base of the stairs. A pretty picture, Leah admitted, and found herself tempted to snatch up one of those apples and bite in.

Taking a deep breath, Leah punched her finger against the bell, listened to it echo through the depths of the house behind the oversize glass and stained-wood door.

The ear splitting wail from inside had Leah stepping back. *What on earth...?*

She barely had time to process the sound before the door was wrenched open. Gil Hamilton, dressed in wrinkled jeans and an even more disheveled and stained gray T-shirt stood on the other side, his mussed blond hair falling oddly sexily over his surfer-blue eyes.

Oh...my.

She swallowed hard. He was a picture. One that had her pulse kicking into uncomfortable ranges. She'd never have believed Gil even owned anything other than chinos and polo shirts, let alone be capable of going barefoot.

"Leah."

It was the mix of confusion, relief and stress that caught her ear and made the anger that had propelled her to his house evaporate into steam. "You look terrible."

His lips twitched. He shoved a hand into his hair, pushed it back in a way that had her heart doing an odd little dance against her ribs. "That's what I like about you, Leah. I can always count on you for the truth. What are you doing here?"

"The council sent me," she fibbed. It had been her idea to confront the issue at the source, but he didn't need to know that. "What's going on? You're never one to miss a meeting, and you haven't been to the office in a week."

His eyes narrowed. "Been keeping tabs on me, have you?"

"Someone has to." Lying was pointless,

at least on this topic. The wailing continued from the back of the house. "What's that?"

"What's what?" He blinked over wide eyes at her and clung to the edge of the door, keeping any clear view into the house obscured.

"You know what. It sounds like..." She stepped forward and he moved in front of her. "Is that a baby?"

"I apologize for being absent, Leah, but this isn't any of your business." The plea in his eyes had her frowning. "I'll be back in the office in a few days. I'm just dealing with a—" The screech that erupted behind him had both of them wincing.

"Gil." It may have been the first time she'd used his name, rather than his title. They'd butted heads so often, it was easier to call him Mayor Hamilton, just to make certain he understood how she saw him. But those dark circles under his eyes, the exhaustion within them... His clothes looked about as anxious to sag to the floor as he did, and behind it all, the crying continued. "What's going on?" She inclined her head, evaluating her options. But only one thing kept popping into her mind.

Gil Hamilton did not have, at least to her knowledge, any children.

"It's a bit of a family crisis." The words didn't seem to strike her as completely truthful. "I'll be back on top of things in a while. I just have some figuring out to do."

"I don't think you can figure out anything with all this crying. Let me come in."

He swallowed so hard she could see his throat constrict. Confusion and doubt had his expression flickering like his system had short-circuited. Instead of arguing, he took a step back and waved her inside to precede him down the long, echoing hallway into the kitchen.

The room, as classy and upscale as she'd have expected of a Hamilton home, with its highly polished wood and crown-molded ceiling, looked as if not one but a whole series of bombs had gone off. Dishes were piled up, and baby bottles littered the counter, along with diapers, teething rings and a half dozen other things she wouldn't have ever expected Gil to buy.

There, in the center of the kitchen table, cradled in a soft-sided basket lay a squirming, vocal and very irritated baby.

"Well, hello." Leah couldn't have tried to stop her heart from tilting if she'd wanted to. The baby was definitely a cute little thing with his rosy cheeks and sloth-themed sleeper.

His ability to throw Gil into a complete state of chaos earned him definite bonus points.

"Leah, this is Elijah. Elijah, this is Leah." Gil rested his hand on the baby's chest and only then did the infant calm. "He's an unexpected visitor."

"Uh-huh." Leah reached out and stroked the tuft of sandy-blond hair. Elijah let out a squeal, kicked his feet like he was running the hundred-meter dash, and let out a definitive gas-influenced sound. She chuckled, shook her head. "Ah, boys."

"This kid," Gil muttered and sank into the chair closest to the basket. "If it's not one end, it's the other. He's like a cartoon, just going, going, going."

"Yes, they do that." She wanted to push, to interrogate, to get to the bottom of the situation, but that wasn't going to happen as long as Gil resembled the walking dead. "How long has he been here?"

"Um, what's today?" He glanced at his watch. "The days have begun to blend and blur."

"You need to clear your head and take a break."

"Sure. Yeah, I'll get right on that just as soon as the kid heads off to college."

It was kind of delightful to see Gil Hamilton felled by nothing more than a baby. "Why don't you settle for a shower and coffee? I'll take care of the latter." Along with getting some of this mess cleaned up. "Go take care of the former and we'll talk when you're done."

"But he'll..." Gil looked down at Elijah.

"He'll be fine." She removed Gil's hand and replaced it with her own. "He needs to know sometimes he'll just be left to cry. Go on, Gil."

He stood up as if in a trance, headed to the door. When he turned back, he looked a bit baffled still. "You're really here, aren't you? This isn't some kind of mirage or hallucination brought about by a lack of sleep?"

Poor guy. He really had been through the wringer. "I'm really here. Go take a shower before you out-stink this guy."

He cringed, nodded and went upstairs.

Leah discarded her jacket, draped it over one of the high-back chairs. She bent over, put her face close to the baby and waited until his big blue eyes—eyes so similar to the mayor's that Leah gasped—met hers. She couldn't wait to hear this story. "How about you give me a few minutes to tidy up, Elijah? Then you and I can get to know each other a little better." She reached across and plucked a small, stuffed raccoon from inside the diaper bag on the table. "He can keep you company, okay?"

Elijah squealed and kicked his feet, grabbed hold of the animal and promptly stuck it into his drooling mouth.

In her former life as a criminal defense attorney, Leah had developed a simple way to form impressions of her clients. She'd visited their homes. Seeing their living environments firsthand, noticing their habits—were they organized, cluttered, sentimental, detached?—gave her insight as to how best to deal with them. It didn't always produce the right results, but as she quickly went room to room, gathering, straightening and sorting, she had no doubt this chaos was not the norm. Thus, there was only one conclusion to come to: Mayor Gil Hamilton had definitely been blindsided by his houseguest's arrival.

While she set the last dish in the drainer and dried her hands, she caught a glimpse of the clock. The shower had stopped running quite a while ago. She checked on Elijah, found him trying to keep himself awake by gnawing on his stuffed friend, so she made her way down the hall.

The photos hanging on the wall didn't surprise her. She knew Gil's history with Butterfly Harbor went back generations. The Hamiltons had been part of the town government from its establishment, which made him at least a fourth-generation mayor.

The pictures of various relations were a visual history of the town going back to Gil's great-great-great-grandfather. There he was as he broke ground on a building that, sadly, had burned down last Christmas Eve. Every image looked as if it had been found in a history textbook and showed the improvement of film techniques over the years. She didn't recognize the faces, only names, including a number of pictures of Gil's father, Morland. A man who hadn't been anything close to successful when it came to finances as well as town management.

Interesting, Leah thought as she approached the curved, highly polished staircase. She didn't see any family photographs of Gil on the wall. Only ones that displayed him in a professional or political capacity. She peeked around the corner into the living room, around another into a formal dining room but found only a minimal amount of furniture and very few, if any, sentimental items. Sympathy flickered inside her. She'd been half joking earlier when she'd thought of this place as a mausoleum, but she hadn't been far off. The entire house felt more like a museum than a residence. A showcase of the Hamilton lineage. As far as she knew, this was the only home Gil had ever lived in and yet…

It felt so cold. So impersonal. One thing Gil possessed plenty of was personality. And charm, she reminded herself. Don't forget charm. But within these walls? The absence of personality was unnerving.

"Gil?" Leah called up the stairs. "Gil?" She took a few steps up, raised her voice.

Gripping the dark oak banister, she walked up, her stomach knotting a bit at the prospect of invading his privacy. When she reached the landing, she wasn't sure which direction to go. A maze of doors awaited her, most of them wide open. Peeking into each, she saw more of what she had downstairs. Impractical, antique furniture that fit the house but not the man who lived here. The hardwood floor had been beautifully maintained and carried that sheen of affluence most homes lost over years of family footsteps and everyday living.

When she came to the only closed door, she knocked. "Gil? Is everything all right?" Was there a secret passage out of this place and he'd made a run for it? He'd looked stressed out enough to do just that. The thought flew out of her head the second she saw him.

He'd all but passed out, face-first, in the middle of his bed, and was fast asleep. The towel he'd slung around his hips was still there. His damp hair uncombed and oddly appealing. She'd never have thought the mayor was a fitness freak, but it was obvious by that shoulder and waist definition he worked out. And yet one itty-bitty baby had him crashing.

Leah covered her twitching lips. She didn't want to be caught being amused. She tiptoed into the room, picked up a quilted blanket off the back of the rocking chair by the window and gently draped it over him. He didn't move. Didn't stir. And in fact, she stood there for an extra moment just to make sure he was still breathing.

On the side board, a framed photograph caught her attention. A young woman with sandy-blond hair and bright eyes, holding a clearly amused Gil in her lap, the ocean behind them. He was, Leah thought as she bent closer to examine the image, one really cute kid. A happy kid.

She crept back, closed the door and returned to the kitchen, where she dug out her cell phone. Elijah let out a squeal of happiness at the sight of her, and smiling, Leah tweaked his toes. "Callie?" Her assistant answered after the first ring. "Hey, I need you to reschedule my morning appointments." She glanced down. "In fact, reschedule the day. I've got...an emergency I need to deal with."

"Anything I can help with?" Callie asked.

"No," Leah said slowly. "No, this is something I need to do myself. I'll be in later and catch you up." She hung up and, after grabbing a dish towel and tossing it over her shoulder, reached into the basket and scooped Elijah into her arms. "How about you and I take a little stroll around the house, Eli?" She cradled his head in her hand, pressed her lips to his temple. "See if we can wear you out while your daddy sleeps upstairs." She took a few steps, swaying as she hummed and bounced him a bit and waited, however long it took, for Gil Hamilton to wake up.

GIL OPENED HIS eyes by degrees. It took his mind some time to catch up with reality as he pulled himself out of the void he'd fallen into. An unfamiliar weight pressed against his back, and he shifted, plucked up the edge of the quilt and frowned. He didn't remember…

He sat up, grabbed his phone off the nightstand and balked. Nearly two in the afternoon? He'd lost practically half the day!

Gil jumped to his feet, patting his hands against his bare chest as if he'd find something resembling clothes, then had to stop, force himself to regroup and think. He grabbed the first pair of pants he found, dragged on a clean shirt and reminded himself to burn the things he'd taken off. Raking his hands through his creatively dried hair, he pulled open the door and hurried downstairs.

The sight that greeted him in the sitting room had him wondering if he was still dreaming.

Leah Ellis, the bane of his existence these past few months and the main reason his job was in jeopardy, was curled up in the corner of the antique couch, working on her laptop while Elijah snoozed on his tummy beside her. She glanced up, crooked an eyebrow and smiled. "Good nap?"

Probably the best one he'd had in his life. "You're still here."

"Of course." She frowned, her dark brows V-ing over her equally dark eyes. "You sound surprised."

"Ah, yeah. I guess I am. Sorry. That was rude." He scrubbed his hands over his face and gave himself a hard shake. Honestly, even before announcing her intention to unseat him from his elected position,

Leah Ellis had made him nervous. She was poised. Elegant. Flat-out gorgeous with that sharp, angled blond bob that accentuated her slightly pointed features. Those eyes of hers didn't miss a trick and that steel-trap mind was as sharp as her wit. In a lot of ways, she was everything he'd ever been told to look for in a woman: smart, affable, capable. Stunning. And yet he knew his father would never have approved of a career woman like Leah.

He didn't need his therapist to tell him that was no doubt part of her appeal.

"Let's start this again." Gil struggled to recharge his charm. "Thank you for staying. I swear I only meant to take five minutes. I hope I didn't mess up your day."

"Days can be rearranged." She clicked her laptop shut as he took a seat on the other side of the aged, polished coffee table.

"How is he?" Gil asked.

She reached over, rested her hand on Elijah's back. "He was a little fussy, but I got him down. Once I got his tummy filled and his diaper changed."

Gil shook his head.

"What?" she asked.

"Sorry." He rested his chin in his hand. "I guess I'm a little surprised you know what to do with one of those."

"With a human?" That unexpected, teasing glint in her eyes had him smiling.

"With a baby."

"I'm the favorite aunt to four nieces and nephews," she told him. "And I'm the oldest of four. Believe me, I've definitely dealt with my share of these. Speaking of—" she slid her computer into the bag she must have retrieved from her car "—are you going to tell me where he came from?"

"The stork?"

She rolled her eyes. "Seriously?"

"It's as good an explanation as any other. Hang on." He retreated to the kitchen, found the note he'd filed with his bills and returned to the living room. "This was in his basket when I found him."

Leah accepted the folded note, read it and looked back at him, her expression unreadable. "It doesn't say you're the father."

"No, it doesn't." He began to pace.

"Are you? Never mind," she added quickly. "None of my business."

"No, it's not." Gil's quick smile softened

his answer. “That wasn’t an election-induced inquiry, was it?” He felt his face drain of color. He hadn’t even considered… Would she somehow try to use this situation against him?

“I left the election on the porch,” she told him.

He wanted to believe her, but doubt remained. She’d been challenging him for months on everything from zoning permits to future plans for various buildings and structures along the length of Monarch Lane. And don’t even get him started on the underdeveloped area up by the old Howser property Declan Cartwright had rented from the city. If he said left, she said right. If he said yes, she automatically said no. “The timing of his arrival, however,” Leah continued. “Is bound to stir up town gossip.”

And there it was. “The change in weather stirs up town gossip,” Gil countered. “But because you asked, no, I’m not his father. But as far as being family—”

“That you can’t deny,” she told him. His brow furrowed. “It’s the eyes,” she added. “They remind me of yours. He seems small for almost six months, but he doesn't look underfed. What are you going to do?"

"Do?"

"About Eli?" She rested her hand on the baby's back.

"I don't know." He shrugged, that confused, almost defeated expression on his face again. "Whoever left him for me wanted him here. With me. She says so in that note."

"And you're just going to take him on. No questions asked."

Oh, he had questions. "What's the other option? Surrender him to social services? Just put him into a system that doesn't always work the way it should. You'd have me do that to him?"

"I'd have you do whatever is best for him," she said quietly. "The system isn't perfect, Gil. I work in family law, remember. I've seen the good and the bad, but the bad isn't a foregone conclusion. There are so many families looking to adopt. Good families who would give him a wonderful home. Heck, I can think of a few couples right here in Butterfly Harbor who—"

"I'm not giving him away." If she didn't believe anything else he said, he'd make sure she understood that. "I'm not abandoning him, too."

"All right." Leah nodded after a moment. "That brings us back to my original question. What are you going to do?"

"You're the family lawyer," Gil said impulsively. "How about you give me a rundown of my options."

Her eyes went wide. She crossed her legs, folded her hands in her lap. "You're asking for legal advice. From me."

"Ironic, I know." He leaned back, his gaze falling on Eli as he slept on. "Can I keep him?"

"He's a baby, Gil, not a lost schnauzer."

"Until she comes back," Gil clarified slowly as his patience strained. "Can I keep him until she comes back?"

"You're assuming she plans to. I'm sorry," she said when he cringed. "I'm a realist, Gil. There's nothing in that note that leads me to believe she has any intention of returning. Sometimes mothers leave, Gil."

"I am well aware." That was one road he definitely was not walking down with Leah Ellis. "She named me as his guardian in that letter. That's one interpretation, right? Me having him now isn't breaking any laws, is it?"

"No." Leah hedged. "And the note could work in your favor should you take this through the courts." She considered him in a way that had Gil shifting in his spot. "Are you sure you want to do this, Gil? We aren't talking about a few days or even weeks but, potentially, years. Is now really the best time to be considering—"

"Now is the only choice I have." Eli, through his mother, needed his help. End of story. "I hear you, Leah. I understand what you're saying and I can only imagine what you're thinking. I can't believe someone would have thought I was the best choice to be this little guy's father, pseudo, temporary or otherwise, but I'm who they chose. He needs me."

"Maybe you need him, too."

Gil blinked.

Before he could respond, Leah continued after taking a deep breath. "All right. I'll get you a list of attorneys I think would best represent—"

"No." Gil cut her off. "No, I want you." Heat flooded his face when she arched a brow. "I mean, I want you to represent me on this."

"I don't think—"

"I do." He took a deep breath, measured his words. "I understand if you don't want to or if you think it's a conflict of interest. And if it is, okay, I'll go through all this again with someone you recommend, but..." He leaned forward, shoved his hands into his hair. "You're good at your job, Leah. You have an excellent reputation both in town and in the courts. You're a straight shooter and you won't steer me wrong. I might not like the fact you're trying to push me into the unemployment line—"

"You started that process yourself," Leah cut him off, then held up her hands in surrender. "Sorry. Couldn't help it. Go on."

He struggled against the surge of doubt and pressed on. "People trust you. And, if what I've heard around town is true, a lot of the people I've known all my life trust you to run Butterfly Harbor better than me. That's the only recommendation I need to know you're the person to handle this. Please, Leah." He wasn't a man prone to asking for favors. Well, not these kinds of favors. The kind of favor that could actually make someone's life—Eli's life—better.

"I need to look into possible conflicts of interest before I agree to take you and Eli on as clients," she said quietly. "I'll let you know in a few days, okay?"

"Okay, yeah. Thanks." His entire body relaxed as if he'd thrown a ten-ton boulder off his shoulders. "I mean it, Leah. Thank you."

"Don't thank me yet. I haven't given you any answers you want." She leaned down, gathered up her belongings and stood. "If you want to get ahead of things, I suggest you look into tracking down Eli's mother."

"How do I do that without alerting social services or the authorities?"

Leah slung her purse over her shoulder and shifted her briefcase into her other hand. "I'm sure there're a few people in town who can help on that account. Maybe even a certain sheriff who excels at staying under the radar?"

"Luke?" Gil blinked. "You think Luke Saxon would help me? We aren't exactly… friends."

"I think it's worth asking him." Leah nodded and headed toward the door. "Luke's a good man, Gil. A forgiving one. You've asked this town to trust you for the past few years. Maybe it's time you started trusting them. I'll be in touch."

CHAPTER THREE

"MUUUFWAAA!"

"You said it, Eli." With the sounds of Motown drifting out of the speakers—the only kind of music that hadn't made Eli howl in protest—Gil took the final turn onto Juniper Lane and parked in front of the picture-perfect cottage house sitting in its own little tree-lined glen.

He turned off the car, rested his hands on the steering wheel and stared through the windshield. Once upon a time, he'd longed for a house like this. Comfortable, cozy, filled with more love and acceptance than he had any experience with. Holly Saxon, Campbell back then, had been a target of his envy thanks to her close relationship with her father and the future she'd embraced for herself. A future that had her running the Butterfly Diner, the town's most successful business.

He and Holly had had their ups and downs over the years, and if he had to qualify their relationship today, he'd label it…strained friendliness. He couldn't blame her attitude toward him. He was the one who had pushed her father out of a job and brought in someone he thought would be more…agreeable to Gil's plans for the town.

"That didn't work out so great for me in the long run, did it, Eli?"

"Pppppp fth!"

Gil laughed and shook his head. He knew better than most that life could change in the blink of an eye, but nothing could have prepared him for the wild ride he was on now. Rather than jumping right into Leah's suggestion yesterday that he turn his attention to finding Eli's mother, Gil had slept on it—or he'd tried to. Eli was definitely not the greatest night sleeper, and he'd been almost as cranky as Gil this morning when it came to eating his breakfast. The little guy had worked himself up into such a state, he'd broken out in a full-on sweat as he'd fought against his bottle.

The longer Gil sat in his car, stalling, the more difficult this next conversation was going to be. It had been almost four years since he'd taken office. A long four years that had him facing challenges he'd never anticipated or wanted. Challenges that had required a certain…finesse to keep the town from slipping completely under. It had also taken a significant amount of his own money to make a dent in the damage his father had caused to the local economy and residents.

"But that'll be our secret, won't it, Eli?"

"Gwwwwaaaaaa!"

As the mayor of a small, tourist town on the verge of breaking into becoming a major vacation destination, he'd had to learn early on to compromise and find the shortest and most effective solutions to the myriad of issues that presented themselves. Taking shortcuts where Eli was concerned, however, wasn't an option. Gil needed to do everything by the book, and no one in Butterfly Harbor was more by the book than Sheriff Luke Saxon.

When he heard the front door open and little feet pound their way down the porch steps, he turned, a smile tipping the corners of his lips. Two-year-old twins, Zoe and Jake, the latter of whom was the namesake of his grandfather, scampered around the side of the house toward the intricate play structure accented with swings and climbing ropes.

"Zoe, Jake, you two be careful!" The calm voice of their father echoed into the cool morning as Luke stepped outside, caught sight of Gil and his car and, after arching a brow, called into the house, "Simon?"

"Yeah, Dad?"

Had Gil not seen Simon Saxon just a few days ago at the diner, he might have fallen over in shock. Not so long ago, the kid needed help climbing onto one of the diner's stools. Now approaching thirteen, Simon almost reached his stepfather's shoulder. He still wore his thick-rimmed glasses and his superhero T-shirts-when he wasn't in his charter school uniform. He also still had that unkempt hair and boyish grin, but he was definitely heading toward adulthood at a breakneck speed. Behind them, Cash, Luke's golden retriever, sauntered out and sat sentry beside his owner.

"Watch your brother and sister for a bit, would you?" Luke said.

"Okay." Simon sighed as only a preteen

boy could and eyed Gil as Gil climbed out of his car. "We're still going to the comic book store, right?" Simon asked his father. "You promised if I cleaned my room—"

"I promised and yes, we are. Did you put the breakfast dishes in the sink?"

"Uh-huh. Wait, Zoe! Let me… Ah, man. She's going to fall on her face again."

Gil couldn't stop smiling as he watched Simon race over to help his baby sister scramble into a too-big swing and plop her butt down with an oversize grin. "Ha!"

"Nice job, Zoe." Simon laughed and pushed her in the swing.

"Your girl's a daredevil, I take it," he said as Luke approached, Cash right on his heels.

"Understatement of the century," Luke said with the affection of a man who adored his kids. "I assumed Jake would be the adventurous one, proving yet again I don't know anything about females. You here on official business?"

Gil heard it, the guarded tone, the waiting-for-the-shoe-to-drop inflection. They'd had a rocky start when Luke first returned to town and had butted heads on numerous occasions since, but in the past few months, they'd settled into an understanding of one another. At least Gil hoped they had. Second thoughts shot through his head like wayward arrows, but needs being what they were, he dodged them. "I called the station, and Fletcher said you had the day off."

"Is that a problem?" Luke straightened, the challenge in his eyes clear.

Gil sighed. He'd really messed things up with people, hadn't he? "No, of course not. I..." He hesitated, then plowed on. "I need your help. Unofficial official help."

Luke's brows shot up. "Okay." He glanced over at his kids, who were laughing and squealing as they played. "That doesn't intrigue me at all. Come on in."

"Uh, yeah, one second. I just have to..." He walked around to open the passenger door and scooped Eli out of his basket. When he turned, Eli held against his shoulder, Gil found Luke standing behind him. This time, his expression was completely unreadable. "This is Elijah. Eli. He's new to town."

Luke stepped around Gil and ducked down. "Hello, Eli." Luke touched a hand to the baby's head. "I'm assuming Eli here comes with a story?"

"I'm sure he does," Gil said, keeping an eye on Cash as the dog stretched up his nose for an approving sniff. "I'm hoping you can help me find out what it is."

Luke nodded, that assessing gaze of his completely unfathomable. "This his bag?" He reached into the car, picked up the basket and the diaper bag Gil had become all too familiar with. "Come on." He jerked his head toward the house. "I'll put on a pot of coffee and we can talk. Simon?" He called again.

"I know, I know," Simon yelled back. "I'll watch them, don't worry. No, Jake, stop eating the dirt!"

Eli let out a little wail when Gil attempted to shift his hold, so Gil kept him where he was, high up on his shoulder, and headed toward the house.

"OKAY, THIS FEELS WEIRD." Leah, seated at the eating area at the almost-completed butterfly sanctuary and science center, leaned back in her chair and eyed Jo Bertoletti. "I'm missing your tiny house." She glanced over to where Jo's forty-foot-long tow-behind house had once sat. The area had since been professionally landscaped and showed no indication it had once held an actual human residence.

"It is strange being without it." Jo, clad in jeans, a roomy flannel shirt and wearing a hard hat over her long blond hair, finished off the chocolate chip muffin Leah had brought her and sighed. "It didn't make sense to keep it when I've moved in with Ozzy. Right, fella?" She reached down and scrubbed Lancelot, the mixed German shepherd, between his ears. "It all worked out. Besides, now this sweet fella has a big backyard to cower in. Alethea's going to make great use of the trailer home while she's traveling back and forth to culinary school in San Francisco, and Calliope's found the perfect spot for it up at Duskywing Farm. It's in good hands."

"Should we be planning a housewarming party for Alethea?" Leah looked over to the food truck painted in bright rainbows and butterflies parked at the edge of the playground. Flutterby Wheels, an extension of Chef Jason Corwin's restaurant at the Flutterby Inn, had developed a cult following in town, thanks to Alethea Costas's imagination when it came to spinning comfort foods into new and interesting dishes.

"If we throw her a party, it means we have to cook," Jo said in a way that told Leah her friend had already considered the idea. "But I've had a talk with Sienna about some of her party-planning ideas. Stay tuned and keep your calendar free." She sat back and stretched out her legs, looking utterly and completely content.

Envy pricked at Leah's heart. Not so long ago, Jo had given up on love completely and resigned herself to embracing life as a single mother after getting dumped by her then fiancé because of her pregnancy. Leah recommending Jo to the town council to fix the debacle of the town's main construction project meant Jo had grabbed hold of the chance to start over. Enter town firefighter Ozzy Lakeman. Jo hadn't been in town five minutes before the two of them had set off enough sparks to warrant a fire warning. Now the two of them were awaiting their winter wedding, which their friend, event coordinator Sienna Fairchild-Bettencourt was happily planning.

"You do realize I was hoping for a few baby snuggles this morning," Leah accused her friend. Spending those hours with Elijah yesterday definitely had her craving more, a craving she'd been able to ignore for most of her thirty-five years.

"Ozzy pretty much ordered me to get out of the house. He said I needed time to myself, but I bet he wanted to be one-on-one with Hope." Jo's face took on a glowing, blissful expression that seemed completely antithetical to the hard-nosed woman Leah had known long before she'd moved to Butterfly Harbor. "So, Lancelot and I headed up here. What do you think?" She gestured to the butterfly sanctuary project she'd been hired to get back on track.

The circular, multilevel structure, nestled in and around a thick grove of eucalyptus trees, peeked out from the cliff's edge, overlooking the ocean. The expansive windows allowed for natural light to complement the energy-efficient solar power system. The building itself, designed by local architect Xander Costas, was sure to be a draw unto itself, with the monarch sanctuary and education center as a bonus. With the official opening scheduled for mid-November, reservations were already booking up at the Flutterby Inn and surrounding motels.

"I'm thinking we'll have the final landscaping finished and the interior touched up maybe three weeks ahead of schedule," Jo continued. "We were hoping to get it finished before migration season started, but that didn't happen. We have seen some butterflies settle into the habitat area, which is fantastic. This time next year, it'll be in full operation for the butterflies and the visitors."

"The sanctuary was built to enhance the system that's already in place in Butterfly Harbor," Leah reminded her. "They aren't losing out on anything, but they are gaining a fabulous vacation home."

"I know," Jo said. "As disappointed as I'm sure a lot of people are, Gil made the right choice, easing back on the festival in favor of the opening ceremony. Even better, as the next mayor, you won't have construction hanging over your head like Gil did." Jo flashed her a smile. "You'll be able to come in free and clear and celebrate its completion."

"Nothing's a done deal until the election is over," Leah reminded her. "Let's not get ahead of ourselves." She didn't like the growing presumption that her replacing Gil as mayor was a given. If she did win, she had no plans to cut Gil out of his due credit. The sanctuary had, like the refurbishment of Liberty Lighthouse, been his idea from the start and, despite the numerous challenges presented, would be a big boon to the town.

"Getting ahead of ourselves?" Jo snorted and settled back again, then closed her eyes. "Try telling that to the Cocoon Club. As far as they're concerned, the election's just a formality. You're in."

Leah sighed. The Cocoon Club. What was she going to do with them? The group of determined senior citizens had become election obsessed, focusing their decades-long frustrations about the town on a man who had only been in office, what, four years? It really wasn't fair, especially considering he'd had to spend a good portion of his term cleaning up the mess left by his paternal predecessors. There must be more to the story than she'd been told, which was one reason she'd put in a request for copies of all board meeting minutes going back to before she'd arrived in town. Not that any information found there would deter the Cocoon Club from their goal of running Gil out of office. "Sounds like I need to have another chat with my favorite seniors," Leah said. "Maybe remind them about maintaining some decorum."

Jo laughed. "Decorum and the Cocoon Club?"

"Do not reside in the same universe, I know," Leah agreed. "But they need to stop with the rumors and speculation. Gil and I both made some inroads with people at the first debate, and I'm sure the same will happen with the second in a few weeks." For the first time since announcing her candidacy, Leah felt doubt creep in. Was she doing the right thing, attempting to unseat a man who knew this town better than she could ever hope to? A man who had literally been born to the job?

All the more reason to boot him out, the cranky angel sitting on her shoulder reminded her. No. She'd done enough research, talked to enough people in the past few months to know that Gil Hamilton's tenure as mayor had run its course. The animosity the name Hamilton triggered wasn't good for the soul of the town. The residents certainly agreed; it was how the special election had been called after all. Of course it had only been able to be mounted because someone—Leah—had finally stepped up to run against him. Now the one-day vote loomed like a storm cloud over a temperamental ocean. An ocean that was making her increasingly seasick.

Leah's status was something that both worked to her favor and reminded people she was still considered something of an outsider. Sure, she'd successfully taken over her uncle's family-law practice in town. She'd even branched out to surrounding areas and had clients within a hundred-mile radius. She'd joined town committees and shopped local and had left all the pressures and memories of her life before well out of reach. She was well-liked. But no Butterfly Harbor insider would have ever dreamed of challenging a Hamilton in a Butterfly Harbor election.

But Leah had.

She frowned, thinking of Gil's protective attitude about Elijah. It had both surprised and unnerved her. Here she thought she'd had the man figured out.

Clearly there were more layers to Mayor Gil Hamilton than she had ever anticipated. "Any other rumors I should be aware of?" Leah asked Jo.

"How would I know?"

"Because you run a construction crew that works all over this town. I have no doubt they've got loads of information to share. Whether it's based on truth..."

Jo's lips curved. "Jed might have mentioned Kyle Knight and Simon Saxon had their heads together lately. This close to an election, that would make me a bit nervous."

Leah caught her lower lip in her teeth. The stories of Simon Saxon, boy genius, were notorious around Butterfly Harbor. Rumor had it he'd infiltrated a neighbor's Wi-Fi and changed all the file names on their computer. To this day, no one was certain of the reason, but at the age of eight, Simon had definitely earned a reputation for eking out inconvenient revenge on perceived wrongdoers, and he was not a fan of Gil's. Leah could only imagine what Simon would be capable of once he graduated from his charter school for top students.

"Was Charlie part of that conversation between Simon and Kyle?" Leah asked. Charlie Bradley, Simon's best friend and daughter of Nurse Paige Bradley and Deputy Fletcher Bradley, acted as part conscience, part motivator when it came to Simon's actions. The two had gotten into enough mischief that they should have earned mention in the tourist brochures as added entertainment.

"Don't think so." Jo shook her head. "She and Simon haven't been hanging out as much together since Charlie started volunteering at the youth center. She's biding her time, she informed me a few weeks ago," Jo added, "until she's old enough to work at the sanctuary. She plans to run it one day, just so you know."

Leah's heart lightened at the thought. "Consider me informed."

"Hey, speaking of rumors," Jo said. "I heard you stopped by Gil's house yesterday to read him the riot act for missing meetings. That true?"

"It is. How did you—"

"It's Butterfly Harbor," Jo said with a roll of her eyes. "Gossip travels faster through this place than fire chief Roman Salazar can suck down one of Holly's blackberry pies. So what happened? Why's Gil been MIA?"

"Not my place to say." Leah's attempt at diplomacy had Jo grimacing at her. "He had a good reason," Leah clarified. "One that I understood. What?"

"What do you mean *what*?" Jo snorted in a way that had Lancelot—his comfort stuffed dragon locked securely in his mouth—jumping up to place his face in Jo's lap. "Sorry, boy. That's my irritated sound and he knows it. You can't stand the guy, Leah. You've taken every opportunity to verbally eviscerate him. Didn't you even create a PowerPoint presentation about all the things he's done wrong as mayor?"

"No, I did not." Leah dug a fingernail into the arm of the chair. "I only thought about making one. I know you and Gil had your battles—"

"Battles might be a bit of an overstatement," Jo said. "I get that he's had a lot on his plate and that mess with his half brother sabotaging this site—"

"And attacking you," Leah added. "Why do you always skip over that part?"

"Because I don't want to remember how close I came to losing Hope. Besides." Whatever anger or pain Jo felt over the incident vanished behind a determined flash. "Gil isn't responsible for his brother's actions."

"He's responsible for his own. He was a jerk when you first met him."

"I work in construction," Jo reminded her. "I'm used to jerks, and actually, by comparison, he was fine. He also stepped up when he needed to and was more than solicitous and concerned when I was in the hospital. Honestly? Whatever issues we had, he's more than made up for them as far as I'm concerned. That doesn't mean I don't think you'll make a better mayor than him. You still have my vote."

"I appreciate your faith." Leah managed a strained smile. "It's going to be a long few weeks until the debate and then the election, isn't it?" Even longer, Leah thought, than it had felt before she sat down.

"I CAN HAVE Matt dust the note for prints," Luke told Gil as Elijah rocked away in the mechanical infant swing Luke had retrieved from the garage. Cash had curled up on the floor beside Eli and kept both eyes trained on him. "My deputies like to keep those talents honed. I'm sure that'll be a good place to start."

"You think?" Despite Leah's suggestion, Gil still wasn't convinced this was the right path to take. But he'd told Leah he trusted her. He had to at least try to follow her suggestion. Sitting in the sheriff's kitchen in the home Luke shared with Holly and their three kids, Gil was reminded of those teenage longings he'd had for a family that had never materialized for him. Everything around him felt like something out of a dream. A dream he'd long given up hoping would come true.

Luke's kitchen was country cozy, with crowded countertops neatly arranged. The rectangular table held not only a bowl of fruit but also a silver cake dome Gil suspected covered some confectionary creation Holly had concocted. A pair of well-used high chairs sat in the corner by the back door, with booster seats stacked beside them, an indication that the twins were in transition from infants to full-fledged little people. On the side counter beside the door sat a red box with "no cell phones at the table" crookedly printed on the outside.

It no longer struck Gil as odd that the guy once dubbed the bad boy of Butterfly Harbor had become not only an admired local sheriff but also a dedicated family man who kept his door open to everyone.

Now that man gazed across the table at Gil as if waiting for him to explain his reluctance to run potential fingerprints against the note Eli's mother had left. "My main concern is raising any alarms," Gil said. "I don't want Eli getting caught up in the system. If word gets out he's been abandoned—"

"You've lived here how long? Holly can't change the diner's brand of ketchup without it circulating. You can't stop a tidal wave like this from hitting, and whatever control you might have is going to be fleeting." Luke stood, retrieved a plastic baggie and slipped the note inside. He then picked up their coffee mugs and refilled them. "I'll do what I can to keep this off the radar, but when it comes down to it, you have an abandoned child in your custody. Note or not, that's a legal issue that needs to be dealt with."

"I know." Gil reached over and reset the timer on the swing as Eli slept. "And I am dealing with it." He purposely kept Leah's name out of it. She hadn't yet called to confirm she'd be taking the case or if she felt obligated to pass it on to a colleague. Dragging her into something potentially damaging definitely wouldn't come across well, especially given the upcoming election. "I also know it isn't fair of me to ask you to keep this a secret."

Luke reached into a cabinet over the refrigerator and pulled out a tin, which when opened, revealed a stash of Holly's homemade white-chocolate-macadamia-nut cookies. "Grab one quick, before Simon sniffs them out," Luke said as he snatched two for himself then replaced the lid and shoved the tin back out of reach. "Kid's appetite has definitely kicked into overdrive. I'll do my best to keep things quiet, Gil." He retook his seat, then leaned over to look out the back window when the sound of excited squeals echoed beyond. "But get ready. You and I both know that once word gets around..."

"The story and speculation will take on

a life of its own," Gil finished. "Yeah, I know."

"So long as you're ready for it."

People had gossiped about him his entire life. It was only recently he'd begun to realize the damage it had done to his psyche. It shouldn't bother him. Gil had spent a good portion of his formative years taking the verbal punches his father had excelled at hurling at him. When Morland Hamilton hadn't been occupied manipulating business deals and driving Butterfly Harbor to the brink of ruin, that is.

That some in town still couldn't distinguish him from his father made him feel physically ill. But he'd finally accepted there wasn't anything he could say to change anyone's mind. Only actions could do that, actions he'd been trying to take for the better part of four years. Actions that had required some tough decisions and creative financial planning to pull off.

Until recently, he'd been able to shrug off the criticism and stay focused on moving forward in an effort to make his own mark on the town his forefathers had helped establish. Well, shrug it off and chalk it up to professional jealousy.

But in the past year, he had to admit, his mindset had definitely begun to shift. That was the thing about almost dying. It changed your life perspective.

He looked at Eli, then back at Luke. "I can't change the past, Luke. But I will be the first to admit I haven't done myself any favors over the years." He took a long drink of coffee. "People are going to think what they're going to think. If they're basing their opinion of me on my past behavior, I'll have to live with that. I'm disappointed people can't see that I've been trying to change, but again, that's on me." It wasn't an easy thing, admitting just how many flaws he possessed. But it was definitely one thing his father had never been able to do.

At least in that way, he could be a better person than his father had been.

"It was the fire, wasn't it?" Luke asked. "That changed things for you."

"Mostly." A man could only blame the past for so long before he needed to own up to his mistakes. And a man couldn't keep family secrets secret forever. His half brother

Christopher's retaliatory actions against Gil and the town had been confirmation of that. "A year ago, I probably would have surrendered Eli to you or social services without giving it a second thought."

Luke inclined his head, narrowed his eyes. "And now?"

"Now it's all different." Gil wasn't entirely sure who or what he was anymore. But he did know there was a baby relying on him to figure it out sooner than later. A baby who needed him.

Need. It was such a new word to him. Someone *needed* him. How had it taken him until the age of thirty-four to begin to understand what that meant? "How old were you when your mother died?"

Luke blinked at Gil's question, his hand tightening around his mug. "Too young." The flinch was one Gil had seen in the mirror himself on too many occasions.

"Your life would have been different, if she'd lived," Gil said. "If she hadn't left you with your father." Like his mother had.

"It would have." Luke nodded, his gaze shifting again to the window to look at his children. "I can't say it would have been for the better. Instead of cancer, it might have been my father who put her in the ground, just like he tried to do to me on many occasions. If it hadn't been for Jake Campbell." He shrugged, letting the thought trail off. His current situation told the entire story.

"Holly's father changed your life," Gil said. "He didn't have to be there for you, but he was. He gave you someone steady to rely on, someone who guided you and eventually brought you back here."

"You brought me back to Butterfly Harbor," Luke reminded him.

"On Jake's suggestion you succeed him as sheriff." Gil was done taking credit for things he hadn't accomplished. "Remove Jake Campbell from your life and where would you be?"

"I honestly couldn't tell you. But I'd bet good money I wouldn't be here with three kids I adore and a wife I honestly wouldn't want to live without."

Gil nodded. He hadn't had a Jake in his life. He hadn't opened himself up to the possibility of asking for help or guidance. He'd been unable to with the overwhelming presence of a father who only saw success and prestige as indicators of a fruitful existence. Despite the mistakes and the enemies Gil had made, a good number of his decisions had done Butterfly Harbor—and its residents well.

He might not have accomplished everything he'd hoped to as mayor, but Eli was a completely separate matter. Someone had trusted their child to him. Someone had seen good in him.

He couldn't turn away from that now because it might put his professional future at risk. He might have been that man once. It wasn't the kind of man he wanted to be now.

"I can be Eli's Jake," Gil said finally. "However this turns out. He's alone in the world. I can make a difference with him. For him. If that means getting tagged as an opportunist so be it. I've been called worse. Heck." He actually laughed. "I've been worse."

"That you have," Luke agreed with a tight smile. "I'll do whatever I can to help you with Eli, Gil. Starting right now." He got up and held up a hand. "Be right back." He walked out of the room just as the front door slammed and the thundering of children echoed through the house.

"Dad, can we go to the comic book—Oh." Simon skidded to a halt just inside the door, causing his baby brother and sister to bash into him from behind. He stumbled forward, caught himself on the table, even as Zoe screeched with laughter and raced around Gil's chair before she slid to the ground as if sliding into home base. Cash bounded to his feet. "I'm thinking we should rename her Wipeout," Simon said with an embarrassed smile.

"I heard you're the odds-on favorite to win the upcoming science fair at the academy," Gil said as he reached down to pick Zoe up off the floor.

Simon puffed out his chest a bit. "Only because I won last year. Elliot Casper's already bragging about his hydrogen-powered robots." He shrugged much the way Luke did, Gil noticed. "We'll see."

"I'll keep my money on you."

"Yeah?" Simon didn't look completely sold on Gil's presence. "Thanks. Where'd my dad go?"

"I'm not sure. He said he'd be back in a minute."

Jake peeked over the edge of the table and pointed at Elijah in the swing. "Who dat?"

"That's Elijah," Gil told him. "Eli. He's come to live with me for a while."

"That's your baby?" Simon's eyes went wide.

"Ah..." Gil struggled for an answer.

"Simon, don't badger our guest." Luke returned carrying two boxes with an infant car seat piled on top.

"He's not badgering me." It was, Gil thought, a legitimate and soon to be all-too-common question. It would be easy enough to explain Eli away, dismiss him as if he was a temporary figurc in his life. It could very well be the way to avoid Luke's concerns surrounding the election. If he was going to have to prove himself and convince people he wasn't the same man who had taken office, this was the perfect place to start. "He is mine, actually, Simon." He dismissed Luke's raised brows and glanced around to where Zoe stood over the swing. Cash remained close to both infant and toddler. "Eli is mine."

Elijah opened his eyes, which instantly went wide as he saw a pigtailed little girl staring down at him.

"Eli." Zoe reached out a hand, and at first, Gil moved to stop her, but Zoe touched the infant's head with feather-soft fingers and so much care Gil's throat tightened. "Baby Eli. Pretty." She crouched down, peeked over the edge of the swing and popped back up. "Peek. I see you!"

Eli squealed with laughter and waved his hands in the air. Cash barked his approval.

"Friend?" Zoe asked Luke, who nodded.

"Eli is our friend. Gil, too," Luke added with a pointed look at Simon. "And friends take care of each other." He gestured to the infant car seat. "If Eli's going to be here awhile, he's going to need the right kind of transportation."

"I—" Gil had been overwhelmed by the choices online, and honestly, he hadn't contemplated having someone to ask. "Thanks, Luke. We both appreciate it."

"But that's Jake's seat," Simon accused.

"Jake has a bigger one now. But you're right, I should have asked," Luke said diplomatically. "Jake, is it all right if Eli borrows your car seat?"

"Yes!" Jake lifted both arms in triumph and looked up at his father, who bent down to pick him up. "I like to share."

"Brothers." Simon rolled his eyes.

"I also found some old baby clothes and toys Holly packed away," Luke said. "They aren't doing any good in the garage. May as well put them to use. I think there's a baby snuggie thing so you can walk him around without your arms getting tired."

"Speaking of Holly." Gil almost hated to ask. "Are you sure this'll be okay with her?"

"Unloading all this stuff? It'll be fine," Luke assured him. "Zoe, be careful with Eli, okay? Be gentle."

"Not hurt baby." Zoe bent down and snuggled her cheek against Eli's. "Pretty friend Eli." She stood straight, turned and looked right into Gil's surprised face. "Friend Gil." She grabbed hold of his arm and tugged his hand over to the swing. "Gil's Eli daddy."

"That's right," Luke said with a widening grin. "Gil is Eli's daddy. Welcome to the club," he added with a chuckle as Gil absorbed the weight of the declaration.

Gil gathered Eli's things and followed Luke out to his car, where the sheriff made quick work of installing the car seat. "He's still pretty little," Luke said as he tugged on the straps. "Depending on how things work out, you won't need to get a bigger one for a while."

Simon came running out of the house waving Luke's ringing cell. "Dad! Phone!"

"Give me a sec."

Luke met his son halfway down the drive as Gil bent down to settle Eli in the seat. "There you go." Gil lowered the buckle and straps over Eli's head, and when Eli squirmed and scrunched his face in a pre-warning howl, Gil crouched and rested his hand against Eli's chest. "You're fine. I promise. This is nice and safe." Eli calmed and blinked wide, trusting eyes at him. In that moment, it felt as if the entire world rested on his shoulders.

Eli's world.

How could anyone just walk away from their child? It was a question that had left a bitter mark on Gil's heart.

"Gil?" Luke called.

Gil stood and looked across the top of his car to the sheriff.

"Yeah?"

"You should get over to City Hall." He clicked off his phone, rested a hand on Simon's shoulder. "Matt's already there."

"What's happened? Is someone hurt? Is it Helena?" His long-time assistant had been dealing with some health issues as of late, and he'd heaped a lot on her these last few days.

"No, nothing like that." Luke approached, lowered his voice as Simon raced to catch up. "Apparently the Cocoon Club is having a bit of a sit-in at your office. Something about a line of trees you plan to have removed from their property?"

"Oh, for the love of Pete." Gil let out a long breath. "It isn't even up to me. But of course they'll see it as my fault. I guess I'd better try to clear things up."

"Or I could have Matt arrest them for trespassing," Luke said with enough of a grin that Gil knew he was teasing. He rested his hand on his son's shoulder.

Yeah, that's exactly what he needed this close to the election. "No, we won't be locking up the Cocoon Club. Not yet anyway," he added under his breath.

"Want me to go with you?" Luke offered. "Help you smooth things over?"

"I knew it," Simon muttered and ducked his head. "No comic book store."

"This is your day off," Gil said quickly and waved off Luke's offer. He'd lost count of the number of days growing up his own father had disappointed him. He didn't want to be the reason why Luke did the same to Simon. Besides, the last person he wanted to annoy was Simon Saxon. Heaven only knew what retaliatory plans the kid could think up. "I'm sure Matt and I can handle it."

"Are you sure?"

"I've been dealing with the Cocoon Club for what feels like decades," Gil reminded him. "Thanks for the baby stuff. And the ear."

Luke nodded. "I'll check with Holly, see what else we have stashed around here. Good luck."

"Oh." He closed Eli's door. "I'm going to need it."

CHAPTER FOUR

"UH-OH. LEMON DONUTS for lunch. We know what that means."

From her spot at Chrysalis Bakery's pickup counter, Leah glanced over her shoulder as Sienna Fairchild-Bettencourt and Brooke Evans walked up behind her. Sienna, who always looked as if she'd stepped off a fashion magazine cover with her thick, dark hair and designer attire, and Brooke, equally elegant-looking but more at home in jeans and an oversize sweater, had teasing glints in their eyes. The two women had joined forces to start Butterfly Harbor's first event planning business and, until Sienna decided on a location for their office, used Chrysalis Bakery as their daily meetup location.

Leah couldn't blame them. Who wouldn't want to call the charming, throwback-cottage-inspired treat factory their home away from home? On the walls, the bright painted butterflies that seemed to swoop in and around the tables added whimsy to an already dainty space. And the air. Leah took a deep breath and held it. The air was thick with sugar and spice baked into everything naughty and nice.

The bakery's café tables were filled with customers gobbling down the tempting treats, from homemade bagels and pastries to donuts that needed their own zip code. Add to that an unending supply of high-octane coffee and this was definitely one of Leah's guiltier town pleasures.

"Sugar is your coping mechanism," Sienna teased as Brooke moved off to order. "Tough morning?"

"On the quiet side, actually." The appointments she'd missed yesterday had been rescheduled throughout the week, which had given Leah the morning to investigate Gil's options were Eli was concerned. She wasn't sure if she was relieved or disappointed not to have a legally defined conflict of interest when it came to representing him, but since she didn't, she'd gathered the documentation to begin the process of naming him as an emergency foster parent. It was, she knew, the quickest and hopefully most effective way to keep Eli right where he was. With Gil.

She tucked the bag of pastries into her oversize purse. "Callie's been going above and beyond lately, so I thought I'd bring her back a surprise. Look at you," she added when Brooke rejoined them. "You're starting to show!"

Brooke rotated her slightly rounded stomach in Leah's direction. "I hit the five-month mark this weekend and I'm eating everything in sight."

"Makes up for the weeks you couldn't keep anything down," Sienna told her with an overly bright smile. "I don't think the town population sign can keep up with all these babies being born. You should look into getting that digitized after you're mayor. Just flip a switch whenever there's a new arrival."

"I'll keep it in mind," Leah said. "Monty back from that trip up to Seattle yet?"

"He's due tonight," Sienna said. "Then I get him to myself for a whole month." She did a little dance in place. "Thank goodness for the slow season for Wind Walkers."

"Might not be as slow as you'd like," Leah reminded her. "Abby Corwin said the inn's already booked up the week before and after the sanctuary opening and she's had a lot of requests for boating excursions, not to mention dining reservations for Jason's restaurant."

"Oh." Sienna's smile dimmed. "Well. It's a good thing Monty's talking about hiring a few more boat guides then."

"Let's grab our favorite table while we can," Sienna suggested.

"The Cocoon Club snagged it from us yesterday," Brooke explained as Sienna moved off to place her own order.

"I thought they usually met at the diner," Leah said.

"I guess they're changing things up." Brooke set her bag in one chair and sat in another.

Leah caught the cashier waving to her indicating her drink order was ready. "Did Jo talk to you about putting together a housewarming party for Alethea?"

"She did. Sienna and I are heading up to Calliope's after this to get a better idea for plans. We're thinking outdoor since the *new* house only holds about three people."

Leah chuckled. "More power to her. Heaven knows I couldn't live in a tiny home." But it made sense as Alethea would be spending a good part of her time in the Bay Area while she earned her culinary degree. Of course, Leah would bet half a year's pay Alethea would be spending most of her time in town with Declan Cartwright at the newly restored and renovated gas and service station on the edge of town.

The former race car driver had taken an unexpected turn in life and was devoting the next year to racing as a kind of farewell to the fans. But after that, he'd be working on his new nonprofit, which was dedicated to helping small-town gas stations and mechanics reestablish themselves in a more energy-efficient world.

Leah's phone buzzed and she waved off, answering as she picked up her cardboard tray of drinks. "Callie, hey, I'm heading over right—"

"You'll need to make a detour to City Hall," Callie told her. "Bobby just called me from his shift at the security desk. He said the Cocoon Club is holding some kind of protest. Matt's already there. Bobby thinks they might have them carted off to the station."

"They can't remove them from public property." Leah sighed, smiled her thanks to the counter girl and after waving to Sienna, headed outside. This wasn't the first time the club had picketed City Hall and it wouldn't be the last. "They're probably picketing because—"

"Oh, they aren't picketing this time," Callie told her in a tone that had Leah stopping midstride. "They're holding a sit-in. At Gil's office. They say they won't leave until he revokes the permit for the tree removal outside their house."

"Awesome." Leah picked up her pace and hurried to her car. "I hope you like cold coffee. They'll last, what? Maybe an hour or two?"

"Longer. They brought snacks."

"Eesh. Where's Ezzie when we need her?"

"The super-duper house mom's on her honeymoon, remember? So when the cat's away—"

"The elderly little mice will find new

games to play. Okay. Tell Bobby I'm on my way." Although who knows what good she could do. When the club had their minds set on something...

"Do me a favor when you get there?" Callie asked.

"Sure. What?" Leah unlocked her car and stashed the drinks in the center console.

"Take pictures. They'll look great on your campaign Facebook page."

"Ha ha." She didn't have a campaign Facebook page. Did she?

She hung up and climbed into her car. "Change of plans yet again." She made a U-turn and, keeping the ocean to her right, sped down Monarch Lane toward City Hall.

SOMEHOW GIL MANAGED to make it to his parking space outside City Hall without so much as a baby squeal from Eli. He seemed content to sleep the day away.

City Hall as a building had become something of a puzzle for Gil. It definitely had historical significance. Originally, it housed two courtrooms, but those, along with the judiciary and town offices, had been relocated to a newer building a few blocks away. Now City Hall felt impractical.

The town literally had only a handful of employees, one of whom was Gil. Because of the financial mess his father had left after his death, Gil had no other choice but to pare down to only essential jobs, which meant turning one-time paid positions into volunteer ones. Positions that, for the most part, went unfilled. Now that the financial situation had improved, he was in a position to rehire, but the task was one of those things he kept putting off.

He was hesitant to make any big changes in case he wasn't here to see them through.

Personally, Gil had preferred the laid-back feel of the old pub they'd moved into during the hall's renovation and code enforcement. But that building had burned down last Christmas Eve. Gil shuddered. If it hadn't been for co–fire chief Frankie Salazar and her team of firefighters, Gil wouldn't have made it out alive.

Now that the renovations on City Hall were finished, he'd moved into the office space his father, grandfather and great-grandfather had occupied. He'd thought the job would feel more…official when he moved in. Instead, it was like having his entire family looming constantly over his shoulder. He'd purposely kept the town records—documents, photographs, furniture—because as far as he was concerned, they belonged to the town. City Hall should be a showplace at the heart of Butterfly Harbor. But it still felt empty.

Except for the ghosts. Even with the new floors, windows and paint, the ghosts remained.

Gil walked around his car and popped open the trunk, dug inside the boxes for the baby carrier Luke had mentioned. He held up the navy blue fabric comprised of straps and cloth. "Reminds me of some weird geometry project from school. Let's see how this thing works." He opened Eli's door, let the fresh air waft in as he twisted the material this way and that, tugging it over his head, then off, turned it around…

He glanced up as Leah pulled into the space beside his. Caught with his arm half out of the straps, his face went hot, but the faster he tried to extricate himself from it, the worse he got tangled.

"Hang on, Mr. Mayor." Leah pushed out of her car. "Let me give you a hand."

Gil let out a breath he hadn't realized he'd been holding. Something about seeing her made the tension in his shoulders ease. "What are you doing here?"

"I have a special Cocoon Club alert on my phone," she said dryly. "Stop twisting around. Just…stop." She placed her hands on his shoulders and looked up at him. The surprise that jumped into her blue eyes vanished when she ducked her head and unclipped the straps to pull the carrier free.

Gil could smell flowers. Summery flowers that reminded him of Duskywing Farm at the height of the season. Lilacs, he thought. Maybe it was lilacs or… He'd never been great with flowers.

She wore a gray suit today with a shimmery silver button-down blouse and heels so thin and high they defied the laws of physics. Around her neck sat the solitary gold charm she always wore, a small scale of justice resting against the hollow of her throat. "Okay, you're free." She stepped back and, after un-clicking a few buckles, turned him around and locked the carrier into place. “Now all you need is the baby. You got him?”

“I’ve got him.” Gil was getting pretty adept at baby handling, and he and Eli had a kind of routine where Gil would dangle him up in the air just for a minute to let his arms and legs relax. Eli gurgled and squealed as Eli brought him toward his chest.

“Ah, nope. Other way.” Leah plucked Eli out of his hold and handed him back. “He’s old enough to need a view. Not that your chest isn’t a…” She trailed off, her cheeks going an unfamiliar yet entertaining shade of pink.

Gil grinned. Who knew he could make Leah Ellis blush?

“Thanks. So you heard?” He did a bit of jiggling to get used to the carrier as Eli kicked his socked feet against Gil’s stomach.

“Heard?” Leah blinked at him.

“About the club in my office.”

“Oh. I heard all right.”

“Trees.” Gil resisted the urge to roll his eyes. “Guess they didn’t think they should consult their attorney first.”

“I represent a number of them in personal matters, Gil. Not litigious ones. You want this?" She reached for the diaper bag. "Nice car seat. Looks like the one that Holly used for little Jake."

"It is." She slung the bag over her shoulder, and while he locked up his car, she did the same with hers. "Luke loaned the seat to me this morning when I stopped by to see him."

"Oh?" Only Leah could manage to sound surprised and superior at the same time.

"I took your advice. He's going to run the note for prints," Luke told her as they headed toward the stone steps to the glass entry door to City Hall. "He's also going to do some unofficial poking around about any missing babies." He pulled open the door and motioned her through.

She nodded. "That goes in line with some documents I have for you to fill out. Emergency fosterage is going to be our best shot—"

"Our best shot?" His voice echoed in the vestibule. "Does that mean you're taking Eli's case?"

"Eli's case?" There went that eyebrow again, and his fingers tingled at the thought of smoothing it back into place.

"I figure he has a better chance with you than I do at this point."

"Maybe he does." She was fighting a grin. "But you're catching up."

"Morning, Jessie." Gil greeted the receptionist at the front desk.

"Morning, Gil." Wearing her usual combination of black and orange, a quirky uniform tradition Gil's grandfather had started when he'd first been elected mayor, Jessie got to her feet and rotated the visitor's log around for him to check, then inclined her head toward the baby. "Um, I don't think he's old enough to sign in himself."

Gil chuckled. "True. Jessie, this is Eli. He'll be a familiar face around here for a while. Eli, you need anything, you come right to Jessie, okay?"

Eli blew a raspberry, which echoed in the mostly deserted building.

A number of the City Hall staff had retired or quit after his father's death, which meant Gil had to pick and choose which positions were vital to running his office. Having a bright, friendly face on the first person people saw when they visited was vital and made Jessie perfect for the job. She'd just graduated college with a degree in political science but had come back home to help care for her grandparents. When Gil's assistant Helena got overwhelmed or needed help, Jessie was ready and willing to jump in. "You doing okay, Jess? They didn't give you any problems, did they?"

Leah nudged him as if in protest.

"I'm fine. Thanks, Gil," Jessie said. "And no. They're more entertaining than a nuisance."

"Don't let them hear you say that," Gil advised and earned a smirk of agreement from Leah. "Matt still upstairs with them?"

"Yes. I told him where he could find some extra chairs after Penny got down on the floor and couldn't get up."

"I doubt *I* could get up if I got down on the floor," Gil said as he checked through the names. "Good idea on the chairs." Six members of the club were waiting for him in his office, including the usual suspects, Myra Abernathe, Alice Manning, and Oscar Bedemeyer, who, supposedly, had a brand new set of high-beam lamps attached to his walker. "Elevator work okay for them?"

“Seemed to. It got them there,” Jessie said. “I bet it was grateful to be used.”

“Want me to sign in?” Leah asked as she reached for a pen.

“Please,” Gil said. “I can give you the full tour before you leave if you want.”

“I might want,” Leah said and scribbled her name. “Or I might wait until my term starts.”

Now Gil did roll his eyes. “Let’s get this over with. Hang on.” The door opened and Kyle Knight walked in carrying two large square boxes with Zane’s Pizza on the side. “Since when do you deliver for Zane’s?” Gil asked.

“I don’t,” Kyle said. “It’s Alethea’s day off with the food truck, so I had to pick up pizza for the crew up at the Howser house. I said I’d drop these off to the Cocoon Club on my way.”

“Good to see you off the crutches,” Leah said. An accident at the butterfly sanctuary back in April had left Kyle seriously injured and needing surgery to repair his broken leg. After months of rehabilitation and hard work, his gait was getting noticeably better. “Jo still keeping you chained to a desk?”

"Mostly," Kyle said. At eighteen, Kyle Knight had managed to claw his way out of a troubled upbringing, thanks to being adopted by Deputy Matt Knight and his wife, Lori. He was on track to becoming one of Butterfly Harbor's youngest-ever licensed contractors and worked steadily for Jo Bertoletti and Kendall MacBride's construction and remodeling business. He'd also been dating Mandy Evans who, rumor had it, was part fish and, when she wasn't in school, worked for Monty Bettencourt as an ocean tour and dive guide. "Can I hand these off to you?" Kyle asked, then balked when he saw Eli. "Ah, maybe you." He grinned and offered the boxes to Leah instead. "No payment necessary," Kyle said when Gil reached for his wallet. "Zane said he's happy to support the Cocoon Club's cause."

"Didn't know he was so into trees," Leah said.

"Don't think the cause matters." Kyle shrugged. "Talk to you later."

"Zane is not a fan of mine," Gil admitted. "I might have suggested he relocate to a smaller space a while back, and he's never forgiven me."

"Ha, I'm aware." Leah lifted the lid to one of the boxes and offered it to Jessie, who eagerly accepted a slice of pizza. "He's given me a fifty percent discount on pizza ever since I announced I was running against you."

"That's also what I get for breaking his nose senior year of high school."

"You did not," Leah shot back.

"Football practice," Gil added quickly. "And it had absolutely nothing to do with him dating Shannon Delco and me wanting to take her to the prom. Okay, maybe it had a little to do with that."

"Wait." She caught his arm at the base of the curving, hand-carved staircase. "Isn't his wife's name Shannon?"

"Huh. Is it?" Gil feigned innocence. "Strange."

"I take it that episode was during your Gil the Thrill stage?" she teased and earned his best irritated glare.

"How do you know about that?"

"I hear things." They climbed the stairs side by side.

"Frankie has a big mouth." All these years later, he was still annoyed by the nickname the co–fire chief had tagged him with in high school. And sure, maybe he'd deserved that and more given his ridiculous attitude, but all these years later, he still couldn't shake it.

"I didn't hear it from Frankie," Leah told him. "I heard it from..." Her gaze shifted to the doors to his office where the distinct voices of the Cocoon Club emanated. "Let's just say I heard about it from a reliable source."

"I bet the Cocoon Club keeps actual records of everything that's happened in this town for the past fifty years."

"More like sixty," Leah said. "They have it stashed in a secret safe under the floorboards."

"Ha. I don't suppose you want to hand those pizzas off to me so I can look like the good guy."

"That depends if you'll relinquish Eli." She raised hopeful eyes to his. In that moment, the world stopped and went silent. Everything ceased to exist except the image of Leah Ellis looking up at him and him imagining what it would be like to kiss those incredible, full, curving lips of hers. Every cell in his body was screaming at him to do just that, and he took a step forward, one hand lifting toward her face. He stopped when a heel of a foot punched him solidly in his stomach.

"Bah! Bah bah bah!" Eli's arms shot into the air as Leah blinked and shook her head. She backed away, her brow furrowing as she turned and stepped into the reception area of his office.

"You and I need to talk about your timing, little man," Gil told Eli, who dropped his head against Gil's chest and babbled some more. Gil couldn't help it. He chuckled and dropped a kiss on Eli's forehead. "It's a good thing you're cute. I bet that's a weapon they aren't expecting to have to battle." With a deep breath, he steeled himself, and followed Leah through the door.

CHAPTER FIVE

"I'M SURPRISED AT YOU, LEAH." Myra Abernathe's narrowed, angry eyes pinned Leah. With her bright orange hair and temper, Myra looked like a lit match. "Surprised and disappointed." She moved out of the way as Harold pulled a slice of pizza out of the nearest box and took a seat on the leather sofa on the opposite side of the spacious office. An office that reminded Leah of Gil's museum of a house. It was all polished and preserved, with very little personality.

A personality Leah was only beginning to see.

A personality that had her almost stepping in for the kiss he'd nearly offered. She ducked her head, hoping the steam from the box would explain the color in her cheeks.

"You're disappointed because of pizza?" Leah tried to feign innocence. Arriving at the same time as Gil had no doubt convinced

Myra that Leah had shifted allegiances and sided with the enemy. "I'm only delivering what you ordered."

"You know very well what I'm talking about." Myra yanked a wrinkled envelope out of her bag and waved it in the air. "What's next? A change in zoning rules? Gil's trying to drive us out of our home and you're helping him. Oh, for heaven's sake, Penny, just pick a slice already. It all has the same amount of cholesterol."

"Not if you eat it slowly," Penny declared before whispering to Leah, "Don't tell Frankie." Penny slid a slice onto one of the paper plates Helena, Gil's assistant, brought in. "She's been keeping an eye on us while Ezzie's away."

"They're doing it in shifts," Harold announced. "First Frankie, then Abby and Paige. Tomorrow morning, it's BethAnn Bottomley's turn and she said something about chair aerobics. I can't wait until Ezzie gets back."

"They just want to make sure you're all taken care of," Leah reminded them. "Abby, especially, since Alice is her grandmother." She smiled at the older woman situated in a top-notch electric medical scooter. Alice's head shook as she grinned and she squeezed the horn on the handle of her chair, making Oscar and Myra jump. "I thought you'd like having them around," Leah said. "Especially since Paige and Abby bring their babies."

"Oh, we love seeing the babies." Penny clasped her hands over her heart.

"Babies are fine, but their mamas think we need a babysitter," Harold mumbled around his slice. Leah pinched her lips into a thin line to stop from smiling. "We did just fine before Ezzie arrived and we can do okay without her."

"You'd be devastated if she left for good," Delilah, a former town council member chided. "Admit it. Having someone be there for us has been a blessing." She swooped around the room in her brightly flowered muumuu, in search of the perfect seat.

"Yeah, well," Oscar grumbled as Penny moved away. "I'm with Harold. I can't wait for her to get back. Frankie made us eat kale for dinner last night." Oscar peered into the box, leaning over so far Leah could see his bald spot. "Do I look like a man who eats kale? That stuff makes my teeth squeak."

"It was better than that squash casserole she made," Harold shuddered and helped Delilah Scoda sit down. "Poor squash never did anything to her. And here I thought firefighters could cook."

"Can we please stop talking vegetables and get to the matter at hand?" Myra's voice shook with anger. "Where is he? Or did he send you in here as a buffer?"

"Gil didn't send me anywhere." Leah set the pizza box down on Gil's desk and grabbed a bottle of water for herself. "Why don't you have a seat and…see. Here he is now."

"Sorry to keep you waiting." Gil flashed an apologetic smile around the room before heading to his desk. "Helena said she'd take Eli, but I can't seem to…" He turned his back and pointed to the clasp.

"Right." Leah reached up. "Got it."

She unhooked the carrier as Gil lifted Eli free. Amid the oohs and aahs, Myra tsked and glared. Gil shifted and pulled the carrier free, dropped it beside his chair and cradled Eli in one arm. "What's wrong now, Myra?"

"You're getting mighty desperate if you think carrying an innocent baby around is going to change our minds about you, Gil Hamilton. We know too much about you to be fooled."

"Myra!" Leah gasped as a good portion of the amusement faded from Gil's face. "That's a terrible thing to say."

"Well, dragging a baby around like this is a terrible thing to do," Myra declared, undeterred by her fellow club members' murmured objections. "Pulling tricks out of your daddy's book now, are you? The way he used to parade you around town, showing off what a great father he was despite being a horrible person. Now you've found some innocent—"

"Myra, that's enough." Leah didn't use her court voice very often, but when she did it was like a gavel being slammed against the bench. Myra, along with her fellow club members, looked stunned.

A soft knock on the door had them all turning toward Gil's longtime assistant Helena. "I can take him now, Gil." Tall and slender, Helena had always reminded Leah of a classic-movie girl Friday with her A-line skirts and rounded collared shirts. Her dark hair was streaked with natural silver and knotted in an intricate bun at the base of her neck. She walked toward Gil, holding out her hands as Gil passed Eli over. "I wouldn't want him hearing any more of this ridiculous discussion or these unfounded accusations. Shame on you, Myra Abernathe." She cuddled Eli close and cupped the back of his head. "Shame on all of you."

She strode out of the office and closed the door behind her.

Myra sat back in her chair and pursed her lips, clearly torn between apologizing and continuing her tirade.

Oscar cleared his throat. "She's just upset, Gil. We all are. And we've been calling your office for the past week—"

"I had a personal matter to deal with." His clipped tone was an indication the man Leah had almost let kiss her out in the hall had vanished. He sat in his high-back chair and folded his hands on top of the antique desk. "You now have my undivided attention."

"What's his name?" Delilah asked.

"Elijah," Gil said.

"Who's his mother?" Oscar asked suspiciously.

Leah sighed and took a seat by the window. This was not going well at all. Maybe she shouldn't have sent Deputy Matt Knight away after all.

"I understand this is about the trees that are scheduled to be removed from near your house." Gil dodged the question with expert dexterity. "You have the letter that was sent?"

"I do." Myra flung the paper out so that it unfolded with a snap. "We've been notified about the removal. No discussion, no way for us to protest—"

"All evidence to the contrary," Leah mumbled and earned a look from Gil. "Sorry." She held up her hands. "I'm Switzerland."

Myra's glare returned.

"First of all," Gil said and held out the letter for Leah to read. "Myra, I apologize you all weren't given any opportunity to protest the removal, but there's honestly nothing you can say in the matter that'll change things." He reached over and pulled open a drawer, dug through until he found a file. "What I can do is show you the results of the recent survey I had done around the city. Given the age of the city's infrastructure and various repairs and upgrades we've had to address, a number of trees all around Butterfly Harbor have been identified as potentially problematic. Some houses already have sewer and drainage problems because of the tree roots. Other trees, like the ones outside your house, are dangerously close to gas lines. All it's going to take to cause a major gas leak or even a rupture is for one of those trees to sheer right through a line. According to the survey, it's only a matter of time before that happens."

"I told you he wasn't trying to push us out of our house," Delilah declared.

"I never put anything past a Hamilton," Myra said.

"It would have been nice if the letter from thc city had stated all those details," Leah said, finding herself irritated at the lack of information in the letter Myra and the others had received.

"The previous letter that was sent did." Gil pulled out a copy and passed it to Myra. "It was my understanding that with Ezzie Salazar—"

"Fairchild," Myra corrected him. "It's Fairchild now."

"You're right. My apologies."

Leah winced at Gil's tone, but she had to admit she understood his mood right now. The Cocoon Club rarely made anything easy, especially if they believed they'd been wronged.

"Your arrangement with Ezzie," Gil continued. "Means all the bills and such come addressed to her, which the previous letter would have. This follow-up notice is simply to notify you all of when the work is going to be done. At city expense, I might add," Gil said. "I'm sorry Ezzie didn't give you any warning, but I'm sure with her getting married recently it probably slipped her mind."

"Well." Myra handed back the copy of the first letter. "I suppose if you'd returned our calls—"

"If you had told Helena what you were calling about specifically, I would have been happy to clear this up quickly. But then if I had, you wouldn't have had an excuse to secretly order pizza in the hopes of avoiding another kale or squash incident."

"Even as a kid, you always did have ears like a bat," Oscar mumbled. "Guess we owe you an apology." He looked pointedly at Myra, who straightened her shoulders and remained silent. “Well, you have mine.” Oscar pushed himself to his feet and held out his hand. “We appreciate you looking out for us, Gil. And while I hate to see those beautiful trees come down, I’d rather that happen than get blown to kingdom come.”

Gil shook his hand, then pushed the pizza closer to the old man. “You all feel free to hang out as long as you like so you don’t have to take the evidence home with you. If you need anything else, please let Helena know.”

“Not sure she’d bring us anything at this point that wasn’t laced with arsenic,” Penny said and earned reluctant nods from her co-protesters.

“If you’ll excuse me.” Gil stood, started to leave, then stopped. “Myra.”

“Yes?” She clutched her purse with both hands and looked over her shoulder.

“I know you won’t believe this, but I’m not trying to fool anyone about anything. I’m aware of who and what my father was, and I’ve been doing everything I can not only to fix what he broke but also to show you I’m not like him. I’m a work in progress, Myra. Everyone is. Maybe you could remember that from here on and we can call a truce?"

Myra blinked away most of the hostility in her eyes. "I'll work on it. Doesn't mean I'm going to vote for you, though."

"Perish the thought." Gil's smile seemed strained to Leah as she stood up to follow him, but he looked at her long enough to shake his head. "I'll be back in the office first thing in the morning."

"Gil?" Leah stepped toward him, wanting, needing to say something of comfort, but found she didn't have the words. "How about that tour you promised?"

"If you don't mind, let's make it another time, yeah?" It was only then she saw the distinct hint of sadness in his eyes.

He opened the door and walked out of his office leaving Leah with the surprising and unsettling desire to go after him.

THE IDEA OF loading Eli back into the car and driving home so soon sat as well with Gil as a spoiled oyster. Since he'd left the baby sling in his office, he stopped long enough to pick up the car seat that had a detachable carrier and he and Eli headed down the hill toward the beach.

Growing up, he'd never appreciated the ocean. He'd never appreciated a lot of things, but there was little now that acted as a better de-stressor than the late morning tide breaking up and over the shore. The fall breeze carried the barest memory of summer, brushing warmth across his face. He set the carrier on the stone wall that divided the beach from the main thoroughfare of his town.

He resisted the impulse to kick off his shoes and sink his feet into the sand. Instead, he watched Elijah's wide eyes brighten at the sight of the ocean and found himself breathing easier with the baby's laughter.

How old had he been, Gil wondered, when his father dropped the weight of familial responsibility on his young shoulders? The Hamilton legacy was on him, but what exactly did that mean?

It was a question he'd been asking himself since the night of the fire, when he'd clung to the sill of the window he'd broken in an effort to draw in enough fresh air to offset the smoke and ash. Just how much was a name really worth? It hadn't, he realized hours later as he'd been treated in the hospital, been worth his life. He'd changed. Maybe not enough to offset his past mistakes but enough to show at least some people he wasn't his father. Or maybe that was just a lie he told himself.

There were those who would always see him as a Hamilton first; nothing else would matter. Myra had certainly made that clear just a few moments ago. Was it even possible to step out from another person's shadow? Was he meant to drag the specter of his father around with him like some kind of ghostly ball and chain? Perhaps he was missing whatever it took to break free of Morland Hamilton's hold once and for all.

His grandfather had been a good man. A decent man who, for the short time Gil had known him, appeared as disappointed in his son as Gil's father had been in Gil. The tension between them had been palpable, especially around the time of Gil's parents' divorce. That year was such a blur. Within months of turning eight, his mother was gone and his grandfather had died.

Gil looked down at Eli, the smiling image of his mother so clear in his mind he almost felt as if he could touch her. "I'm so sorry your mother left you." He caught Eli's socked foot in one hand and squeezed. "I can't tell you why she did, but she must have had a good reason." It was what he'd told himself all his life. It was the one lie he let himself continue to believe.

"Eeeeee! Babba bab." Eli scrunched up his face and hiccupped a sob.

Gil recognized that sound and dug into the diaper bag for one of the bottles of formula he'd stashed inside. He uncapped it and held it to Eli's mouth. Eli shoved it away, his face turning red. He let out a gasp, and in an instant, his face cleared. For a moment, Gil thought he saw a tinge of blue around the baby's lips, but Eli grabbed hold of the bottle and dragged it up.

"Fussy little things, aren't they?"

Gil glanced over his shoulder. With her hands shoved into the back pockets of her jeans, wearing a bright pink T-shirt with the Butterfly Diner logo embroidered above her heart, Holly Saxon looked as if she'd been standing there for a while. The wind caught her dark ponytail and whipped it around her face, a face that was devoid of an expression Gil could decipher.

"He is a bit of a mystery," Gil confirmed. "I take it you talked to Luke?"

"I did. Mind if I sit?" She pointed to the wall he was resting on. He nodded and she joined him, stretched out her legs and rotated her sneaker-encased feet. "There are days I really need to take a few minutes." She leaned her head back and closed her eyes. "Then there are days that come as a complete surprise." She peeked a look at Eli. "He's cute."

"Not going to argue."

She assessed him, those dark eyes of hers as effective as an X-ray. "What's going on with you, Gil?"

"Going on?"

"Don't be cagey," she warned. "We've known each other most of our lives. This... baby thing."

"His name is Elijah."

"Right. Elijah." Her lips curved. "Come on. What's really going on, Gil?"

"It's a family thing" was the only explanation he could come up with without spilling all his secrets. "His mother needed some time and she left him with me." He shifted the bottle and tilted it up higher for Eli. "It's been… I don't know. Fun."

Holly laughed. "There's one word for it. You're a natural, according to Luke. He should know since he was, too. Not an easy accomplishment given how he grew up."

"No," Gil agreed. "No, it's not."

"I see it in you, too. I couldn't at first, when Luke dropped the news. Gil Hamilton playing daddy." She shook her head. "Who would have thought?"

"Gil the Thrill you mean."

"No." Her brow furrowed. "I don't see you that way anymore. I mean, yeah, we've had our differences."

"I took away your father's job." He sighed.

"Yes, you did." Her nod was slow. "But if you hadn't, if you hadn't hired Luke in his place, my life wouldn't be what it is now. I forgave you a long time ago, Gil. About Dad. About a lot of things. It probably would have been nice if I'd told you before now, but I'm not sure you were ready to hear it." She reached out and rested her hand on his arm. "You've changed. I can see it. It started a while ago, but since last Christmas, you can't hide it as well."

"Hide what?" He didn't like the idea of being read so easily.

"The regret. We all do the best we can at the time. When the bank went under and the town started to suffer, there wasn't anything you could do about it, not as long as your father—"

"Was alive?"

"—was mayor," Holly corrected and nodded at Eli. "I think he's finished."

"Oh. Right." He set the bottle down and scooped Eli onto his shoulder. Holly dug into the diaper bag for a cloth to drape under him. "You were saying?" The question came out even as he wondered if he wanted to hear the rest.

"Morland Hamilton was a difficult man. We all saw that. We all knew it. It was as if we had our own town villain and it gave us someone to blame when things went wrong."

"Easy enough to do." Gil's gut twisted. "He was responsible for a lot of what went wrong."

"He was," Holly agreed. "But I don't know that any of us stopped to think what it was like for you. As his son. I'm sorry I didn't see how difficult that must have been."

"Guilt by association," Gil explained away. "I understand."

"That doesn't make it right. This election, the recall. I've had a lot of time to think and I've come to the conclusion it isn't about you. It isn't *all* about you," she corrected at his skeptical look.

"It's enough about me," Gil said. "Just ask The Cocoon Club. Just ask Myra."

"Myra." Holly let out a strained laugh, reached over and wiped Eli's chin when he hiccupped, burped and drooled. "Tell me something. When you became mayor, how deep did you dig into what your father was involved in?"

"Deep enough I needed a delousing shower," Gil admitted, then came clean. "Not as deep as I probably should have."

"Myra and her husband lost their life savings when your father called in those loans through the bank. Sixty years of saving for a retirement her Dennis didn't live to enjoy because of the stress. Myra blames your father. Morland saw the bank's collapse coming and did nothing to stop it. A lot of people still believe—"

"That he triggered the collapse in the first place? Yeah." Gil tightened his hold on Eli. Feeling that little heart beat against his chest was the only thing keeping him calm. "He did that. And a lot more. As he tried to dig himself free of the hole, the deeper he sank. I want to say he had remorse for what he did, but he didn't. He only felt bad because he got caught. I told him that the night he died. I told him a lot of things," he added with an unexpected laugh. "Twenty-eight years of pent-up anger and disappointment just blew, and the next morning he was gone."

"Leaving you to deal with the fallout of what he'd done."

He didn't particularly care for the sympathy he heard in her voice. "Don't make me out to be some kind of hero in all this, Holly."

"Oh, I'm not." She stood, reached out and took Eli from him, settled the baby against her own shoulder and patted his back in a way that allowed him to produce an epic burp. "You were caught up in the riptide of being a Hamilton and you played your part to the hilt. That said, you could have easily slipped down that same path Morland took. But you didn't. You came close." She turned her head, pressed her lips to Eli's temple. "But you didn't. And that makes you more of a man than your father ever could have hoped to be."

Something akin to hope bloomed inside his chest. As much as Myra's words had hurt, Holly's could almost heal. "Why are you telling me all this?"

"Because I think you needed to hear it from someone who has known you a long time. The Gil I knew for the past two decades never would have accepted a baby being left on his porch. He would have turned him over to the authorities and never looked back. I see who you are now. And you're someone I can consider a friend. Especially since you're keeping such adorable company." She slid Eli back into his carrier. "Don't let your father continue to define you, Gil. You've started coming into your own and you're still mayor. Maybe only for a few weeks. Maybe for another term. Election or no election, mayor or not, you're in the position to be someone's entire world now." She stroked Eli's head and smiled at

Gil. "Believe me, there's nothing better than that."

A weight he hadn't realized he'd been carrying lifted. He sat straighter, felt lighter. "Thank you. I can still do better."

"You bet you can," Holly said with a determined snort. "Oh, there was one other thing I wanted to tell you when I came over here."

"Yeah?"

"Yeah." Her smile widened. "I'm going to be needing that car seat and those boxes back by next spring."

"You are, huh?" Gil arched a brow. "Not according to Luke."

"Luke doesn't know everything. Yet," she added. "I'm telling him tonight. Don't want to give you the chance to ruin the surprise. It's just one baby this time," she added when he opened his mouth to ask. "I had them check on that first thing. I'm sure our town's baby whisperer Calliope would have been happy to confirm there aren't twins in here, but this time, I thought I'd do it the old-fashioned way." She hesitated. "You going to be okay, Gil?"

Gil nodded and got to his feet. "I think I just might be. Thanks, Holly."

"You're welcome. Now, how about you and Eli come in to the diner for some pie."

"Blackberry?" he asked and picked up Eli's carrier. "With ice cream?"

"You've got it."

CHAPTER SIX

"LEAH, JUDGE RAMOS's office is on the line," Callie called out from her desk in the reception area of Ellis Family Law. "She can see you at two, but you'll have to make it quick. She's heading out for a long weekend with her family."

Leah opened her mouth to respond, but she was too stunned to eke out a sentence. She blinked, rereading the page in front of her, and then sorted through the subsequent pages that had been sent over with the requested minutes from the town council meeting. This wasn't possible.

"Leah? You hear me?"

"What?" Leah blinked, then processed. "Sorry. Right. Two o'clock." Leah glanced at her phone and cringed. "It'll be tight, but I'll take it." She shoved all the papers into the envelope they'd arrived in and got to her feet.

In the days since she'd acted as unofficial mediator between Gil and the Cocoon Club, she'd been playing catch-up. She'd written two wills, a family trust and consulted on a new partnership agreement that could bring Butterfly Harbor its first IPA brewery if everything fell into place.

Her days now were a far cry from those spent as a criminal defense attorney, a career she'd happily walked away from, thanks to her uncle. But she had to admit, there was a familiar ping of excitement when it came to applying her skills in an effort to make sure Gil could keep Eli. It wasn't a done deal. Not by any means, but the road was paved. Now all she needed to do was extricate herself from the situation before her emotional involvement compromised things.

"Compromise you, more like," she muttered as she picked up the manila envelope containing the foster care paperwork and stuffed it, along with the board records, into her bag. Gil Hamilton's sudden parental predicament had wiggled its way under, around and over her defenses. Her face warmed at the memory of Gil leaning in, stepping toward her, the desire in his eyes clear. He'd almost kissed her.

And she'd almost let him.

"No. No, no, no." Not going to think about that. Not going to think about how much she'd wanted to know what it was like to feel his mouth on hers, to confirm that he was as good a kisser as she'd imagined him to be. And she had imagined it. A lot in the last few days.

It didn't make sense that she had feelings, actual *feelings* for Gil Hamilton.

Except it might. If what she was reading in those council meeting minutes was accurate, then he really wasn't the bad guy so many in town believed him to be. "It's not true." But even as she mumbled to herself, she knew it was. "I'm not going to let myself believe it."

"Believe what?" Callie poked her head in the open door. "Did I miss something with the Pavarels' living trust?"

"No." Leah looked away before Callie could ask more questions. "Just talking to myself. You have lunch plans with Bobby?"

"You know it." Callie grinned. "Thursday

is roast turkey and stuffing day at the diner. We never miss it."

Leah felt her stomach growl, just thinking about it. "I'm probably going to work at home the rest of the day. Why don't you forward all the office calls to me and take the rest of the day."

"Seriously?" Callie's eyes brightened and she sat up straight. "You sure? No, wait. Never mind." She waved her hands as if she could erase her question. "You never offer unless you're sure." She picked up the phone and hit a few buttons. "There. Done. Too late to change your mind."

Leah smiled as Callie gathered her belongings. The young woman had been just out of college as a prelaw student when she'd responded to Leah's posting looking for a paralegal and office administrator. They'd gotten along immediately, and after hearing of Callie's desire to stay close to home to be near her family and take online classes toward her law degree, the fit was perfect. She wore her red hair cut straight to her shoulders and had a permanent sparkle in her green eyes. A sparkle Leah hoped wouldn't fade the further she went into her chosen profession.

"I'll walk to the diner with you." Callie locked the door behind them. The hanging sign in the front yard identifying "Ellis Family Law" squeaked against the cool breeze.

Leah had had the sign made over in bright white-and-gold lettering when she took over the practice. She'd also had the one-story bungalow repainted white and yellow with accents of gray. It was a better match to the rest of the town than the dark brown she imagined her uncle had found on discount somewhere. The space served a small family lawyer well, with its homey atmosphere and laid-back, beach-friendly design. Situated just around the corner from Monarch Lane and only a few blocks from City Hall. Her uncle Benjamin Ellis had done well in establishing both himself and the practice, and taking it over had been somewhat of a breeze.

Last year, she'd finished prettying the place up by hiring Lori Knight, a woman whose gardening talent made Mother Nature look incompetent, to redo the landscaping. Now the office bungalow burst with bright color. The whole project had been completed with one of Charlie Bradley's homemade butterfly baths—bird baths filled with marbles and water for the insects and bees to use. That and the plethora of lavender, milkweed and other pollinator-attracting plants had Leah feeling as if she—and her office—truly belonged in Butterfly Harbor.

"Can I ask you a question?" Callie slung her purse over her shoulder as they headed down to the corner of Monarch Lane.

"Better than anyone else I've ever met." Leah crossed her arms over her chest against the chill in the air. "Always an excellent talent for a lawyer."

"Thanks," Callie chuckled. "What happens when you become mayor?"

Leah blew out a breath. She shouldn't have been surprised. The election was all anyone wanted to talk about these days. "There's no use asking that question until it happens, Callie."

"Actually, there is. If you win, there's only, like, three weeks before you get sworn into office. What happens to the law practice? Are you moving to City Hall? Do I need to find another job?"

Okay, Callie had a point. They hadn't had an in-depth discussion about what would happen if Leah was elected mayor. Mainly because until a few weeks ago, Leah honestly hadn't anticipated winning. She did wish, however, that Callie had asked this when Leah had more time to talk.

"I have to answer some questions of my own before I can answer yours," Leah said carefully. "But I can put your mind to rest that I don't foresee any situation where I wouldn't want you working with or for me. You've made yourself invaluable, Callie. Wherever I end up, whether you want to look for another job is going to be entirely your decision."

"Okay, great." Leah would bet good money Callie had been holding that breath she released for weeks. "Bobby said that's what you'd say, but I wanted to be sure."

They made a left on Monarch Lane, and Leah picked up her pace toward City Hall. She'd chosen a bad day to walk to work and an even worse day to wear new shoes.

"Are you heading over to talk to Gil about his emergency foster parent application?" Callie asked.

"How did you know about that?" She'd purposely kept all the paperwork to herself.

"I'm good, remember?" Callie's cheeky grin made her eyes spark. "You were on a tear the other morning when you went over to his house, but that didn't last. Next thing I hear around town is that someone left a baby with Gil and that's why he's been AWOL from work. Then there was the whole Cocoon Club thing..." She shrugged. "You forget I clear the office computers' browser histories. You were investigating conflicts of interest between political rivals. Math wasn't exactly my strong suit, but I can manage simple addition."

"On second thought, maybe I should just turn the practice over to you outright." Leah tried to sound teasing. "I've drawn up the initial paperwork. Gil doesn't want Eli to end up in the system and I agree with him."

"It's good to be mayor," Callie said as they reached the diner's front door. "If Eli had been left with anyone else—"

"But he wasn't." It had occurred to her last night that that may have been Eli's mother's intention. Leaving Eli with the mayor could be the mother's means of circumventing child protective services. Should she come back, it would be easier to regain custody from Gil than it would be from a government agency, and Gil would just hand him over to avoid any kind of scandal. Leah's mood soured. Sometimes she hated thinking so ill of people. "I can only work with what I've been given. As his attorney—"

"It's your job to find a way to protect Eli according to the law but to do whatever's truly in his favor." Callie shrugged. "I get it, don't worry. I just think it's interesting, is all. Eli's mother couldn't have picked a better person to leave him with. Logistics-wise, at least. Could she?"

No. She really couldn't have.

The conversation ended as Callie entered the diner to meet her boyfriend. Leah walked away, her heels clacking against the sidewalk en route to City Hall. It wasn't just the documents she needed him to sign for his emergency foster parent application, but the list of family attorneys she was recommending. While she hadn't been able to pinpoint any conflict of interest per se, she wasn't comfortable with the situation. She wasn't comfortable with most situations where a lot of emotion was involved. Criminal law had taught her that.

Baby Eli was already becoming a problem for her. And, okay, maybe it was a good idea to put some distance between herself and the mayor. It was a lot less complicated being his opponent than being his friend. It was also a lot easier to think badly of someone when you didn't know them very well. "Or when you don't know their secrets."

Yep. Better to cut things off now and step away before her heart got any more tangled and confused than it already was.

By the time she reached the check-in desk, her feet were screaming almost as loudly as the infant inside the building. "That been going on for long?" Leah had to raise her voice as Jessie rolled her eyes.

"About an hour. I'm ready to wave the white flag and surrender."

Leah chuckled. "Hang in there." When she reached Helena's outer office, she found herself scanning the room for Cocoon Club members, just to be safe. Instead, she saw Helena pry off a pair of noise-cancelling headphones just as Eli let out a screech that could have attracted dogs. "Does he have a minute?"

"He has as many as you need. Go on in." Helena replaced her headphones and settled back into her typing.

Leah knocked before opening the door, then poked in her head, as if waiting for something inside to explode. "Gil?" She rapped her knuckles on the frame again, saw him turn from his place in front of one of the giant plate-glass windows overlooking the back courtyard. Eli was resting against Gil's shoulder and howling so hard he was vibrating.

"Leah." The relief in his voice had that sympathy she'd been feeling for him kicking up a few notches. "He won't stop. He's been fussy all morning, but this is...." He shook his head, rubbed a hand against Eli's back. "He barely drank any of his breakfast. I don't know what to do. He's breaking my heart."

And with the helpless, concerned look on his face, Gil slid right into hers.

Gil definitely wasn't the only one in over his head.

She set her bag down on the sofa and approached, reaching out to check if Eli had a fever. The baby blinked at her, hiccupped a few more times, then quieted, shoving his fist in his mouth and gnawing. Ah.

"Are you serious, little guy?" Gil brought his chin into his chest to look at the baby's tearstained face. "I offered to buy you a pony and you kept going. All it took was her?" He let out a slow breath. "I should have called you hours ago."

The idea that Gil thought of her as an infant lifeline had her shifting her gaze away from the mayor. "Sometimes a baby just has to cry." And it sure looked as if Eli had been having a whopper of a day. She located the diaper bag and dug around inside until she found one of the gel teething rings she'd seen the other day. She held out her arms. "How about I give you a break for a few minutes?"

"That would be great, thanks." Gil handed off Eli, expertly maneuvering the cloth diaper over Leah's shoulder as she cuddled the baby close and offered him the ring. The second he had it in his mouth, he began to chew. Gil's expression shifted to mild embarrassment. "You're kidding me."

"You aren't a mind reader, Gil." She swayed back and forth. "And there is a learning curve for parenting. Most people get a good nine months to prepare. You can't expect to excel at it right out of the gate."

He was definitely a man drowning in blink-and-I'm-a-parent syndrome. That said, the office had gotten a serious shift in decor since she'd last been here. He'd moved a lot of the furniture over to one side of the room and arranged a playpen and crib in their place. He'd made a makeshift changing station out of an antique dresser and she wondered how long it would be before he regretted that choice. Put all of it together, however, and it signaled that Gil really was taking fostering seriously.

Which only added to her growing confusion about the man and whether anyone—herself included—really knew him at all.

"Maybe I can't excel at parenthood," Gil said with a bit of envy in his voice. "But it sure seems like you can." Someone definitely needed a nap, and it wasn't the baby in her arms.

"Give Sebastian at Cat's Eye Books a call," she suggested. "Have him set aside a few books on parenting for you. He's been reading up on them anyway, since he and Brooke are expecting."

"They already have Mandy," Gil frowned. "What does he have to read about? Do things change that much?"

"In sixteen years?" Leah offered a less-than-sympathetic smile. "I think there's probably some new information to consider."

"I have to write that down to remember to call him." He sat behind his desk and scribbled a note. "Nothing has been sticking in my brain these days."

"You'll find your footing," she assured him as she quietly hummed to Eli.

"I'm just glad you turned up when you did." He looked up at her. "What did bring you by?"

"Paperwork." His gratitude had her swallowing hard. *Keep it professional. Keep things calm. Do not let yourself think about that almost kiss in the hall.* "The emergency foster parent documents. I have an appointment with Judge Ramos in about an hour." She shifted her hold and let Eli snuggle in the crook of her arm as he slurped.

"That was fast." Gil blinked in shock.

"The word *emergency* opens a few lanes

in the red-tape race. I agree we should get Eli protected as soon as possible." She pressed her lips against the top of Eli's head. He wasn't warm. He didn't have a fever, but his breathing seemed off. He was occasionally taking short, uneven breaths. Probably just overexerted himself, screaming the place down. "It's not the best timing, I know. I'm sure you're not feeling as committed to him at the moment as you once were."

"I have no intention of being a fair-weather parent."

Leah's eyes went wide. "All right." The sharpness in his voice belied issues she couldn't begin to fathom. "I meant that as a joke, but good to know."

"Sorry." He shook his head. "I'm all over the place today. I guess maybe we both are."

Sometimes babies just needed to cry, she thought again. And sometimes their surrogate fathers needed to talk. Whether they wanted to or not. But that would only lead her into trouble. Instead, she shifted to the one subject she could safely control.

She walked over to the sofa, dug out the envelope and handed it to Gil, then re-adjusted the teething ring for Eli when it slipped out of his hold. “It’s all pretty standard.” Gil opened the envelope and pulled out the papers.

She stepped closer to the desk. “All it needs… Oh. All right.” She sighed when he flipped the pages to the sticky note. His pen barely seemed to have time to touch the paper before he signed. “That’s one way to do it. You really should have read it first.”

“If I can’t trust you with this, then I can’t trust anyone about anything,” Gil said and flipped the pages closed. “So what’s next?”

“Next I get the judge to sign off, and it’ll be expedited through social services.”

Gil flinched. “No way around that, I suppose.”

Callie’s comments about it being good to be mayor echoed back at her. “No, there’s not. Not if you want to solidify any kind of future with him.” Everything needed to be kept on the up-and-up if Eli was going to have real stability. “They’ll assign you a caseworker and they’ll do a few evaluations, but, in the meantime, Eli will be able to stay with you. Unless they find something wrong.”

“Like what?” Clearly the idea of that happening hadn't crossed his mind. "I have a nice house, a good job..."

She did her best to keep her face expressionless.

"I have a good job for now." There was an odd tone in his voice, one she couldn't identify no matter how hard she tried. She glanced up to try to read his face, but he was back on his feet and wandered to the other window.

"Potential employment issues aside." Leah attempted to break through the tension circling the room. "As far as Eli's guardianship is concerned, you're in a really solid position here, Gil. But there are a few things that could help."

"Something other than surviving my recall vote?"

Refusing to be baited, she sat in the chair on the other side of his desk and settled Eli on her lap. "You could turn one of those bedrooms in your mausoleum into a nursery."

"Mausoleum?" Was that humor or offense in his voice? "My house? That's how it feels to you?"

"It's a bit—" she struggled for the least inoffensive word "—cold."

Gil laughed, one harsh sound that told her he didn't think she was wrong. "Hamilton houses have never been known for their warmth. All right. Criticism noted and taken under advisement. Add a nursery. Got it."

"Nothing fancy," she added quickly. "Just something a bit more child oriented. The room closest to your room would be best. And babyproofing. Even at this age, may as well get a jump on that to show you're serious about the future." Again, she wondered if he had any idea what he was getting into. A lifetime was really a big promise to make to someone. One of the many reasons she'd never made that promise herself.

Gil nodded, turned and seemed to have blinked away the doubt as he grabbed a pen and added to his note from before. "The stuff Luke and Holly loaned me is a good start, but I'll need more of this—"

"Don't get carried away," Leah warned. "Keep things simple. Low-key. Don't—"

"Don't throw money at the problem?" Okay, now she heard the bitterness. "Don't worry about that. What else?"

"The sooner you settle into a routine, the better. For both of you."

"Right." He glanced up, expecting her to go on.

"You should get him on to your health insurance as soon as possible. And established with a pediatrician here in town." She hesitated before plunging ahead. "Character references would go far to bolster your case."

"Character references." He arched a brow as if she didn't see a glaring problem with that suggestion. "I don't see that working out the way you think it should. I'm trying to keep Eli, not shine a spotlight on why I shouldn't be able to."

She wished she could argue, but considering Myra's reaction to Gil's sudden parenthood, she couldn't dismiss his doubts. "I'm sure there are some people… Helena, for example?" She indicated his receptionist on the other side of the closed door. "Jessie downstairs. Maybe BethAnn Bottomley?"

"The fact you can only name three people in this entire town who might be willing to vouch for my character and ability to parent says everything about that idea."

It wasn't hurt she heard in his voice. But

disappointment. Resignation. Regret. And there wasn't anything she could do about any of those. "How about we focus on what you can control. Routine, a good home environment. A good support system wouldn't hurt. Family—"

"Uh, the family I've got left really isn't worth mentioning."

"There isn't anyone else other than your brother?"

"You mean the *half* brother who's in jail and has been charged with felony arson and assaulting Jo Bertoletti and Declan Cartwright? No." He shook his head. "There's no one."

The fact he was essentially alone in the world explained so much about him. "What is going on with Christopher?"

"The sheriff in Durante's a friend. He's kept me up-to-date. Christopher has a public defender, and his first hearing is coming up. The day after our next debate, actually." His flash of a smile didn't come close to reaching his eyes.

"Are you going?"

"I hadn't planned to. He doesn't want me

there, or so he told his lawyer after I requested to be put on the visitor's list."

Now, that surprised her. "You want to see your brother?"

"*Want* to? No. But there's a number of topics the two of us really should discuss. Not the least of which is our father."

Leah looked back down at Eli. "I know the situation with Christopher is complicated."

"*Complicated* is about ten miles in the rearview mirror," Gil said. "He believes it's my fault my father never acknowledged him or was a part of his life. Funny how I can be blamed for a situation I knew nothing about until after my father was dead."

"You don't owe me an explanation, Gil."

"I know. But it's not like you haven't already heard some of my biggest secrets." He made an attempt at a laugh even as Leah glanced guiltily at her bag.

"How my father dealt with or didn't deal with Christopher is one mistake of my father's I'm not taking ownership of. I can fix a lot of things he did, but I can't go back and stop him from abandoning Christopher and his mother." The pained expression struck her hard. "I didn't know about him, Leah. I didn't know anything about him until after my father died and I was going through his papers."

"But Christopher knew about you," Leah said softly.

"Oh, he knew. And from the one meeting I did have with Christopher after his arrest, it's clear he's chosen to blame me for everything that's wrong with his life."

"Maybe because it's easier to blame you than to admit your father never cared about or even loved him."

Gil started to respond, then went very still. "You do have a way of cutting right down to the bones of things, don't you? You have an appointment soon with Judge Ramos, right?"

"Right." Leah stood and walked Eli over to his crib and laid him down.

When she returned to the desk, Gil picked up the documents he'd signed to hand to her. He looked down and frowned. "What's this?" He flipped through the pages. "A list of family lawyers?"

"Oh, that. Yeah." She blew out a breath. Passing him on to another lawyer would be the easy—and cowardly—thing to do. "Just…here." She reached over and snatched the paper free of the clip. "Contingency plan. Disregard." She couldn't believe what she was saying as she gathered her things. She wanted distance from him. She needed distance. And yet…

And yet she couldn't bring herself to walk away either from Gil or Eli.

"Well, that's good to hear." The relief on Gil's face was almost comical. "I know it sounds crazy, but the idea of working with another attorney on this—" He shook his head. "That might just push me over this teetering edge."

Something tight inside of her uncoiled. Whatever it was, she didn't want to identify it. She was helping someone in need. Two someones. Maybe she really had turned that corner and now considered Gil a friend, but that was all he was. A friend helping a friend. Despite the fact she was probably going to push him out of his job.

Despite her inability to get that almost kiss out of her head.

"I'll email you copies once I'm back in my office," she told him as she headed to the door. “If anything else comes up, I’ll give you a call.”

“Okay.” He walked behind her, held open the door when she pulled it open. “Thanks, Leah. For…everything. It almost feels as if I’m not in this thing alone.”

She nodded, mainly because, while she wasn’t cowardly enough to send him to another attorney, she was definitely leery enough not to admit the truth.

That she was 100 percent on his side.

CHAPTER SEVEN

"THANKS FOR HELPING me with all this, guys." After grabbing three beers from the fridge, Gil handed one to Hunter MacBride and the other to Ozzy Lakeman and kept the third for himself. Eli was settled once more on the kitchen table, this time in his carrier, batting at the hanging stuffed octopus Gil had rigged over his head.

"I'd say it was no problem, but something tells me my back is going to be giving me fits tomorrow." Hunter attempted to stretch out a few kinks, then seemed to think better of it and just accepted the beer.

"Come running with me tomorrow morning," Ozzy goaded as he raised his bottle in a toast. "Guaranteed to work out all the aches and pains."

"I've seen you run on the beach," Hunter said. "I've no need to train for a triathlon, thanks."

Gil grinned and glanced over at Eli, who was happily kicking up a storm.

Hunter and Ozzy had been the only two people he could think to call to help him move the furniture out of the room located next to his. Now that furniture and other pieces that suddenly felt impractical had been stashed in a number of the other bedrooms. Not his father's, though. Morland's room was one he had no desire to go into at all. Something he'd made very clear when Hunter had accidentally popped open the last door at the end of the upstairs hall.

He'd met Hunter, a photojournalist turned suspense author, in college, and last year, Gil had hired him to document the refurbishment of the Liberty Lighthouse, one of Butterfly Harbor's many neglected structures. Not only had the legend of said lighthouse shifted Hunter's career path, Hunter subsequently fell head over heels for recent arrival Kendall Davidson, who had been doing all the restoration of the lighthouse herself. Now the two were married and raising Hunter's orphaned niece, Phoebe, as their own.

Funny, the twists life took sometimes. Hunter aside, Gil never would have thought

Ozzy would be someone Gil could reach out to for help. It should have. Ozzy had always had a reputation for being a person everyone could count on, in good times and bad. Ozzy, the deputy turned firefighter, who was now an almost-married father of one.

"Well." Gil raised his bottle. "I thank you and so does Eli."

"To the little man of few words," Hunter echoed and toasted the baby.

"I'm just glad they don't make furniture like that anymore," Ozzy semigroaned. "Morticia and Gomez Addams might come calling on you to buy it all."

Gil grimaced, recalling Leah's comment in his office. She didn't like his home. That much had been made clear. And if she didn't feel comfortable here, how would Eli? "Does this place feel like a mausoleum to you?"

"What? No." Ozzy said quickly, then leaning over to look down the hall, shrugged. "Maybe a little. It's got its own personality. Just not very—help me out here, Hunter. You're the writer."

"Nope." Hunter shook his head. "You have to dig yourself out of this one."

"It's that bad?" Gil asked.

"No. Not bad. Just..." Hunter let out a breath. "Okay, fine. It's very angular. Sharp. Polished. It reminds me of—"

"Your father," Ozzy finished for him with a dark glint in his eye. "Definitely has a Morland Hamilton feel to it."

"Well, it was his house." Why, with everything he knew about his father, did he continue to defend him?

"It's still his house," Hunter said. "He'd be so pleased to know you kept a shrine to him."

"Oh, come on," Gil tried to laugh, but the words had struck deep. "That's not—"

"Exhibit A." Ozzy stepped into the hall and pulled down one of the framed photos off the wall. "Who's this?"

"Ah, that's my father," Gil said slowly, looking at the black-and-white photograph with a critical eye. "And that's..."

"Someone you can't name. Let's try again." Ozzy set his beer down and walked farther down the hall, this time coming back with a stack of pictures.

Something jumped inside Gil at the idea of those pictures coming down. Something odd and uncomfortable.

"Where are you in these pictures?" Ozzy asked.

"Here." Gil pointed to an image of his father and BethAnn Bottomley's husband, the late senator. "I'm right here in the corner."

"A bit out of focus, aren't you?" Hunter narrowed his eyes and leaned forward. "Where are your school photos? Graduation pictures? Heck, what about your senior football portraits? Weren't you the high school quarterback for a year?"

"Try three," Ozzy muttered under his breath. "He was also class president and prom king."

And none of it, looking back, despite outward appearances, had brought Gil even a shred of joy. He knew very well why his father didn't display any photographic evidence of Gil's youthful achievements. Because to Morland, Gil hadn't accomplished anything of value despite being the one to push Gil into all those activities in the first place.

"As someone who almost had to take on extra hours to pay for Phoebe's second grade pictures," Hunter said, "I've got those suckers all over the house. And yet here? The only place we see you is standing right in front of us."

"I had to upgrade my cell phone to fit all my pictures of Hope. Oh!" Ozzy dug into his pocket. "Speaking of which, I've got new ones—"

"What we're trying to say," Hunter said as he accepted Ozzy's phone and scrolled through the new images of Hope. "Gosh, she's a beauty. Anyway, what we're trying to say, Gil, is that your father's gone. And even when he was here, he was always more about his own accomplishments than yours. Speaking as a father, any shrine in this house should have been to you, not himself."

"I didn't need that," Gil lied defensively, even as he remembered the endless hours he'd spent wishing his father would once, just once, say how proud he was of something Gil had done. "That wasn't the kind of man he was."

"It's good that you know that," Ozzy said. "But given we both just fractured our spines moving furniture around for Eli, maybe think about what atmosphere you plan to raise him in. Hunter's right. Your father's gone, Gil. He has been for more than four years. Maybe it's time you let him stop dictating your life."

LEAH HAD PROMISED herself she'd stay away. From Gil, from Eli, and from the temptations both of them presented.

Good thing she wasn't being held to account for self-promises, because she clearly had no intention of keeping them.

Here she stood, this time on a Sunday morning, on the front porch of Gil's house, avoiding the overbearing glare of carved jack-o-lanterns in seemingly sinister moods. She set the gift box down by the door. She stood up straight, hands on her hips, debating whether to ring the bell. She knew what she should do. She should leave.

But her feet—or maybe it was her heart—didn't seem inclined to follow orders today. After leaving Gil's office with his paperwork signed off on and then processed, she'd sworn she'd keep their contact limited to legalities about Eli. She had people relying on her, people who had invested a lot of their time and energy, determined to get her elected as mayor. She'd made a commitment and she had plans for the town. Ones that hadn't changed just because she'd begun to see Gil in a different light.

Leah was not going to let guilt push her

out of the election. If social services decided to reject Gil based solely on his lack of employment, that said more about them than Gil. But would they?

Maybe. She chewed on her bottom lip. Maybe they would. If he lost.

Yeah, she shouldn't be here. Leah pivoted, took a step, only to have the front door open and Gil appear.

"Leah." Did he have to look so happy to see her? And did he have to look so unapologetically appealing with Eli strapped to his chest? He wore cargo shorts today and deck shoes along with a simple white T-shirt that had no business looking as good as it did on him. She'd often heard him compared to a surfer-movie extra without a script, and she saw it now, with that sandy-blond hair of his and that endless dimple that had her own lips twitching. "I was just about to take Eli for his first walk on the beach. Join us?"

"No, that's okay. I just wanted to drop this off." She pointed to the box. "It's one of those diaper-disposal things. My sister swears by it and I thought you could use it."

"Well Eli can, that's for sure." Gil chuckled. "That was really nice of you. Thanks."

"I'll just—" She stepped around him, picked up the box and set it inside. "That was all." She gave him a quick wave and moved toward the steps.

"Please, why don't you come with us?"

Go with them? On a family beach outing? Oh, that was really going against every promise she'd made to herself. "Ah, I really shouldn't." But darn it, she wanted to. Eli kicked both feet as if jump-starting a transportation device.

"Why not?" Gil asked. "It's a gorgeous day and Frankie's hosting a youth water-safety class. Thought I'd make an appearance and lend my support for the program she's proposing to the town council." He stepped back, looked her up and down. "You're already dressed for it."

"Um, yeah." She tugged her baggy sweater tighter, crossed her bare legs and rocked forward on her heels. "On Sundays, I give my wardrobe a rest. Elastic waists and oversize shirts and sweaters." She felt her cheeks warm and wondered why discussing her wardrobe had her blushing.

"You have actual legs. Great legs," he added with that adorable grin of his. "I would have bet a year's salary you didn't own a pair of flat shoes."

"I like to surprise people," she said. "You seem to be doing better today."

"Better? Hang on." He stepped inside long enough to grab the diaper bag along with a larger tote containing what she could see was a blanket, drinks and a small fabric cooler for Eli's formula. "Sorry. Better than what?" He pulled the door closed behind him and locked up.

"Better than you were doing at your office when I saw you last." She didn't want to bring up the subject of his brother again or anything else that might dim the lively light in his eyes. She'd been worried. That's what had really brought her here this morning. There was only so much one person could take, and despite his protests to the contrary, she was certain Gil's overburdened shoulders couldn't carry much more.

"Oh, that. Yeah, I am. Hunter and Ozzy came by yesterday to help me move stuff around. I have a furniture delivery coming later this week for the nursery. And I even ordered a new sofa for the living room. It has actual cushions and padding."

Leah laughed. "You really are making some changes."

"You sure you don't want to come with us? Nothing better on a Sunday than a walk on the beach. Come on. Loosen up. Have some fun," he urged when she opened her mouth to refuse again. "You don't want to miss Eli putting his toes in the ocean for the first time, do you?"

As if waiting for his cue, Eli squealed and threw his hands in the air.

She had work to do at home. Work that could wait until tomorrow when she was back in the office. Work she'd set aside last night when she'd buckled down and read through the records of each and every single council meeting of Gil Hamilton's tenure.

"*You're* telling *me* to loosen up?" She eyed him as her resolve slipped. "You aren't exactly known for your love of frivolity."

"I think Eli brings it out in me. Or maybe you do." Gil's smile was pure charm. No wonder so many people fell under the Hamilton spell. "I'll even treat you to a mocha shake at the diner on the way."

"Eli's feet in the ocean and now a shake?"

Leah feigned being impressed. “How can I possibly say no?”

“And now we know how to win you over.” He put his hand on her arm. “There’s just one thing…” He trailed off, lifted his free hand and tucked her hair behind her ear. She shivered against his touch, the barest, softest touch of his skin against hers. She watched, her breath caught in her chest, as he leaned toward her and pressed his mouth to hers.

It was, Leah thought as her mind emptied and her system jolted, quite possibly the most perfect kiss she’d ever experienced. Gentle, coaxing, teasing and utterly, completely divine. She’d always believed kissing had been overrated but clearly she hadn’t been presented with the right partner. A partner who had her taking a step closer, rising up on her toes and kissing him back.

An excited squeal broke them apart and for a moment, they stood there, staring wide-eyed at each other even as their lips twitched.

“I’m going to take that as a squeal of approval,” Gil said. Eli reached up and grabbed hold of Leah’s hair.

She laughed, bent down and pressed a kiss

to the baby's forehead. "You little matchmaker."

"Bah! Gah ba ba ba!" Eli finished his response with a big wet raspberry.

"The king has spoken," Gil pronounced.

"Gil, wait." Leah grabbed his arm when he moved away. "The kiss was nice, but—"

"Nice?" Gil's eyes widened in disapproval. "I must be losing my touch."

Hardly. One thing she did not doubt was his romancing capabilities. She needed to get this out before she overthought things or, worse, talked herself into surrendering to what she was beginning to want more than anything. "Gil, we need to keep things friendly. You know what I mean," she added with a laugh she couldn't contain. "Things are more complicated than you want to admit right now. You have a lot going on, and I'm sure you see me as a nice distraction—"

"You keep using the word *nice* as if it means something else."

"Gil, if we let things get...complicated between us, people are going to talk, and we don't want that."

"Maybe you don't."

"I know you don't want to have to consider it, but the election is still happening. And I'm sorry, but I'm not going to withdraw from the race." There. She'd gotten it out. Finally.

The humor faded from his eyes. "Is that what you think I'm doing? Running some kind of seduction scheme to make you drop out?"

"Well, no, of course not." She looked away and flexed her fingers because she couldn't think of anything else to do with her suddenly shaking hands. "But I mean, yes, it occurred to me." She crossed her arms over her chest and looked up at him, wishing he could somehow read the jumble of thoughts she couldn't seem to keep together.

"What was it you said the other day? That you'd left the election on the front porch?" He took a step down, then another until he was on the walkway to the house. "It's recently been brought to my attention that I haven't done a lot things that have made me happy in life. I woke up this morning determined to change that," Gil admitted. "Thing one was taking Eli to the beach. And thing two was kissing you." His smile returned.

"The election? That's on the porch. At least for today."

"And what about tomorrow?" Why, oh, why did she have to ask such questions when she didn't want to hear an answer?

He took a deep breath, looked around the street of houses that surrounded them. Houses that created this wonderful little town she'd decided to call home. The town he'd spent the past few years fighting for in his own way. It was, she thought, a bit like watching a prince surveying his inherited kingdom. But she no longer saw any superiority or entitlement on his face. She saw…

Pride. Appreciation. Love.

"Tomorrow the campaign begins again," he told her. "And for the record?" He bent his face close to hers and smiled until that twinkle sparked in his blue eyes. "I'm going to win."

She couldn't help it. She laughed. "You think so, huh?"

"I have to." He reached down and caught one of Eli's hands in his. "For him."

THE SPRING MONTHS were Gil's favorite time of year but fall was making a pretty big play for second place.

This year, at least. Normally he'd be neck-deep in Monarch Festival plans, where the parks and streets were lined with weekend vendors selling all sorts of handcrafted items and treats, when tourists crowded stores and eateries and the beach. Between his office being inundated with vendor-license applications and booth-placement demands and scheduling events that would appeal to all ages, not to mention booking entertainment acts and catering services for the private events, he hadn't had a chance to truly appreciate the relaxed season for what it was.

Maybe his affection for the homemade apple cider Calliope sold by the gallon up at Duskywing Farm was getting the better of him. Or perhaps it was the salty ocean air carrying an unexpected hint of cinnamon and promise. Or he could be honest with himself and admit the elements of said season had nothing to do with how he was feeling—as if he could set all his cares aside. It was more likely the company he was keeping.

As he and Leah rounded the corner, the crowd outside the Butterfly Diner had him rethinking his offer of a mocha shake, but a promise was a promise. He guided Leah ahead of him, beneath the winding trellis of Monarch butterflies arcing over the door. She glanced back at him and he jutted his chin toward the take-out counter.

"Be with you in a sec." Twyla, Holly's long-time server, acknowledged them as she motioned for a table of six to follow her to the back corner, the streak in her long dark hair a neon green this week.

"Place is hopping." Leah craned her neck to look around.

"It's been like this since we opened at six." Holly strode by and set a now-empty tray on the counter under the pass-through window. "You two in a rush?"

"Nope." Gil grinned. "We're just headed to the beach to check out Frankie's new swimming class. Thought we'd stop by for a couple of shakes."

"Shakes, great. Mocha?" Holly took a moment to hold out her finger to Eli, who immediately tried to shove it into his mouth. "Teething, huh? I bet that hurts."

"Mmmmfffth!" Eli confirmed.

"Sorry about that. Leah, could you hold this?" Gil shifted the diaper bag around so Leah could grab it, then pulled open one of the pockets to produce the teething ring he'd almost forgotten to pack.

"Kevin, two mocha shakes, please," Holly called over her shoulder when Eli finally relinquished his hold. "Be about five minutes."

"We'll get out of the way," Leah said.

"You're fine. Unless you'd like to join the Cocoon Club," Holly said with a warning glint in her eye. "They haven't stopped staring at the two of you since you walked in."

"Told you," Leah muttered, but as she turned, her smile appeared and she waved at the table filled with suspicious seniors. "I'll be right back." She slung the strap of the diaper bag over his shoulder and made her way through the crowd.

"Did you tell Luke?" Gil asked Holly once they were alone.

"About the baby? I did." Holly couldn't take her eyes off Eli. "He should be coming out of his shocked state any moment now. Speaking of, he said something about needing to talk to you."

He swallowed hard. Only one thing Luke would be wanting to talk to him about. "Should I stop by the station?"

"No, he's out on the beach with Simon. He

wanted him to take Frankie's water-safety class now that he's been swimming more. Twins are hanging out with my dad and Serena at her office today. She has a litter of puppies to entertain them with."

"Serena always has a litter of puppies, it seems," Luke said of their local veterinarian. "You aren't getting another dog are you?"

"No," Holly said firmly. "But I wouldn't be surprised if my father snatched one up. He's spending more time in his RV, driving around and trying out the best fishing spots, and as long as Serena's still in business, she thinks he needs some company. Works well for me. The kids get to play with the pups and I don't have to do the caretaking. Oh, thanks, Kevin." She slid the large paper cups across the counter while Gil pulled out his wallet. "You'd best get over there and save her," Holly warned. "Heaven only knows what they're planning next."

"Just my political demise, I'm sure," Gil said with a reluctant smile. "Thanks for these. And for the other day. The talk," he added at her furrowed brow. "I'm feeling… clearer about some things."

"Good to hear. Have a blast at the beach.

Bye, Eli!" Holly waved to the baby before heading over to the sink to wash her hands and confab with Ursula, the diner's cantankerous cook, who was glaring at him through the order window.

"Oh, Gil, there you are." Leah took a step back to make room for him as he approached the table the Cocoon Club occupied. She accepted the shake Gil offered and took an immediate loud slurp. "Heaven in a straw. Thanks. Myra was just telling me—"

"Was not," Myra cut her off, her overly bright red lips pouting.

Gil's eyebrow arched.

Leah aimed a look at Myra that Gil knew he never wanted to be on the receiving end of.

"Myra and Oscar were just telling me," Leah said more slowly this time, "That they think a truce is in order."

"A truce?" Now, that surprised him. "That's not something I'm adverse to. What are the terms of surrender?"

Leah shifted and planted her foot right on top of Gil's. "Not helping," she muttered out of the side of her mouth.

"Terms are negotiable, Mr. Mayor," Oscar

Bedemeyer said with a glint of amusement in his eyes. "Elliot, Harold and I can draft up a document."

"Not on that infernal computer thingy," Harold countered. "Ezzie's due back from her honeymoon this week. We thought we'd have you and Leah over for dinner to welcome her and Vincent home. So we can clear the air once and for all," he added in a tone that sounded more like a dare than an offer of hospitality.

"We think it's time we had a civilized discussion," Delilah held up a perfectly manicured finger to stop Myra from interrupting. "Rather than a surprise confrontation."

"I suggested it might be a good idea to air all grievances well before the election rather than letting issues continue to stew," Leah told him. "And just to keep things going in the right direction, Ezzie and I will mediate."

After a couple of decades of ill will, Gil had little hope a solitary dinner with the Cocoon Club was going to make a dent in the built-up resentments, but if Leah was going to be there…

"All right." He nodded, clearly surprising the club members. "I'll need a couple of days' warning so I can find a sitter for Eli."

"Or you could bring him," Delilah said with hope in her eyes.

"It probably would be best if Eli remains out of earshot this first go-around," Leah countered. "But maybe if there's a next time and you all behave, he can come with Gil. You let me know the night and time and if we can contribute anything. Gil? I think Eli is ready for his first dip in the ocean."

"I think you're right. I'll see you all one night this week, then." He slipped his hand down to the small of Leah's back and guided her out of the diner. "It crossed my mind to pay their bill, but I figured they'd take that the wrong way."

"Good call." She had another long drink of her shake. "You handled that pretty well, terms-of-surrender comment aside," she added.

"Couldn't make it too easy, could I?" Gil countered as they crossed the street to the shore. "They have every right to their feelings. Maybe this dinner will make them see that I'm not the person they're really mad at."

"Asking them to get over being angry with your father won't be an easy get."

"I don't plan to ask them to get over it." Gil's uncertainty shifted into determination. "I'd just like them to stop lumping me in with him. I know I've messed up a lot, and I've regrettably done a few things the same way he did, but that doesn't make me him." He stopped by the entrance to the beach, caught her arm and waited until she looked up at him. "I'm not my father, Leah."

"I know you aren't," Leah said softly. "But I'm not the one you need to convince." Leah set her cup down and reached for Elijah, tugging off his socks before lifting him out of the carrier. "Ooh, look at that cute little whale on your onesie. So stylish. Enough about the club and the election. Let's get this boy into the ocean, yeah?"

She waited until Gil disentangled himself from the carrier and shoved it into the diaper bag, then, juggling that, the cooler and his shake, he followed Leah and Eli to the lapping waves.

CHAPTER EIGHT

"I HAVE BECOME that guy."

"What guy? Nope." Leah reached out and stopped Eli from shoving a handful of sand into his mouth. "I bet he's hungry." She pointed to the tote bag.

"I'm spending all my time taking pictures of him and not enjoying the scenery."

"But you got the money shot," Leah told him as he handed her one of the bottles. She held it out to Eli, who shook his head and shoved it away. "The look on his face when that wave lapped over his feet was priceless. Yours was, too," she added with a laugh. He'd had to wade out in the water to the point he'd pretty much soaked his clothes.

Cheers and shouts echoed down the nearly empty beach. Leah shielded her eyes and looked to where Frankie Salazar, her red hair glowing beneath the fall sun, was demonstrating various floating techniques to more than a half dozen kids under sixteen. Overhead, a burst of color flashed against the blue sky. Leah's lips curved up at the sight of Duchess, a parrot who had arrived in town with Sienna Bettencourt. The pretty bird arched through the air probably on her way back to the marina.

With the Monarch Festival on the back burner, the crowds Leah had come to expect at this time of year were negligible, giving the locals the continued run of the place.

That wouldn't be the case next year. The butterfly sanctuary and education center would be open and there would be a fully scheduled festival that included live performances and a food and crafts fair in Skipper Park. Chances were pretty good the town would have plenty of tourists, for sure. Great for the economy and local businesses and hence the residents. But she'd miss this. Leah sighed. She'd miss days like this a lot.

"Did you say you needed to talk to Luke?" she asked Gil when she caught sight of the sheriff and Matt Knight, one of his deputies, standing by Frankie and her students.

"Apparently he needs to talk to me." Gil

tossed his phone into the tote and pushed to his feet. "Thanks. You got him?"

"More like he has me, but yep. We're good." She continued to try to coax Eli into eating, only to come up against thirteen pounds of stubborn six-month-old. Being around the baby helped ease the longing she felt for her nieces and nephews. It had been the trade-off she'd made, moving across the country, but the change had been necessary. Starting over took sacrifice, her sister had told her, even as she'd promised to load up the entire family and come for a visit. A promise she had yet to fulfill. Maybe next year, Leah hoped. When she was mayor.

"Okay, let's try this another way. Come here, you." She set the bottle down and scooped Eli into her arms, dangling him in the air for a moment as was their new routine. She settled him onto her lap so he could look out at the water. "You need to keep up your strength so you can learn to swim like Charlie and Simon and their friends." She shifted her focus once again to the group of kids who wouldn't be kids much longer.

She couldn't believe how much Charlie and Simon, not to mention Phoebe McBride,

Willa MacNeil and Stella Jones, Calliope's young sister, had grown. Pretty soon they'd be trading their bicycles for cars, zipping down the same roads they raced down now. Part of her wanted to stop time and keep them all as they were. Young, innocent and full of hope.

But the other part of her couldn't wait to see what they—and all the rest of the young people of Butterfly Harbor—became. "Hopefully that'll include you, little Eli."

He popped open his mouth to laugh, and she took advantage to nudge the bottle between his lips. He gave her a look not unlike one Gil had given her before, as if he'd known what she'd done to trick him and he wasn't happy about it. But after struggling for a moment, he heaved out a sigh, grabbed hold of the bottle and began to drink.

"I DIDN'T EXPECT to see you down here," Luke called out to Gil as he made his way slowly across the sand to where the parents of Frankie's students lined the beach. "Is that Leah with you?"

Gil cringed, noting a few curious faces turn toward Leah and Eli. Just a matter of time, he supposed, before the gossip mill ramped up to overdrive. "Thought it was a good idea to introduce Eli to the ocean," Gil said. "Leah came along."

"Nice." Luke's grin was quick but not as sly as the one Matt Knight had on his face. "How's Leo doing?" Luke asked his deputy.

"Hanging in there. He likes a challenge," Matt added. "I had to convince him he could still swim without his prosthetic."

"Don't they make them waterproof?" Gil asked.

"Not ones we can afford," Matt said, looking down at his own artificial leg, which had replaced the one he'd lost in Afghanistan. "Guess I'm going to have to take the plunge myself so my son doesn't show me up. Speaking of." He moved toward the shore as Leo, supported by Frankie, sucked up a face full of water.

"You look relaxed," Luke said when he and Gil were alone. "Laid-back. Taking a day off from work must agree with you."

"Who would have thought?" He couldn't recall his own father ever taking a day off. Not even for Gil's high school or college graduation. And taking him to the beach to swim? Morland would have considered that an utter waste of time. This was definitely a nice way to go about proving he was not his father's son. He wasn't ever going to be, especially when it came to Eli. "The emergency foster application's been filed," he told the sheriff. "Leah said I'll probably be getting a caseworker in a few days, since she pushed for an expedited process." He hesitated. "Holly said you wanted to talk to me about something."

Luke nodded, shoved his hands in his pockets.

It wasn't just that he hedged but how he hedged. As if Luke wanted to do anything else but talk. "You found Eli's mother." Gil swallowed hard, trying to think if he'd even considered Luke being able to track her down. "She wants him back, doesn't she?"

"Not exactly, and I'm betting not." Luke cocked his head. "Let's walk." He started off down the beach, away from Leah and Eli, leaving Gil to follow.

"What's going on, Luke?" Gil's heart was beating double time when he caught up. "What did you find out?"

"The good news is I didn't find any reports of missing or abducted babies that fit Eli's description. I went wide. Statewide, just to be sure."

"Okay." So far that sounded...good.

"Since I didn't get any answers," Luke continued, "I started looking at this in another way and asked myself why you?"

"Why me what?"

"Why did his mother leave Eli with you?"

"No idea," Gil stated emphatically.

"It's the big question, though, isn't it? The note said you were his only family and for you to keep him safe. I sent the prints to a lab tech I know in Sacramento. Tammy works primarily in major crimes and has a soft spot when it comes to complicated family situations."

"Meaning?"

"Meaning now I owe her big-time," Luke said with a forced chuckle. He was trying so hard to keep things light, which told Gil there was bad news looming. "Tammy ran the prints for me, nationwide, found a match to a Sylvie Edison, age twenty-four from the Phoenix, Arizona area. A criminal record matched."

"Okay." Gil added that information to his overloading brain.

"Sylvie's had a rough time," Luke said. "Mostly when she was a teen. A couple of shoplifting arrests. Nothing violent or dangerous. But it gave me a place to start. I ran her name through a program Ozzy helped me create, one that searches through multiple databases across the board. Her name popped up once. A marriage license filed three years ago in Arizona. From there I found Eli's birth certificate." Luke stopped walking, looked out at the water for a long moment before he faced Gil. "Gil, Eli's father..."

"His father what?" Gil pressed, but even as he asked, his entire body went cold.

"You're not going to be able to avoid this or him any longer, I'm afraid." Luke's guarded expression shifted into one of acceptance. "It's Christopher, Gil. Eli is your half brother Christopher's son."

"Gil!"

It took Gil a moment to process his name being carried along the ocean breeze. He turned, barely registering Luke's information, scanned the beach behind him and found Leah standing up, waving frantically, Eli in her arms.

Cold draped over Gil's body. Leah didn't do frantic. Even from a distance he could register panic not only on her face but in her voice.

"Something's wrong."

"Go!" Luke ordered. "I'll get Frankie."

Gil didn't wait to be told twice and raced to the blanket. "What is it? What's wrong?"

"I don't know." Leah was holding Eli, who was huffing and puffing, trying to breathe. "I thought he was just being cranky about eating, but he's sweating like crazy."

"Okay, okay. Let's lay him down. Maybe he has some kind of heat issue with the sun."

Leah dropped to her knees and started to lay Eli on the blanket, but he screamed when her hold loosened.

"Oh, Eli," Leah whispered. "Sweetheart, what is it?"

"What's going on?" Frankie Salazar, Butterfly Harbor's co–fire chief skidded to a halt next to Gil, rested a hand on his shoulder, her simple black swimsuit glistening along with her long red hair.

"He's not breathing right," Leah told her.

"Okay. Lay him down." Frankie crouched as Luke and Matt joined them. Gil didn't have to look behind him to know a crowd was forming, but all he could do was stare down at the innocent, helpless baby he'd been given. When Eli's howls continued, Gil walked around and knelt beside Leah. Together, they rested gentle hands on Eli's chest, trying to get him to calm down.

Frankie pressed her finger against Eli's neck. "His pulse is fast." She skimmed her hands down his body, checked his arms, his legs, unsnapped his octopus onesie and looked at his tummy. She pressed her fingers into his skin. "His arms and legs are slightly swollen." She angled her head, leaned in, smoothed a hand down his feet. "And I see a blue tinge to his skin." She looked up, then over her shoulder. "Luke, call for an ambulance."

"On it." Luke pulled out his cell, turned his back, signaling for the kids Frankie was teaching to come out of the water.

"What? An ambulance? Why?" Gil felt the warmth of Leah's hand on his arm, the only part of him that felt alive at the moment. "What's wrong with him?"

Even as he asked, Eli began panting and wheezing. Gil flexed his hand and tried to will whatever was happening to go away.

"I'm not a doctor, Gil."

"You're the closest thing we have right now. What's happening to him?"

"I can't be certain, but..." Frankie cringed. "I think there's something wrong with his heart."

LEAH HAD BEEN in emergency rooms before. She'd been in this particular emergency room only a few months ago when Jo had been attacked up at the butterfly sanctuary's construction site. Emergency rooms were never a pleasant experience for anyone.

But there was something particularly nightmarish about having to bring an infant into one.

And if *she* felt that way...

Catching sight of Gil stepping out of the curtained cubicle down the hall, Leah jumped to her feet, ready to race toward him, but stopped when Dr. Phillips appeared. Feet glued to the floor, she watched Gil nod, shake his head, run his hands through his hair. Even from a distance, she could feel the anxiety and worry cascading off him.

He must feel so alone.

Leah leaped when a gentle hand touched her arm.

"Sorry," Paige Bradley, Charlie's mother and ER nurse, offered a gentle smile. "Didn't mean to startle you. Here." She pushed a cup into Leah's hands. The two had become good friends years before when Paige had asked Leah to draw up legal documents to protect her daughter Charlie after their past had caught up to them. Paige's love for her older daughter knew no bounds. So much so Paige had been willing to give herself up to protect Charlie from mistakes she'd made. Having Paige here now, Leah realized, knowing she was with someone who wouldn't sugarcoat anything, was a bit of comfort.

"Water?" Leah eyed the liquid suspiciously.

"The last thing you need is caffeine." Paige followed Leah's gaze down the hall. "Dr. Phillips is the best. Eli's in good hands."

"He's so little," Leah whispered, letting a fraction of the fear and doubt slip free. "Paige, how serious—"

"I'm not one to speculate," Paige said in a

firm but gentle tone. She wore blue scrubs with bright white flowers today, in honor of new daughter Lily who had recently made her appearance. "Just keep those good thoughts circulating, okay?"

"I'm trying." But it was impossible to erase the image of Eli struggling for breath against the fresh air of the ocean. She hadn't noticed the tinge to his skin or the swelling in his chubby legs. "I thought he was just being fussy," she whispered. "How did I not see something was wrong?"

"Because babies don't come with instruction manuals." Paige stepped in front of her and met her eye to eye. "One thing about this town, you call for help, it's right there. Frankie was absolutely correct with her instincts because she could see Eli objectively."

"Frankie." Leah let out a laugh. "She's always in the right place at the right time."

"Speaking of." Paige inclined her chin toward the woman walking toward them. "We were just talking about you."

"No wonder my ears are burning." Wearing a pair of shorts and a BHFD hoodie over her swimsuit, Frankie offered a tight smile. "I couldn't stop worrying. How is he?"

"Gil's talking to the doctor now." Leah waved a hand in his direction.

"How about you?" Frankie asked, her concern showing. "I know that was scary."

Leah's shoulders slumped. "How do they sneak into your heart so fast?" Despite her best intentions to keep it together, tears burned her throat and flooded her eyes. "He's not even mine."

"He's not Gil's, either," Frankie said.

"What's that supposed to mean?" Leah asked.

"Nothing." Frankie frowned. "I didn't mean it the way it came out. I didn't," she insisted. "Look, I'll admit Gil isn't one of my favorite people—"

"Says the woman who dubbed him Gil the Thrill," Paige reminded her dryly.

"I've apologized to him about that. Multiple times," Frankie added grudgingly. "In my defense, he'd more than earned that nickname. And don't forget he did try to cut the fire department budget to the quick just last year."

"But he didn't," Leah said.

"Only because he got an up-close-and-personal look at what it is the department does," Frankie said. "He could have died in that fire last Christmas. Both of us could have. Why is it some politicians only shift their viewpoint when whatever it is suddenly affects them?"

"And why is it everyone else in this town gets a shot at redemption except Gil Hamilton?" Leah snapped.

"Leah." Paige sounded shocked.

"That's not true," Frankie protested.

"Isn't it?" Whether it was the stress of not knowing what was wrong with Eli or the way this picture-perfect day had been marred, or maybe it was seeing Gil standing at the end of the hallway trying to absorb whatever the doctor was telling him, she'd had enough. Enough of the judgment and the anger. He'd done more for this town than anyone realized. But it wasn't up to her to share what Gil obviously wanted kept quiet.

But she did know that he'd been working day and night to clean up the mess his father had left. That Gil had put up the Hamilton house as collateral to secure the funding to build the butterfly sanctuary after multiple banks turned Butterfly Harbor's application down.

She wanted to tell Frankie that the only

reason the fire department's funds hadn't been cut was because Gil had stopped taking a salary in order to cover it.

But she couldn't.

If Gil wanted people to know what he'd done, he wouldn't have presented his offer of solutions behind closed doors.

"How is Gil supposed to make any kind of difference around here if everyone in town never sees him for who he is? He's not his father. And whether you want to believe it or not, he's done a lot of good for Butterfly Harbor."

"He has," Frankie said reluctantly. "I know that. So does everyone."

"If they did, then this recall wouldn't even be happening," Leah reminded her.

Paige took a step back, her brow furrowing. "Leah, why are you—"

"Because I'm sick of everyone in this town treating him like he's some kind of villain out to take over the world." She set her cup on a nearby table. "And you know what? Given what I've heard about Morland Hamilton, it's a pretty darn big miracle he isn't just like him."

"Why are you angry at me?" Frankie's

befuddlement seemed as acute as Leah's. "You're the one running against him for mayor."

"I know." The snap in her own voice had Leah blinking. "I know," she said again with a sigh and shoved her hands through her hair. "I'm sorry. He's—" She broke off when Gil turned around, his searching gaze halting only when he found her. "He's hurting. He's hurting and he's scared about that little boy. He's human," she said after she cleared her throat. "And he's doing the best that he can." She offered Gil the only thing she could. A smile. Her heart stuttered when she earned a small one in return. "Just...give the guy a break, okay?"

Frankie nodded, worry and confusion shining in her eyes. "Sure, okay."

Leah had run out of words. When Dr. Phillips moved off, she didn't hesitate to head in Gil's direction, didn't feel her heart stop racing until she reached his side. "Hey. How are you doing?"

"Fine. Good." His breath sounded almost as shaky as Eli's had. "You didn't have to stay."

"Yes," she said firmly and took hold of his

hand. "I did." For Eli. And for him. "What did the doctor say?"

He held on to her so tight her fingers tingled. "They're waiting on the first round of blood tests and Dr. Phillips ordered an echocardiogram. He thinks Eli is showing the symptoms of something called VSD." He shook his head as if to clear it. "I'm not entirely sure I processed all of it."

"It stands for Ventricular Septal Defect." Paige said from behind them.

Leah and Gil turned. Frankie stood just behind her, the silent apology bright in her eyes.

"It's not all that uncommon in infants. It means there might be a hole in his heart. Usually it's between the lower chambers and disrupts the flow of blood." She tapped two fingers against her chest.

"They're admitting him overnight. There's fluid buildup they want to take off and…"

"Okay, that's good." Leah squeezed his hand to remind him he wasn't alone. "That means they know how to treat him. How to help. Can we go see him?"

"Of course. Yeah. Come on." Gil tugged

her into the room, Paige and Frankie following.

It hadn't occurred to Leah, at any time, that there could be a reason for a crib to exist in an emergency room. But here one sat in front of her. It was metal, sterile, cold and housed a baby who suddenly looked even smaller than she remembered.

Eli's eyes were drooping, as if he were fighting to stay awake. He'd been stripped down to his diaper. Even his socks were gone.

"He has to be cold," Leah whispered and turned to Paige.

"I'll get a blanket." Paige reached over and touched Leah's arm. "You'll get through this." She looked to Gil. "You all will. I promise."

"Thanks, Paige." Gil's smile didn't come close to reaching his eyes. "Frankie. Sorry. I should have… Thanks for helping us at the beach."

"I'm glad I could." She stood next to Leah, looked into the crib and touched a hand to Eli's forehead. "He looks better already. The blue tinge I saw is gone. And he's breathing better. That's a good sign."

"What's the treatment for VSD?" Gil asked.

"Oh." Frankie shook her head. "I don't think I'm the right—"

"You're the perfect person," Gil told her. "You've never lied to me, Frankie. You've always been straight with me, so don't change now. Worst case."

"Surgery." She said the word as quickly as she could, as if she wanted to spit it out of her mouth. "If the hole is significant, they'll need to perform surgery to close it up. A lot of kids outgrow it—it heals on its own—but there are more complicated cases that require invasive intervention. The echo they've ordered will determine the next steps."

"Okay." He took a deep breath. "Okay, I just want to know what I'm dealing with. Would you mind staying with him for a while? Both of you?" Gil asked. "I need to call my insurance company and see about getting him added on. The paperwork we filed will help with that, right, Leah?"

"Yes, absolutely." It felt safe to discuss a topic she actually knew about. "As your attorney I can take care of—"

"No. Thanks, but I need to do this myself. He's mine." There was a vehemence that wasn't there before, an intensity that had chills racing down Leah's spine. "I need to take care of him. I'll be back in a bit."

Leah watched him leave and choked back the tears that threatened again.

"You were right," Frankie said as Leah accepted the soft, small blanket Paige brought in. "The snark comes naturally where Gil is concerned. It always has. I'll keep it in check. And not because of Eli," she added when Leah eyed her. "Because maybe if anyone's earned their shot at redemption around Butterfly Harbor, it is Gil." Her lips twitched before she grinned. "Don't you dare tell him I said that. I'd hate to ruin our relationship."

"Don't worry," Leah assured her and draped the blanket over Eli. She rested her hand on his chest, the same way Gil did, and tried to take some comfort in the now-steady beat of Eli's heart. "It'll be our secret."

CHAPTER NINE

GIL'S HAND CLUTCHED his cell so hard his fingers went numb.

He'd spent his life learning how to work a deal. How to fix things. How to turn opportunities to his—and others'—advantage.

He knew how to plan, finagle, how to barter, to argue. He knew when to push and when to back off. He knew, better than most, that throwing money, while solving some problems, tended to exacerbate others. He'd also learned that not every arrangement was good and sometimes giving in meant winning in the end.

But one thing he did not know, could not fathom, was how to fix Eli.

There wasn't anyone to bargain with, no deal he could offer to smooth things out. All he could do was stand back and hope the people caring for Eli could help him.

Exhaustion crept over him when he hung

up, and he sank onto one of the outdoor benches that allowed for better cell reception than the inside of an emergency room. He'd been spinning like onc of Charlie Bradley's garden pinwheels—unable to stop and catch his breath or his thoughts against the never-ending winds of life.

Familiar and not familiar faces passed by him. Medical personnel, town residents coming and going for appointments or to take advantage of visiting hours. He could hear the light trickle of the waterfall in the back corner of the meditation garden and waiting area. Round redwood tables with Adirondack-style chairs were scattered about, some with sun-blocking umbrellas, others allowing for a full day's dose of vitamin D. A small café cart near the exit to the parking lot offered drinks and snacks.

"There you are." Leah's voice carried both irritation and relief as her shadow moved over him. "You really know how to disappear, don't you?"

"Sorry. Just needed a couple of minutes of quiet to think." Why did it feel like a struggle to breathe?

She sat beside him, crossed her bare legs

and huddled over as if the fall air was too chilly for her. "Did you get things settled with the insurance company?"

"Supposedly," he said, not wanting to belabor the issue. He'd deal with things as they came. "How is he?"

"Better. Paige says his numbers are already improving and that they'll probably let you take him home tomorrow. She and Frankie said they'd stay with him until I found you. Hey." She reached over, covered his hand with hers, and finally, finally, he felt warmth return to his system. "He's going to be okay, Gil. We got him here in time and he has excellent care."

"I should have brought him in to see a doctor sooner. If I had, they would have found this."

"You've only had him a couple of weeks," Leah said. "It's taken you time to adjust."

"I thought I was protecting him. I was afraid—"

"You were afraid if you brought him to the doctor before you applied for temporary legal custody you'd lose him. No one's blaming you, Gil. Eli looks perfectly healthy. There's no reason—"

"You said you thought he was underweight. That day you came to my house—" Gil remembered. "You said you thought he was small for his age."

"Babies develop at different rates, Gil. And continuing to blame yourself for something you can't change is only going to tick me off. Stop wallowing and get it together. Eli needs you strong and focused."

Her words felt like a bucket of ice water straight to the face. But instead of taking offense, he found himself smiling. "You always tell it like it is, don't you, Leah?"

"Professional habit." She shrugged. "I learned early on in my trials that the worst thing you can do is waste time. State your point, prove your point, move on. Hovering over things that literally cannot change only delays justice. Or in this instance, looking forward."

"You used to handle criminal cases, didn't you?"

"I did. But I don't anymore." When she blinked it was as if she'd dropped a thick curtain between that life and now. "Time's short enough. I don't like to waste it on what-ifs and I-wish-I-had-dones. If I'd been that concerned about Eli's weight, I would have pushed for you to take him to a doctor.

I didn't. So if you're determined to blame someone for all this, add me to the list."

"I have nothing to blame you for." Heck, if it wasn't for Leah's presence, he wasn't entirely sure he'd have gotten through the last couple of weeks.

"Then, we move on. Move on, Gil." That warning tone she possessed had his self-doubt melting away. "Before we go back inside, what did you find out from Luke?"

"Luke?" Gil blinked. "Oh, right. Luke." All the information the sheriff had dropped on him moments before Eli's crisis flooded back. "He found out who Eli's parents are."

"He did?" Leah sat up straight and snatched her hand away. "Who are they?"

"His mother's name is Sylvie Edison. She's twenty-four and sounds like a bit of a drifter. In and out of trouble over the years, mostly when she was a kid. Eli was born in Arizona six months ago." He hesitated, not entirely sure how to present the other tidbit of information Luke had imparted to him.

"You're hedging." Leah reached out and stroked her index finger against the creases in his brow. "Whenever you're uncertain about something, you show it. Right here."

Her finger stopped over his lips. Their

eyes locked. Gil's breath caught in his chest. He could feel her pulling away and caught her hand in his, brushed his mouth against the back of her knuckles before weaving his fingers through hers.

"Tell me," Leah whispered. "Tell me what you don't want to say."

"Does my case get stronger if I'm Eli's blood relative?" Gil asked because if he didn't say something, he was going to kiss her again. Right here out in the open where anyone could see.

"That depends, but usually stronger. Why? Are you and this Sylvie related?"

"No." Gil shook his head. "Eli is Christopher's son."

"Christopher." She blinked. "Well." She looked down at their linked hands, but instead of tugging herself free, she clung harder. "Does he know about Eli?"

"No idea." Gil stood, pulling her with him. "But I'm going to find out."

"You're going to see him."

"I am," Gil vowed. "Whether he wants me to or not."

"OKAY, THERE IT IS."

Leah narrowed her eyes at the screen, trying to see whatever Dr. Phillips saw. They'd brought the echocardiogram machine to Eli, who had apparently let everyone in the pediatric wing know he was awake shortly after dawn. Waking up to Eli's healthy wails had been, according to an exhausted Gil, one huge relief.

Eli followed up his morning scream fest with a full bottle of formula, which for once, he didn't fight. The swelling in his legs and arms was significantly reduced, and his color was back to normal. He looked utterly and completely healthy.

It had been, Leah thought when she'd arrived with coffee and bagels from Chrysalis Bakery shortly after nine, the perfect start to the day.

"What am I looking at?" Gil asked as if reading Leah's mind. He kept one of his hands gently around Eli's arm as the baby kicked and squirmed beneath the wand pressed against his chest.

"This right here." Dr. Phillips pointed to a pulsing on the screen. "The rhythm is off. You can hear it. That uneven swooshing instead of a steady beat. That's what's causing the heart murmur."

Leah glanced at Gil, who, when he met her gaze, shrugged. "I'll have to take your word for it. What does it all mean?"

"Well." Dr. Phillips moved the wand around more, clicked a few images. "I'll have to consult with a couple of my colleagues, but the hole doesn't seem to be as large as I anticipated."

"So that's good news," Leah pushed.

"It means we'll take the time and monitor his condition before making any invasive recommendations."

No surgery. Leah let out a long breath. That was good news.

"But it's a hole. In his heart," Gil said in disbelief. "Won't it get bigger? Isn't there, I don't know, pressure or something?"

"Holes rarely if ever get bigger. In fact, most of the time these types of conditions heal as the child grows. The stronger he gets, the better his chances of it resolving itself."

"But—"

"Gil." Leah touched his arm. "Dr. Phillips wouldn't be recommending anything that isn't in Eli's best interest."

"Right. I know." But Gil still didn't look convinced. "So is there medication he needs to take? Food he should or shouldn't eat?" Gil looked far more uneasy now than that first day Leah had shown up on his doorstep.

"I'd like to see him gain a few pounds." Dr. Phillips wiped off the wand and hooked it onto the portable machine. "You can start him on baby food a few times a day, along with his formula. Watch his fluid intake and bring him back in a week for a new round of lab tests. Gil—" Dr. Phillips reached out and rested a hand on Gil's shoulder "—I know this is scary, but Leah's right. It is good news. And now both of you know what to be on the lookout for. If you see any signs of what happened yesterday recurring, you bring him back in. Okay?"

"I can really just take him home?"

"You really can." Dr. Phillips moved aside as one of the nurses came in to wheel the machine away. "I'll let the desk know to process his discharge summary. You have my number."

"And Paige's," Leah added. "She said to call her day or night if you had any questions or concerns, Gil."

Gil nodded and, after the assisting nurse cleaned off Eli's chest of the test gel, lifted

Eli into his arms. The baby snuggled in and rested his head under Gil's chin, letting out a sigh of contentment so perfect, Leah blinked back tears.

"It'll be a few minutes. Drink your coffee. Have something to eat," Dr. Phillips suggested. "Then go home and get some sleep. Eli's going to be just fine." He touched Eli's head affectionately and left.

"Thank you, Doctor." Leah called after him as she moved around the exam table and rested her hand against Eli's back. "You can take him home."

"Home." The way he said it, with a longing she suspected he wasn't aware he'd conveyed, had the invisible bands around her chest loosening.

Bureaucracy, it soon became clear, wasn't relegated to town management and operations. Discharging someone—even a small someone like Eli—seemed to take forever. By the time Gil carried Eli into the sunshine of the parking lot, it was almost noon.

"I hope you don't mind, but I stopped and picked up your car. Helena gave me the spare keys you keep in the office."

"Helena gave you my keys?"

"I needed them anyway to get Eli's car seat, but I was afraid I wouldn't install it properly in my car, so it made sense to bring yours. If you wouldn't mind dropping me off at my office on your way home?"

The expression on his face wasn't one she recognized. The stress was there, displaying itself in those tiny lines around his eyes, and the shadows beneath them was clear evidence he hadn't gotten much, if any, sleep.

"Something wrong?" she asked as he clicked off the alarm and pulled open the back door while she stashed the diaper bag and other belongings in the trunk.

"I guess I'm just surprised you spoke with Helena." He clicked Eli into his car seat with surprising efficiency.

"She was worried. About you and Eli," Leah told him. "Word spread pretty quickly about what happened at the beach, and when she couldn't reach you..."

He patted his pockets, a mild panic crossing his face. "My phone."

"It's here." She plucked it out of the diaper bag where she'd tossed it yesterday. "I threw everything together when the ambulance came."

"Right. Thanks." He took it back, turned it on, then stared down at the screen as his messages and voice mails bleeped their delivery. "I guess I have a lot of catching up to do."

"Not as much as you might think." She gestured to the car and they climbed in. "I made a list of what I discussed with Helena. I can run through it for you while you drive."

The silence in the car pressed in on her when he didn't respond. Backing out of the parking space, he maneuvered them quickly onto the road toward town. Ignoring the uneasy clutching in her stomach, Leah dived in.

"Helena was able to reschedule your meeting with the town planning commission to Friday morning. It'll also be a video conference instead of in person. Just worked out better that way for everyone, apparently." She glanced up, saw his jaw tense.

"She's forwarded you copies of the various committee reports for the upcoming town council session." Leah skimmed through her phone. "There's been some updates to the schedule for the sanctuary's opening ceremony, but nothing too wild. The permit proccss for food salcs and charity organizers can be expedited with the proper paperwork. She's processing applications for the new town attorney position you're looking to refill, and she put on hold the other job listings you've compiled. I didn't realize so many jobs had been eliminated in the last few years."

"Budget necessity" was all Gil said.

"Oh, before I forget, Jo's fielding questions from her construction workers about establishing a new workers' union. It could impact future projects in town."

"Is that everything?"

"Um." She scrolled through her notes. "Nothing that can't wait. I guess at the last council meeting it was decided the annual budget would be presented a week later than normal. Any particular reason?"

"Two of the council members will be out of town on our normal meeting date."

"Have you considered hiring a town manager to take a lot of this off your shoulders? I see things listed here that the council members really shouldn't be— What are you doing?" She glanced out the windshield as Gil pulled the car over to the side of the road. "Something wrong with the car?"

"No. Nothing is wrong with the car." He shifted slightly, checking on Eli before he looked at Leah. "You haven't won yet, Leah."

"What?" It took her a moment to understand what he was talking about.

"You aren't mayor. Not yet. Maybe not ever. And while I appreciate everything you've done to help me with Eli, I don't need your assistance doing my job."

"But I—" She clicked her phone closed and lowered it onto her lap. "I was only trying to help. Helena needed some guidance with the schedule and I just..."

"I know what you were doing and it wasn't necessary."

"Clearly it was," Leah countered. "You were out of communication and your office had questions that needed answering. I offered to help. Everyone understands about Eli. No one's angry about this, Gil. No one except you."

"I'm not angry."

"Tell that to your face. I'm happy to back off, Gil. I have plenty of work of my own to do. I was trying—"

"I know what you were trying to do and you don't have to. I meant what I said the other day, Leah. I need this job. I have to keep it if I'm going to have a fighting chance to keep him." He jerked his thumb to the back seat. "How do you suppose it'll look to people in town if you're stepping in to cover for me?"

She stiffened in her seat, pulled her gaze from him and stared straight ahead. "I didn't think about that."

"Because you don't have to. Look, you've been great. And thank you for being there where Eli is concerned, but from now on, let's keep our relationship on his side of the line, okay?"

Their *relationship*? It was on the tip of her tongue to press the issue, but that would only drop her farther into the hole she'd begun digging. "All right." She pushed her phone into her bag. "If that's what you want."

"It is." He pulled back onto the road, but the tension was still circling inside the car. Eli's baby babbling was the only source of comfort she could find.

"This wasn't me trying to sabotage you or get behind-the-scenes information I can use against you in the election." She glanced at him in time to see his brow arch. "It wasn't. Nothing I discussed with Helena—"

"What else did you discuss with her?"

"Nothing important." The suggestions she'd made to his long-time assistant were just that. It was up to Helena as to whether she ran with them or not. "By the way, I tried to reschedule the furniture delivery this afternoon, but it was too late. The only other option was to cancel and that would have incurred a significant charge. They'll be at your house sometime before three today."

"Good to know." He glanced at his watch. "Thanks."

"This recall election isn't my fault, you know."

"I know." That tic in his jaw returned.

"Whether you want to believe me or not, I was only trying to help you navigate the choppy waters you and Eli were in. No ulterior motive."

"Noted."

Since she'd already ticked him off, her qualms about asking after his brother evaporated. "Are you going to see Christopher this week?"

"I plan to. Why?"

"I thought you might want someone to go with you. An objective third party who also happens to be a lawyer."

"I appreciate the offer, but I think it's best I approach him myself."

"All right." She pinched her lips together to stop herself from telling him he was making a mistake. "What about Eli?"

"What about him?"

"Are you planning to take him to jail with you or are you going to get a sitter?"

Oh, yeah. He was sending out Morse code with that jaw clenching of his. "That depends."

"On what?"

"On whether I can pry my foot out of my mouth long enough to ask if you'd be up for it." He cringed, but finally his hands eased up on the steering wheel even as he took the turn onto Monarch Lane and buzzed past the diner. "I do know you were trying to help, Leah. Hearing about you talking with my assistant just felt as if—"

"I was trying to slide into the job I'm running for ahead of schedule?"

"Pretty much." He made the right turn and double-parked in front of the cute bungalow that housed her practice. "I was out of line and I'm sorry."

She nodded, suspecting that apology probably dinged his ego harder than anything else she could have said. He'd had a lot land on him in the last day. Heck, he'd had a lot land on him in the last few weeks. But that didn't justify him snapping at her. Especially not when the election hadn't even crossed her mind. "Apology accepted. And for the record, yes. I'd be happy to watch Eli when you go to Durante to deal with your brother." She looked back at the baby. "You good with that?"

"Gwwwwwhaaaaa!" Eli shoved his fist in his mouth.

"You're going to have to buy more teething rings," she told Gil. "Give me a call when you need me. For Eli," she added at the glint sparking in his eye again. "We want to make sure to keep things on that side of the road, right?" She shoved out of his car, grabbed her bag. "Have a good afternoon, Gil. Bye, Eli." She closed the door and turned away, feeling oddly alone as Gil drove off.

CHAPTER TEN

"Boy, I sure messed that up, huh, Eli?" A glance in the rearview mirror left Gil on the receiving end of a look of confirmation he had to be imagining.

Gil knew what had happened. He was tired and angry. Adrenaline and panic were battling for control of his body and he'd realized at about three this morning that there was a very good possibility he was going to lose the election.

Why did things always seem most dire in the middle of the night?

"Because it's the only time your mind is quiet enough to hear the warnings," Gil told himself as he pulled into the driveway of his house. When he climbed out of the car, he spotted Helena's parked on the street. He'd no sooner turned toward the porch when his front door opened and his assistant stepped out. "Helena. What are you doing here?"

Unlike Leah's carefully thought-out reactions to his borderline rude inquiries, Helena didn't miss a step or the opportunity to glare.

"Someone needed to be here for the delivery. Leah wasn't sure what time you'd be coming home with Eli." Helena stormed down the steps and along the walkway to the car, her sturdy heels sounding as determined as she looked. "How is he?"

He still had a hole in his heart, something Gil wasn't certain he'd ever be able to accept. But rather than focusing on the negative, he bent down and lifted Eli out of the car. "He's much better."

"Oh, I can see that now." Helena rested her palm against Eli's cheek. "What's his prognosis?"

"We're in wait-and-see mode. Would you mind taking him for a minute?"

"Not at all. Oh, this brings me back." She settled Eli into her arms while Gil emptied the trunk of the car and headed inside. "Makes me wish I didn't live so far away from my grandchildren."

Guilt struck him square in the heart. Helena and her husband had been able to ride out Butterfly Harbor's economic flatlining.

Unfortunately, her daughter and son-in-law weren't able to. In order to find work—and a livable income—they'd had to move north to Washington state. Now Helena was lucky to see her three grandchildren a couple of times a year.

"You're welcome to play surrogate grandmother anytime you'd like," Gil offered as he waited for her to precede him inside.

"I would love that." Helena's face went brighter than the town's Christmas tree at the height of the holidays. "You hear that, Eli? Oh, you aren't going to be spoiled at all." She pressed her lips to his cheek and rocked him back and forth.

Gil came up short in the living room. "The delivery's already been?"

"About an hour ago. I hope that's where you wanted the new sofa." She lowered herself onto the deep turquoise cushion. "I love the color. So bright and cheery. And that new coffee table's lovely and practical. No sharp edges for him to bump his head on."

"Where's the old—"

"In the back bedroom with your moth—with the other old furniture," she added quickly. "They made quick work of the nursery. It would have been nice if you could have painted the room ahead of time, but it should suit him for a while."

He dropped the diaper bag and beach tote on the floor and headed upstairs. He had to stop halfway as his leg stiffened up on him. All the walking around and being on his feet had both loosened things up and made him think he'd overdone. He bypassed his own bedroom and clicked on the light to the nursery.

He'd chosen white—along with the brightest colors he could find—in order to bring some light into the otherwise dour décor. Dark wood paneling and trim matched the equally dark floor. The ceiling was an eggshell color that had clearly seen better days. The new crib—one that could easily be transformed into a toddler bed when the time came—sat perfectly between the two windows currently bare of curtains. He'd also purchased the matching changing table, dresser, open-shelf storage unit, and a comfy chair and footstool to round things out.

It was still missing personality, a theme and, okay, it needed a lot of work, but it already felt more homey and welcoming than the rest of the house. A house that Gil was determined to make into a home for Eli. He heard Helena's footsteps coming up the stairs.

"What do you think?" he asked her.

"I think it's an excellent start. I hope you don't mind. I went ahead and made up the crib and did some arranging of the items in the boxes."

"Those are on loan from Holly and Luke," Gil told her.

"Loan?" Helena's eyes went wide before she smiled. "Well, isn't that lovely. Another playmate for Eli down the road." She settled him on the blue-and-green-striped-covered mattress. "Why don't you come downstairs and let him sleep a bit."

"All right." Gil stopped to look down at the baby, found himself once again laying his hand against his chest. Eli gurgled and cooed, kicked his feet even as his eyes drooped. "We'll get you fed again when you wake up, okay?"

He left the door open and joined Helena downstairs.

"This is for you." Helena handed him a small handheld speaker. "It's the baby monitor that's hooked up in his room. There's an app you can install on your phone as well. I've left the instructions in your office."

"I can get them tomorrow when I come in," Gil said.

"Oh, not that office." She crooked her finger. "This way, please." She led him down the hall and off the kitchen. "I know it might have made more sense for you to use your father's old home office, but this felt like a better solution."

Gil stared. He recognized the desk from his grandfather's old room. And some of the bookcases that now lined the wall of the dining room. "Helena, how did you—"

"Well, the home-office suggestion was Leah's. She thought you should have the option of working from home until you find a good schedule that works for both you and Eli. She came over this morning and helped me go through the rooms."

"You two didn't—"

"Move all this? Heavens, no. Leah and I chipped in and paid the delivery men to do it. I figure if there's something you don't like, you can have Ozzy and Hunter come over again and readjust. I've called your cable company to come out and upgrade your internet and Wi-Fi, and Ozzy will be by tonight to network all your computers so you aren't tied to one office or the other."

"This is amazing. And look at all this light." The dining room bay window behind his desk allowed for so much sunlight he could turn the room into a greenhouse. "I don't know what to say. Thank you, Helena."

"You're welcome. But don't just thank me. Leah's responsible for most of it. It was her idea." She clasped her hands behind her back and held his gaze for a moment. "She's a lovely woman, Gil. It's a shame the two of you are at odds in this election."

"Yes," Gil murmured as he looked out the window to stare at the courtyard. "It really is. I understand you two reevaluated my schedule for the week."

"I didn't want you getting stressed over things easily remedied. I've updated your online calendar and kept things as fluid as possible. I wasn't sure if you're planning on getting help with Eli, a nanny or daycare provider—"

"No." Gil pulled himself away from the sterile backyard. "No, nothing like that. I'm sure I can find sitters when and if I need them."

"All right." Helena nodded. "I'll head on

back to the office, then. I'll be a phone call away if you need me."

"I'll always need you, Helena." Gil couldn't help but feel he had to reassure her. "You've been invaluable to me these last few years, just as I know you were to my father. I'm sure we haven't made it easy on you."

"Well, one of you didn't," Helena said with a quick smile that faded almost instantly. "I know what Myra Abernathe said the other day must have hurt."

Gil attempted to wave off her concern. "It's fine."

"No," Helena said in a tone that had always reminded Gil of his battle-ax of a high school history teacher. "No, it's not fine. She was wrong. She might not see that, but I do. You've had your challenges, but you're nothing like your father. In time, and it might take longer than you'd like, everyone else will see that, too."

"I hope so," Gil said. She picked up her jacket and purse and headed out to her car. "For Eli's sake, I really hope that's true."

"DELIVERY FOR YOU."

Leah glanced up from her screen as Callie sang and boogied her way into the office. Leah's mouth dropped open at the elegant arrangement of peach, yellow and red roses interspersed with various types of lilies.

She'd spent the past couple of days caught between stewing over her last conversation with Gil and rationalizing his behavior. After going back and forth while slogging through multiple requests for her mediation services as well as a child custody proposal for one of her divorcing clients, she'd landed somewhere north of she couldn't blame him and south of being hurt he thought her surrendering to ulterior motives.

"What on earth?" She stood as Callie set the clear glass vase on her desk. "Who are they from?"

Callie pointed to the bamboo skewer holding the card displaying Lori Knight's new business. "It's sealed, so I couldn't peek." She bounced on her toes like a little girl waiting for Christmas. "Go on. Open it."

Leah tossed her pen down and plucked up the envelope. She slid the card free, her lips curving into a smile. After she finished reading, she slipped the card into her blazer pocket and carried the flowers to the side table by the door.

"Are you going to keep me hanging or tell me who they're from?" Callie whined.

"They're from Gil and Eli." She turned the flowers a bit, stepped away to evaluate, then adjusted them one more time. "Just thanking me for my help." His note assured her he'd successfully removed his foot from his mouth and he'd appreciate the opportunity to apologize—genuinely—in person.

"That's more than a thank-you bouquet," Callie told her.

"Maybe it is," Leah agreed. "Now, let's hope I can keep it alive long enough to enjoy it." The flowers were lovely, but it was the note that touched her heart. She'd missed them. Both of them. Enough that the idea of mending fences overrode any doubts she had about remaining in their lives. "What's the rest of my day looking like?"

"Wondering when you can get away to thank Gil personally for the flowers?"

"I'm just asking a question," Leah said innocently.

"Uh-huh. You have Manuel Chitterdon

coming in at three to sign his new will. After that, you're done for the day."

"Excellent." She smiled down at the flowers. "Definitely most excellent."

The phone in the outer office rang and Callie, clearly irritated, left to answer it. A few seconds later, she was back. "It's Ezzie Salazar. Something about a welcome-home dinner doubling as a mediation session?"

"Got it, thanks." Timing is everything, Leah thought, as she circled back around her desk. "Ezzie, hi. Did you have a good trip?"

"Glorious," Ezzie gushed. "I saw parts of the Mediterranean I didn't know existed and I have pictures. Boy oh boy, do I have pictures."

The joy in the older woman's voice had Leah's smiling spreading. "I can't wait to see them. You up for this dinner with Gil and the club?"

"Up for it? Heck I'm thinking about selling tickets," Ezzie said. "My husband, on the other hand, is planning to get out of the danger zone. Vincent's making plans to rent one of Monty's boats for a guys' night. Can you imagine that man of mine organizing something like that?"

"No," Leah said, having to bite her tongue. "I really can't." Vincent Fairchild had spent most of his life keeping those he cared about most—including his daughter Sienna—at arms' length. Now, after following Sienna to Butterfly Harbor and meeting Ezzie Salazar, the now-retired CEO was one of the town's transformation stories. "I was thinking around five for dinner? What can I bring?"

"Just yourself and Gil, and Eli, of course. I've heard so much about him. I'm in need of some baby time since Roman and Frankie haven't made me a grandmother yet."

"I'm sure they're working on it," Leah laughed. "I have to leave Eli's attendance up to Gil. Thanks for doing this, Ezzie. It'll do a lot of people a lot of good."

"There's enough ill will in the world," Ezzie agreed. "If we can get the Cocoon Club and Gil to call a halt to their feud, then there's hope for everything else."

After she hung up, Leah sat back and turned her chair to face the flowers. It wasn't just that Gil had sent them as an apology. He'd used the town's new florist—a woman whose storefront was frequently filled with residents snapping up Lori's creations.

While Lori wasn't a gossip, it wouldn't take much for word to get out about the mayor sending his political rival flowers. Odd. The idea didn't make her as uneasy as it did just a few days ago. At some point, her concerns about public perception had been resolved.

Leah twirled in her chair. Wasn't that just lovely?

"WHAT DO YOU THINK?" Gil asked Kendall MacBride as she made notes on her clipboard. Kendall was old-school through and through. "Is it doable?"

"Everything's doable," Kendall replied without looking up. She walked over to the dining room window, ran her hand down the dark wood trim with something akin to wonder in her usually jaded eyes. "This is really excellent work. Antique-style craftsmanship. Seems a shame to cover it up."

"I'd like Eli to grow up in a house that doesn't scare him."

"Scare him?" Kendall glanced over her shoulder.

"You ever take Phoebe into a store, someplace where you're petrified she's going to touch something and break it or knock it over?"

"Hunter and I have learned not to take Phoebe into any place with breakables," Kendall said on a laugh.

"My point exactly." Gil admired his home office that only yesterday had housed a massive dining room table with a fancy candelabra and, before his father had died, displayed a set of china belonging to Gil's great-great-grandmother. "I spent my youth worried that I'd break something if I closed a door too hard. I want Eli to run around this place. I want to see him bouncing off the walls, slamming doors. I want to hear him laughing and playing and sliding down that banister—"

"Okay, you do not want that," Kendall warned.

"Yeah," Gil argued, "I do. Because I never could. The second I walked in that front door every day, it was like I was at military attention. The only safe space I had to relax was my own room. It was like living in a bubble. I want better for—"

"Your son." Kendall finished for him.

Gil crossed his arms over his chest. "He isn't that." He needed to keep tethered to that bit of truth. Eli might be in his custody at the behest of Eli's mother, but Eli had a father. He was behind bars at the moment, but Eli was still Christopher's son.

"Maybe not legally," Kendall said. "But in the ways that matter? From what I hear around town, that little boy has already made a big impact on your life."

With most people, that statement would be a subtle inquiry into the truth of the situation with Eli. Kendall, on the other hand, was where gossip went to die. She didn't feed the monster; she ignored it. And if she wanted an answer to a question, she straight out asked it.

"So, what do you think about the house?" He said in an attempt to steer them back to the reason she'd come over.

"I think you've presented an interesting challenge." Kendall stepped away from the window and carried her clipboard—she was a co-partner in the construction, renovation and remodeling business with Jo Bertoletti—into the living room. "Given the house is considered an historical landmark—"

"That I still own," Gil felt compelled to remind her.

"Doesn't matter." Kendall shrugged. "Landmark status limits what we can do, beyond the safety standards most buildings require. Still, we can soften the place up pretty easily without losing anything that would counter those legalities."

"Yeah?" The doorbell rang. Gil cringed, glancing at the baby monitor in the hopes Eli wouldn't wake up. "Take a look at the kitchen and see if that theory holds up." He headed to the front door and pulled it open. "Leah." He blinked. Somehow she'd gotten more beautiful in the days since he'd last seen her, but that didn't seem possible. "Hi."

"Hi." Her suit was a deep, rich sunset red today, offset by a white blouse and lethally pointed-toe heels. "I finished early at the office and thought I'd stop by and say thanks for the flowers. And that I accept." She hesitated as if suddenly uncertain. "Your apology. Again."

"And the dinner invitation?" Gil asked hopefully.

"And the dinner invitation." Her cheeks went bright red, something Gil found absolutely incongruous considering her normally stalwart presence. A presence he had definitely come to appreciate.

"Come on in and we'll talk details." Gil stepped back to let her inside.

"Gil, I'm not seeing a lot that needs doing in the kitchen… Oh. Hey, Leah." Kendall slipped a pencil behind her ear and tucked her clipboard under one arm. "You mind if I take a look upstairs? I'll be quiet."

"Go on ahead." Gil told her. "There's also significant attic space that I'm open to suggestions about."

"What's going on?" Leah asked as Kendall disappeared up the stairs.

"I'm looking into doing renovations," Gil told her. "You know, shifting from mausoleum chic to something more livable."

Leah winced. "I didn't mean to suggest you redo the entire house, Gil. Just add some color. Maybe a few throw pillows. Like this." She pointed to the new sofa and set her purse down. "Now this looks like something I want to fall into at the end of the day."

He'd love for her to do just that. "It's good to have furniture I won't crack my head on," he agreed.

After a long moment, Leah said, "Eli's sleeping, huh?"

"Afraid so. You're welcome to look in on him—"

"No, it's fine. I wanted to let you know I talked to Ezzie a little while ago. Dinner on Thursday night's a go."

"You mean the Butterfly Harbor peace summit?" Gil said with more amusement than he expected to feel.

"That works." Leah tucked her hair behind her ear. "Five o'clock all right?"

"Should be." Gil frowned. "I plan to be back by then."

"Back?"

"From Durante. I talked with Christopher's lawyer. He's agreed to put me in the room with my brother. Whether my brother's willing to talk to me or not—"

"Don't worry about it until you have to," Leah said. "Does he know about Eli?"

"Part of me hopes that he does. The other part—" Was it wrong to hope that his brother's potential ignorance could make it easier for Gil to obtain permanent custody one day? Then again, Eli could end up being the least of his worries. Who knew what skeletons were going to come flying out of the family's closet once he and Christopher had an actual conversation?

Kendall seemed to accentuate her footsteps on the way down. "Don't let me interrupt," she said as she joined them. "Furniture showroom aside, upstairs will take a lot more discussion." Kendall pointed her finger at the second floor. "If it's okay with you, I'd like to set up a time for me and Jo to come over here together and brainstorm."

"Has Phoebe decided on her Halloween costume yet?" Leah asked Kendall before she left.

"She keeps changing her mind," Kendall answered. "I told her she has to decide soon because I'm not buying a costume for every whim. She's currently got it narrowed down to a princess, a mad scientist or a race car driver."

"A race car driver?" Leah snort-laughed at the idea of the almost eight-year-old decked out in coveralls and a helmet.

"Phoebe has a crush on Declan Cartwright," Kendall admitted. "Don't tell Hunter. I'm not sure his heart can take her growing up any faster than she already is. I'll give you a call, Gil."

"Great. Thanks for coming out." He walked her to the door, then he turned back to Leah. "Guess we're all alone now."

"I guess we are." Leah looked into the new home office. "All of this working out all right?"

"It is, thanks. You and Helena make a good team."

Leah's eyes narrowed.

"I mean that in a good way," he said quickly to avoid another misunderstanding like the one they'd had in the car the other day. "I was totally out of line with my accusations."

"Not totally," Leah said after a minute. "It was understandable you'd feel like that, given what I'd done. I overstepped. I like fixing things and I thought I was helping."

"You were. You did. You saw matters in a way I don't tend to. Case in point, my office now has natural light." Because his hands itched to touch her, to hold her. Because the desire to kiss her again nearly had him diving toward her, he shoved his hands into his pockets and walked into the room. Sunlight streamed in. Now the antique desk and matching chair, the lawyer's bookcase and side table didn't have the intimidating, cold look they'd had in the original office on the other side of the hall. "I'm hoping Kendall and Jo can figure out how to lighten more things up around here."

"They will. It'll also build up new equity in the house."

"New equity?" Gil shifted as she came up behind him. "What are you talking—"

"You own the deed to the house, Gil, but you put it up as collateral against the loan for the butterfly sanctuary. The bank that's paying for the sanctuary holds the note."

He opened his mouth to deny it, but she shut him down with a look.

"I've seen the closed-session council meeting minutes, Gil. There's no point in telling me I'm wrong."

Clearly not. "How did you—"

"I had requested the council meeting minutes as the representative of the small business association. Whoever put the file together apparently didn't realize there was a difference between open sessions and closed."

"Jessie." Gil squeezed his eyes shut for a moment. "Helena has her help when she's afraid of letting something sit for too long." He did not want this information getting out as general knowledge. "You haven't told anyone, have you?"

"That you essentially paid for the sanctuary out of your own pocket? No. I have not." Leah touched his arm. "I'm more curious as to why you haven't. Gil, if people knew then, the recall probably wouldn't even be happening."

The election. What he wouldn't give to have that over with in this moment. "I ran on the promise of bringing something new and important to Butterfly Harbor, and that's what I've done. How I went about doing it shouldn't make a difference."

"It was supposed to be done using town funds, not your personal bank account."

"Yeah, well, there wasn't all that much in it when I took office." This was definitely not the conversation he wanted to have now that they were alone, but he also knew she'd keep digging. Heading her off at the pass was the only route to keep her from finding out other information he definitely wanted to keep to himself. "My father made promises he never kept. It was always *I'll get to it later*, or *it's on the list*, or *after looking at the numbers, it just isn't possible.* I needed to show them I wasn't the same kind of mayor without shining a giant spotlight on how I was getting things done. But when I took over and saw how much damage my father had done to the town's treasury and the bank..." Shaking his head, he moved away. "I wasn't about to make the same mistakes." He'd known it would be bad, but seeing for himself that his father had siphoned dollars out of the town's operating budget in an attempt to save the bank that was doomed to fail... "There wasn't any money to pay for anything, Leah, let alone the sanctuary project. I've been scrambling since I was sworn in to scrape every penny together to keep this town going. The money he lost—it wasn't mis-invested or shifted around. It was gone. Last year, I had to decide between funding emergency services or keeping the elementary and high schools open."

"Gil." The sympathy in Leah's voice had Gil stepping farther away.

"I found a temporary solution and pushed

for outsourcing emergency services in a way that would keep the fire station open. But that created a danger I hadn't anticipated. One I learned about firsthand." One that had nearly killed him.

"At the time, I knew if the school closed, it was game over for Butterfly Harbor. Those families with kids would have moved away, or if they didn't, they'd have to arrange to get their kids to Durante, which is a ninety-mile drive each way. That wasn't practical let alone affordable for anyone. Can you imagine walking down Monarch Lane and not seeing Charlie Bradley on her butterfly bike? Or Mandy Evans not racing down the beach toward the marina? Jake Campbell's done wonders with the kids' community center. He's given youth and the younger children in this town someplace to learn and go to when they're bored... That's who Butterfly Harbor is supposed to be for. The future. The generations to come. Taking out a mortgage on this house seemed a small price to pay to ensure what comes next." A pressure built in his chest. Was purging truths supposed to ache this much?

"But that's not all you did, though, is it?" Leah challenged. "It doesn't come close."

"You need to stop." Gil tried to keep his voice even. "None of this is any of your business."

"Oh, yes it is. Not only because I live here but because I care about you." Leah lifted her chin. The defiance, the challenge, the spark in her eyes had him wanting to fall into her arms for eternity. "You stopped taking your mayoral salary."

"I didn't need it," he said, transfixed by what he thought might be admiration in her eyes. "I have a trust fund from my grandfather." Even as he said the words, he had to look away. He hated lying to her, but he'd made enough confessions today to ease a thousand souls. "I won't take more from the town than it can give. Let this go, Leah. Let things run their course. Please."

"You're fine letting everyone in this town believe you've only been in this job for yourself. They're recalling you from office because of it, because they think you're an egomaniac and incompetent."

That she was outraged at the thought was more than enough balm for his wounded heart. "They're recalling me because my father nearly ruined all their lives," Gil corrected. "Nothing I've done changes anything. Not really. My father hurt this town. People moved away. They lost their businesses, their jobs, their livelihoods. People died because of the stress. People like Myra's husband. Leah, when you consider all that, what I've done doesn't add up to a drop in an ocean."

"It matters to me."

"Why would I need more than that?" The idea that anyone, but Leah especially, was willing to fight for him despite everything that had happened, truly did feel like a win for him.

"Maybe I need more." She kissed him. Not just to shut down his protests, he thought, because he could feel the tension coursing through her as she held on to him. There was more to how her lips moved over his, as if demanding he pay attention to her, to what she was trying to tell him. She was showing what she felt. Her hands clasped his face as he kissed her back, his fingers gripping her hips until finally, as he breathed in that intoxicating scent of her, she pulled her mouth free.

"You are a good man, Gil Hamilton," she murmured. "A good man who seems determined to pay for sins that aren't his. You are not and never have been responsible for your father's actions." She kissed him again, softly this time, gently, and in so doing, he felt something broken inside of him stitch back together. "You asked me why all this matters."

"Why does it?" His voice hitched, the depth of emotion telling.

"It matters because I want people in Butterfly Harbor to see you the way I do. Behind the walls you've built. Behind the mask you refuse to take off. You've worked so hard to rebuild this town, taken on so much that people don't know or understand. If they knew—"

"If they knew, they'd think it was just another Hamilton ploy." As much as he appreciated what she was trying to say, he was a realist. He'd known these people all his life. Their deep-seated resentment and anger couldn't be cracked open by his secret good deeds. "Just as Myra thought I was using Eli to win sympathy votes and come off as reasonable."

"The past has a tendency of blinding people to what's really in front of them."

"Maybe," he whispered and stroked a finger down her cheek. "Maybe I'm all right with that." He wasn't. But he didn't want Leah putting any more focus or energy on this. Not when they had important issues to think about. Like Eli. Like Christopher.

Whatever was building between him and Leah, because something was building, he didn't want it to stop.

As if hearing his thoughts, the telltale sounds of an infant waking echoed out of the monitor. "Saved by the baby. I don't want to talk about this anymore, all right?"

"But—"

"I don't want to talk about this anymore. Please."

She pursed her lips, her brow furrowing. He knew she was attempting to find some way, any way, around his statement.

"Thank you." He pressed a kiss against her forehead, stepped away and held out his hand. "Come with me to get him? I'm getting pretty good at the feeding thing, especially now that he has a high chair."

She sighed, nodded and took hold of his hand. "Lead on."

CHAPTER ELEVEN

IMPULSIVE DECISIONS MADE at three in the morning rarely, if ever, turn out to be the right thing to do. Despite being well acquainted with that crumb of knowledge, Leah found herself pulling into Gil's driveway shortly after nine o'clock. She parked and, before she talked herself out of it, grabbed the extra-large satchel she lugged around on day trips and exited.

There was more to Gil's secretive management of Butterfly Harbor than he was letting on; she'd bet serious money on it. She knew when someone was deliberately keeping something from her, and that knowledge was like an itch that couldn't be scratched until she found out the truth.

She headed for the walk, her lips twitching at the all-too-familiar morning wails. And no, she thought with a chuckle to herself, it definitely wasn't Gil. She knocked once, then pushed open the door when she heard the muffled "come in."

"Surprise!" she called from where she stood in the foyer, waiting for another screech to tell her which direction to head.

"Up here."

Eli added his very loud two cents and Leah dropped her bag and climbed the stairs. The nursery had seen better days. Clearly it hadn't been a good night for man and baby. Toys had been flung and discarded, blankets were wadded up on the floor, and the crib-side lamp had been toppled. Gil, similarly, looked as if his day had gotten off to a rough start. He was wearing striped pajama bottoms and a dark tank, and his hair looked as ruffled as Eli's. Gil Hamilton, neat and put together on a normal day, in normal light, garnered feminine appreciation in spades.

Rumpled and disheveled Gil, on the other hand, had her plan of action threatening to skid right off the road. Wow, the man was nicely built. Of course she knew that after kissing him on impulse the other day. Her inability to resist temptation had only confirmed what their first kiss had proposed:

she and Gil were a potent combination. Maybe this wasn't such a good idea after all.

"Someone break in last night and wreck the place?" Leah stooped to scoop up the various items and dropped them into the plump, cushioned chair.

"No such luck," Gil grumbled, then sighed and rested his hands on the railing of the crib. "You are in one serious mood this morning, little guy." He shook his head. "I've tried to put this thing on him three times and he keeps kicking out of it." Gil flipped a yellow onesie in the air.

"Maybe you're offending his sense of fashion." Leah retrieved a pair of elasticized shorts and matching T-shirt, depicting an octopus and dolphin holding tentacle to fin. "I'm betting it's not a giraffe kinda day. Hey there, Eli." She hip-bumped Gil to the side and bent down to blow a kiss on Eli's bare tummy. She waited until he was in midgiggle before quickly dressing him. "There you go. All ready for the day. Your turn," she said and looked at Gil.

"I'm all yours." Gil said the words in a way that had Leah's cheeks warming. "Thanks for the assist."

"No problem." She slipped her hands under Eli and scooped him into the air, grateful for someone else to hold on to.

"You're early. I wasn't expecting you for another hour or so."

"I'm actually right on time. I'm going with you. To Durante," she added at his blank expression. "You said your meeting with Christopher's at noon, right? That gives us enough time to stop for a quick breakfast at the food truck and be on our way."

"We talked about this the other night over dinner," Gil argued. "We agreed you'd come over and stay with Eli while I went."

"Uh-huh, that agreement doesn't work for me. You don't need all that alone time to spin your wheels, emotionally, I mean. Think of me as a distraction. Well, think of both of us that way," she added when Eli squealed and bopped her on the chin. "He can enjoy the ride and we can talk about all kinds of things." She batted her lashes at him. "I have a feeling there's even more to learn about you."

"You do, huh?" Gil's mouth curved. "Funny how that information stream hasn't been running both ways. You're right." That grin of his had chills racing up her arms. "Seems a good time to remedy that."

Now it was Leah who blinked. "That wasn't what I—"

"Too bad." He kissed her, quick and hard and had her seeing stars. "Offer accepted. He's already had his breakfast. Sweet potatoes, peas and half a bottle of formula. I, on the other hand, am starving and have my hopes set on one of Alethea's breakfast burritos. If you want to pack up his bag, I'll grab a quick shower and meet you downstairs. There's coffee if you want," he added as he backed out of the room.

"Thanks." She blew her hair out of her face. "Caffeine might be the last thing I need at the moment." Gil Hamilton first thing in the morning was definitely a jolt to her system. "Let's see what you'll need today, huh, Eli?"

AS THEY NEARED the turnoff for Durante, a little more than an hour northwest of Butterfly Harbor, Gil tried not to eavesdrop on Leah's discussion with her paralegal, but given the confines of the car, the task was near impossible.

"Go ahead and access Mr. and Mrs. Delaney's file on the system," Leah said as she offered an apologetic smile to Gil. "They can call me if they have any questions. How's that information coming on the LLC application for Seth Masters? Uh-huh. Okay, yeah. Make a note of that and put a sticky on my desk. I'll take a look at it tomorrow when I'm back in the office. Have a good day, Callie." She clicked off and tucked her phone in her bag. "Sorry about that. She still gets a bit nervous when I'm out of the office for more than a few hours at a time."

"No apology necessary. I had a similar conversation with Helena before we left." Not that his long-time assistant got nervous. About anything. "Sounds like you've got your hands full with clients."

She sat back with what he'd learned amounted to a relaxing sigh. "Having an attorney look over various life-affecting issues gives people peace of mind. I think I can recite life insurance contracts in my sleep by now." She stifled a yawn. "Callie's handling it all pretty well."

"Must be a big difference. Switching from criminal cases to family law."

"Worlds apart." She tucked her hair behind her ear and looked out her window, but not before Gil saw the tension pulsing in her jaw. She'd found a wardrobe balance today. The jeans she was wearing looked brand new and the oversize turquoise sweater, one he recognized from Needle and Thread, one of the newer town shops, appeared comfy and warm. She'd ditched the heels in favor of boots.

The fall weather seemed to be having an identity crisis and alternated between light showers and sunshine playing peek-a-boo with the cloud cover.

"You don't miss it? Isn't courtroom excitement pretty addictive? You ever think about going back?"

"To being a defense attorney? No. Not happening in this or any other lifetime." Her terse tone snapped through the car before she apologized. "Sorry. Suffice it to say criminal law was not for me."

"I take it neither was Boston." He'd have to be careful how hard he pushed and how deep he dug.

"No. I don't like snow."

"Well you definitely don't get that here."

Gil glanced in the rearview mirror to check on Eli, who appeared to be having a fascinating silent conversation with his fingers.

"Gil, I'd really rather not—"

"Is it anything like what they show on TV?" Gil asked. "Being a lawyer?"

"No."

He'd dealt with stubborn people in his time, but Leah was proving more of a challenge than he expected. "I'll tell you what. I bet I can guess the date of when you won your first case. If I do, you have to answer at least some of my questions with more than one syllable."

Leah smiled. "And what do I get if you don't?"

"I'll let the subject of your past career drop. Come on, Leah. You know way more about me than I'd prefer. Give me a chance to even the playing field."

"Fine. If you guess, you can have five questions."

"Ten," he countered.

"Seven. Final offer." She folded her arms over her chest. "Month, day and year." She smirked. "Go."

"What, no exact time?" But as soon as he

teased her, he rattled off the date and felt a surge of pride when she looked at him, eyes wary.

"Anyone can use the internet."

"Are you accusing me of cheating?" He feigned shock.

"Perish the thought. You've had this entire conversation planned out since I said I was coming with you."

"Only somewhat true," Gil admitted without a scintilla of guilt. "My answer has absolutely nothing to do with online research and everything to do with the day your uncle Benjamin bought nearly everyone in town dinner at the Butterfly Diner to celebrate your victory."

"You're making that up." The tension in Leah's face eased. "He did?"

"He went in for his usual early bird dinner and stayed until closing. Paid for every bill and bragged about you to anyone within earshot."

"Must be why it felt like everyone knew me when I first moved to town." That information was enough to soften her expression. "He was my biggest cheerleader. He paid for my first year of law school. Since he never had children of his own, he was excited when I told thc family about my plans. He confided in me that he'd never been so happy to write a check that big. One of the reasons I took the bar both back in Pennsylvania and in California." The glimmer of joy in her eyes dimmed. "I hope I didn't disappoint him given how it all worked out."

"You bought him out and allowed him to head off to Florida for the retirement he always dreamed of," Gil said. "Where's the disappointment in that?"

"He used to tell me he imagined me arguing in front of the Supreme Court."

"Did you? Have that dream?" Gil asked.

"No. No, my dream was a bit on the smaller side. Although it did have to do with fighting for and defending the wrongly accused and persecuted. I was so naive."

That definitely sounded like a story. "What happened?"

"Gil—"

"Hey, you started this by uncovering my secrets. Turnabout is fair play."

"Is not," she muttered. The silence stretched for a long moment before she sighed and rolled her eyes. "All right, fine.

Maybe I'm no longer naive. It just took me longer than most to learn what a lot of defense attorneys discover early on. Most people lie."

"People or clients?"

She smirked, looked back out the window. "Do you remember hearing about the Brock Russell case? The private investment director who was accused of embezzling from his mostly elderly clientele?"

"Sure. That trial was headline news for weeks. He was charged with stealing over eight million dollars. One of the podcasts I follow micro-commented on the entire thing." Gil caught up with his own thoughts. "Don't tell me you were one of his attorneys."

"Second chair." Leah flashed him a less-than-humorous smile. "My first big case as a junior partner. I spent more than eight months listening to Brock Russell protest his innocence, that it had all been a horrible mistake, and that his late mentor had actually been responsible and he was just trying to protect the business after his mentor died. That's the angle we used for his defense and, hey, who could really argue it because the guy who was to blame was dead. Brock was just another one of his victims." Her words dropped from her lips like chunks of ice. "It took the jury less than four hours to find Brock innocent."

He glanced over and noticed she had clasped her justice scale pendant between her thumb and forefinger. She was moving it back and forth along the gold chain around her neck. "You did your job, Leah."

"Yes, I did." Her tone made him shiver. "And I did it really, really well. Despite the fact that everything he ever told us was a lie. Not only had he stolen the money but he had no qualms about throwing his mentor under every bus in the Philadelphia area."

"Well." Gil took a deep breath. "That explains it."

"Explains what?"

"Your instant dislike of me. Don't look at me like that. Now I know why. Brock Russell and I have a lot in common."

"Hardly."

"No?" Gil arched a brow. "I listened to that podcast. They dissected his life. Russell came from money, same as me. He was only in the job he had because of the family legacy and business, same as me. Everything probably came easy for him or, at least, appeared to."

"But it didn't for you," Leah countered.

"No," he admitted, "it definitely did not. How did you find out the truth about Russell?"

"I can't say specifically." Leah pressed her lips into a thin line. "Let's just say that once double jeopardy was attached, the real Brock Russell made an appearance and I did not like what I saw. Either in him or in the mirror. It made me physically ill to think I'd helped him get away with robbing those people."

Gil could relate. Far more than he cared to admit. "Did I hear something about the money being found recently? Or did I imagine that?"

"A little over two years ago," Leah confirmed. "A private investigator hired by some of the families tracked down the various offshore accounts where Russell had stashed it."

"Talented PI."

"The civil case is going to be a slam dunk from what I hear." It didn't escape his notice that she shifted the subject slightly. "Of course, a lot of Russell's victims have passed away now. It's their families who are left to deal with the mess. A mess I had a part in creating."

"You were doing your job," Gil repeated. "We need representation on both sides of the aisle, Leah. You chose a side and found it didn't fit. Live and learn."

"Yeah, live and learn."

He understood her so much better now. It was as if this one small revelation opened up a lot of closed doors he hadn't even seen before. It also explained why she was determined to stick her neck out not only for the members of the Cocoon Club but for the town as a whole. She'd seen him as someone she could defeat and help to make things better. How could he not like her for that? "I guess it turns out I'm not the only one who's been looking to atone."

"You sound like my therapist," Leah said, only now her voice had finally lightened.

"You talked to your therapist about me?"

"No," she laughed. "It's just something she would have said. And don't think I haven't been keeping track. You only have one question left."

"I'll save it for when you're least expecting it." He reached over and took hold of her hand. Not only because he sensed she needed something—someone—to hold on to but because he did as well. He took a deep breath and veered off the freeway into Durante. "Guess confession time is over."

Durante was significantly larger than Butterfly Harbor and boasted at least four times the population. While Gil had made certain to continue his town's dedication to small business and preventing large chain and box stores from setting up camp, Durante had embraced it all, leaving a number of their mom-and-pop stores empty along the main thoroughfare.

"There's a park about two blocks down from the police station," Gil told Leah. He retrieved the new collapsible stroller from the trunk while Leah unbuckled Eli from his car seat. It felt—and no doubt looked—as if they were a family taking an outing to a neighboring town. But an everyday outing didn't come with a swarm of anxious hornets buzzing in his stomach, looking for a way out. He stood on the sidewalk, staring down the street toward the police station and dreading what came next.

"You okay?" Leah touched his shoulder.

"You were right." Gil shifted so he could slip his arm around her waist and pull her close. Just for a moment. Just long enough to lose himself in the comforting floral scent of her that danced through his senses. "Making that drive alone would have only had me spinning in circles. Talking helped."

"Probably because we were talking about me most of the time," Leah said slowly. "I can still come with you to see Christopher," she said. "I'm sure there's someone in the station who could keep an eye on Eli."

"No. This time I mean it. Take him to the park. Enjoy the fresh air and the sunshine, now that it's on full blast." The sun had indeed managed to burn its way through the clouds and bathed the bustling downtown Durante area with light. "I'll text you when I'm done."

He gave her waist a squeeze and moved away, only to have her tug him back and put a hand up to his face. "None of what he's done is your fault, Gil. His behavior is on him. He needs to accept responsibility if he's going to have a chance at any relationship with either you or his son."

"He doesn't want a relationship with me," Gil reminded her. "And I'm not sure I want him to have one with Eli. Go on, Leah." He pressed his lips to her forehead. "Thank you. But go."

Leah scrunched her face. He recognized that look. It was the one that said she thought someone was making an error in judgment. Not a mistake, Gil thought as he walked away. Leah would never be so tactless as to call what he was doing a mistake, but this was something he had to take care of himself. Whether he wanted to or not.

"THEY'RE BRINGING HIM out now." Perry Chandler, the public defender assigned as Christopher's attorney, rifled through his overstuffed, soft-sided briefcase. He was younger than Gil had expected and had a surprising amount of optimism on his round face. Optimism that Gil suspected might fade one day, given Leah's comments about the job. "Don't mind me, but he's going to be seriously ticked off to see you, Mayor Hamilton. Not that he needs much of an excuse. Christopher's got himself a temper."

"Gil," Gil corrected for the second time since they'd been escorted into the private meeting room in the police station. Gil and Durante sheriff Sean Brodie went all the way back to high school. It was one of Gil's few surviving friendships, one he'd appreciated even more in the past few years. No doubt their connection was part of what earned Gil the special arrangement he currently found himself in. "If you want to leave now, I'll understand, Perry," Gil said. "No need for him to be mad at both of us."

"Well, I do still have to work with him after this." Perry shook his head after taking a moment to think. "Nope. I'll stay. I think it's best you two clear the air. He needs to get rid of all that mad somehow. If he carries it into court with him, he'll end up with a sentence longer than a person's expected lifespan."

Gil stood at one of the blind-covered windows and looked out to the smattering of desks and computers and uniformed officers. The building was brightly lit and spacious, unlike the sheriff's office in town, which felt more like a cabin in the middle of the woods. Surrounded by redwoods and poised at a lookout over the ocean, Gil definitely knew which law enforcement location he preferred. The meeting room he currently stood in had as much character as an abandoned motel room. Small, no windows that allowed for outdoor light, and mismatched furniture that had probably been tossed in here as an afterthought.

Definitely not an ideal space for a family reunion.

In the distance, a heavy door slammed shut and an officer emerged from a hallway, his hand locked around the arm of an orange-jumpsuited young man. The handcuffs around his wrists had Gil cringing. Head down, hair overgrown and his shoulders slumped, Christopher Russo didn't come close to resembling the photograph on the wanted-for-questioning flyers that had been circulating through the county.

"Last chance to leave," Gil said to Perry without looking away. Those hornets that had been buzzing in his belly picked up speed. He'd been dreading this moment forthe past few days. He'd reworked what he'd planned to say a thousand different times in order to convey a thousand different thoughts. Only now…

Now he didn't know that there was anything to say that would ever be enough.

One hard rap signaled the officer's arrival. The uniformed man pushed open the door and ushered Christopher through, angling him to one of the chairs, but before Christopher sat, he caught sight of Gil. Angry, betrayed eyes flashed over to Perry. "You set me up."

"Christopher—"

"Take me back to holding," Christopher demanded of the guard, who shook his head.

"Sheriff's orders. Not until you hear him out." The officer jerked a thumb in Gil's direction. "Brodie says this makes you two even now. Slate's clean."

"That's what he thinks." Gil couldn't help but chuckle.

"Hamilton payback," Christopher spat. "Typical. Like father, like son."

"You should know," Gil shot back, then, in the back of his mind, imagined Leah's disapproval. Even with her not being here, she was still…here. "Sit. Please, Christopher," he added, noting his brother's glare. "You're the one who came here to California. You're the one who spent months trying to get my attention in Butterfly Harbor and ended up hurting innocent people in the process. Well, you have my attention now. All of it. Let's talk."

"You really think talking is going to fix anything?" Christopher demanded but did as Gil suggested and claimed one of the chairs. "You're the reason I'm in this mess!"

"I'm not responsible for the choices you've made." He hadn't believed Leah when she'd said those words to him, but seeing his younger brother now, handcuffed and dejected, he understood. "I didn't know about you," he said quietly. "Not until after our father died. I didn't know, Christopher," he said again, hoping the truth would seep in. "I get it that you don't want to believe that."

"It's not a matter of want. I don't." Christopher whipped his head back, sending his too-long hair behind his shoulders. He looked like their father. The chiseled, granite jaw, the more angular features. He had the same sturdy build, not as lanky as Gil, but then Gil took after his mother in most respects. Lucky Christopher, Gil thought. But it was Christopher's eyes that caught Gil's attention the most. He had the Hamilton blue eyes. Just like Eli.

Gil's heart twisted into a knot.

"You're a liar," Christopher said, "just like our father."

"Why would I lie?" It was the one thing that had never made sense to him. "Christopher, if I'd known—"

"He told me you knew. After my mother died, he came to Arizona. I didn't have anyone left. I was eighteen and I was alone and I had to figure out how to bury her. I thought, finally, he wouldn't have a choice. He'd bring me home with him and—" Christopher seemed to catch himself, sat up straighter, and the hard ice in his eyes returned. "I thought we'd be a family. Instead, he sat me down and told me the truth. That when he told you about me you swore you'd never accept me. That you didn't want to have anything to do with me. And that as far as you were concerned, you didn't have a brother. He said you told him to choose and he had to choose you."

For an instant, Gil saw the boy Christopher must have been. The innocent, lonely boy who had been as starved for their father's affection as Gil had.

"None of that happened, Christopher." So much of what had occurred with his brother since then now made sense. An awful, heartbreaking kind of sense.

"He gave me a check." The loathing in Christopher's voice was couched only by pain. A pain Gil was all too familiar with. "He gave me a check, enough to cover my mother's burial expenses and a couple months' rent. Then he left and came back home to you. I never saw him again."

Gil turned away, unable to face the accusation evident on his brother's face. Lifelong rage that had never found an outlet circled inside of him, screaming for release. His fists clenched and he lifted them, wanting to smash into something, anything that would bend to his will. Until an image shifted through his thoughts, cutting through the hurt and the pain and resentment.

Leah.

Beautiful, smiling, no-nonsense Leah, who didn't let him get away with anything.

Leah, who saw who he was but also who he was trying to be.

Leah.

Suddenly, the anger popped, like a dud of a firecracker dying with the snap of a finger. Anger wouldn't do anyone any good. Not Christopher. Not Gil. And certainly not Eli. Letting resentment and hatred dictate his actions was what their father would have done. And Gil was done following in anything resembling Morland Hamilton's footsteps.

"Gil?" Perry spoke from his seat beside Christopher.

"No more," Gil whispered to himself. "No more." He turned, relaxed his hands and strode to the table where he faced his brother. "I need you to listen to me. I need you to *hear* me," he insisted in as calm and rational tone as he could muster. "Our father lied. About everything, I imagine. But if you don't ever believe anything else I say, believe this. I did not know about you until after he was dead."

Christopher blinked but didn't give any indication he'd heard a word.

"She was right." Gil shook his head, almost laughed. "Heaven help me, Leah was right about this, too. It's just easier to blame me, isn't it? You want to believe the lie because it's easier to accept than our father wanted nothing to do with you." There! He saw it. A flinch in Christopher's eyes. The words had hit their target. He'd cracked the defensive shield. Now he just needed to shatter it completely. "I don't know what I would have done had I known about you sooner. I'll readily admit that, because our father did just as big a number on me as he did on you. But who I am now? The man I'm trying to be. I'm not walking away from you. I'm not leaving you alone. Whatever happens, you're my brother and I'm done hiding behind Morland Hamilton's secrets."

"Whatever. We finished?" Christopher stared at him as he rose to his feet until they were eye to eye. "Can I go now?"

Gil would not flinch. He would not look away. This felt like a test. One he had to pass if any of them were going to move on from here. "If you want to go, yes." Gil remained where he was, his fingers gripping the table as failure circled. He couldn't let things end like this. He couldn't let this be the last time he spoke to his brother.

He couldn't be the wedge that came between another father and son.

He waited as Christopher made his way to the door, his heart pounding painfully in his chest. "Just answer me one question before you go."

"What?"

"Elijah." Gil waited for his brother to stop and look at him. "What would you like me to tell Elijah when he asks me about you?"

"OKAY, LITTLE MAN." Leah lifted Elijah out of the stroller and trudged through the sand to the infant swings. She'd recognized the pre-fuss sounds during their walk. He was probably feeling cooped up. Or he was picking up on Leah's anxiety, as she was carrying around buckets of it.

"He can do this on his own just fine," she told her baby companion as she settled him in the swing seat.

Eli raised wide eyes to her as he pounded his hands on the rail. "MMmwwwwha!"

"Someday you're going to have to tell me exactly what that means." She sat down in the sand and curled her legs under her so she could gently push Eli. Watching the delight and joy flash across his face brought a smile to her own, but it didn't do much to ease her nerves. As much as she tried to tell herself she was concerned about Gil and the meeting he was having with his estranged half brother, the emotions rioting through her went deeper.

She prided herself on being practical, down-to-earth. A realist in the strictest sense. She wasn't particularly romantic or fanciful. She was straightforward and honest, because she found it the easiest way to exist. She'd never been one to get her head stuck in the clouds or fill her mind with fantasies and wishes she knew would never come true.

And yet…

She let out a slow breath and wondered. "Yet you're doing both by falling in love with him." No, she corrected herself. Not just him. Not just Gil Hamilton. She was falling fast and hard for both of them. "This is all your fault, you know," she chided Eli who squealed and giggled. He reached his fists up to grab handfuls of air and kicked his feet as if trying to make himself go faster.

She'd moved beyond her desire for a family of her own years ago. Her education, the law, her career, they had always come first. She'd wanted as many options open to her as she could juggle. She'd chosen her path but now…

Before she'd moved to Butterfly Harbor, she'd been surrounded by her siblings and their children. Since she'd made her transition, she'd found herself embraced by friends who shared their families as well. She was godmother to Jo and Ozzy's baby, Hope. She'd tag-teamed slumber parties and babysitting duties with Alethea Costas and attended countless events filled with the laughter—and sometimes crankiness—of the town's children. Her life was full.

Or, she thought it had been. Now that Elijah Hamilton had sneaked into her heart and pretty much taken root there, she knew she hadn't come close to filling the capacity of her desire for a family of her own. For people to love. To claim for herself.

That was within her grasp. She knew that now. How could she not accept it when her waking thought every morning was whether she was going to see Gil and Eli? When she had to stop herself from texting Gil before she went to sleep just to see how he was doing?

She saw him so much more clearly now. It was as if he'd been existing in some kind of rumor-caked fog that prevented her from seeing past the ill will that had followed him around all his life.

There was no denying it. She was falling completely and utterly in love with Gil Hamilton. The scary thing was, she didn't have any means to stop it.

The scarier thing?

She wasn't sure she wanted to.

CHAPTER TWELVE

"ELIJAH."

Had Gil any doubts that Christopher knew about his son's existence, they disappeared with the whisper of Eli's name. There was a reverence, a desperation that couldn't be faked.

Christopher's cuffed hands dropped away from the doorknob as he stepped toward Gil, the animosity replaced with a longing Gil had only recently become acquainted with. "You know about Eli. You've seen him? You've seen Sylvie? Where are they? Are they okay?"

It was like looking at a different person. But this man, unlike the Christopher who had been brought in from holding moments before, seemed willing to have a conversation.

"Let's talk. For real this time, Christopher," Gil added when the suspicion crept into the man's eyes again. "Perry, you want to go out and get coffees?" He glanced at his brother.

Christopher nodded and Gil looked to his attorney, who took the hint with surprising ease. "Sure. I'll be back in a bit. Any preferences?"

"No." Gil just wanted the next few minutes to be between him and Christopher. Once Perry left, Gil shifted his attention fully to the man across from him.

"Eli's fine," Gil said. "Sylvie left him with me a couple of weeks ago." The relief on his brother's face, sadly, only presented more questions than answers.

"Where is he now?"

"With a friend," Gil answered. "Tell me about them. Tell me about your family."

"It's a mess." Christopher shook his head. "It always has been. Sylvie and I, we aren't really good for each other, but it was enough, you know? Or maybe you don't." He weaved his fingers together so tightly his knuckles went white. "After Mom died, me and Sylvie got married because it made sense. Sylvie's family situation was worse than mine, and beyond that, she had…problems. But we were making things work. I promised to take care of her and I had a good job. Kids weren't supposed to be part of this. With all the medications she was supposed to be taking..." He shrugged, as if that explained it all. "She wanted someone to love. Someone to love her, but Eli was so much work and she didn't cope well either during the pregnancy or after he was born. The only thing I could think was if we only had enough money, things could be better."

"You're wanted for questioning in Arizona regarding a string of break-ins and car thefts," Gil reminded him. "And there are the unsolved burglaries here in Durante they're looking at you for."

"I'd lost my job," Christopher said. "And our medical insurance. I had friends who helped me over a rough patch, but it wasn't enough. That's when I decided to come out here and talk to you. To ask for help. I was going to go back, just as soon as I could, but..." He stopped, as if afraid of saying too much. "What did Sylvie tell you?"

It would be easy to lie, but there had already been enough lies between them. "She didn't tell me anything." He reached into his back pocket. "I never saw or spoke to her. She left Eli on my front porch along with this note." While Christopher opened the folded paper, Gil brought out his phone and tapped open one of the dozens of pictures he'd taken in the last few days. "My friends helped me put the pieces together. We found your marriage certificate and Eli's birth record. I don't know where Sylvie is now, Christopher. I can have people start looking for her—"

The paper rattled in his hands. "If she left Eli, she doesn't want to be found." He looked down at the screen Gil turned around for him. "He's gotten so big. Look at that face of his." The affection was clear and eased Gil's uncertainty a bit. "I should have followed through. I shouldn't have let the anger take over, but when I saw you walking around town, talking with people, reminding me so much of our father… I wanted to hurt you and the only thing I knew you cared about was the town and that new building project. I didn't mean to hurt anyone other than you. Everything just snowballed."

The fight in him evaporated like steam. "My lawyer said the woman I hurt was okay."

"Jo's fine. So's her baby, thankfully," Gil

added to remind his brother there had been more than one innocent person affected. "More damage was done with that machinery you sabotaged. One of the workers was seriously injured and more could have been."

"I only wanted to—"

"I get it." Gil held up a hand. "But you didn't stop. You kept going. Kept hiding out and...then there was what happened with Declan Cartwright. What were you thinking?"

"That's the guy with the big work shed next to the house? I was just trying to find things to sell, to get enough money for a bus ticket back to Arizona. Sylvie had stopped answering her phone and I was just...stuck."

"You had a way out," Gil reminded him. "The biggest mistake you made in all of this was not coming to me like you originally planned. I would have helped, Christopher. None of this, *none* of it, had to happen."

Christopher grimaced. "I know. I have to fix all this. I have to, for my son." He lowered his hands, turned pleading eyes on Gil. "I know I have no right to ask, but can you bring him to me? Can I see him?"

"That'll depend," Gil said. "Eli is why I'm

here, Christopher. I think there's more to Sylvie leaving him on my front porch than just her feeling overwhelmed." He debated how to say it, then realized there was no good way other than to spit it out. "Eli's sick. He has a heart condition."

"A—what?" Christopher blinked. "Is it serious?"

"Potentially. He has a hole in his heart. The doctors are monitoring him, and some day it might require surgery. Or he might just outgrow it. Either way, he's going to need consistent care. He's going to need a stable home."

"You aren't going to turn him over to social services are you?"

"No. My attorney's gotten me approved as an emergency foster parent."

"Wait, you're his parent?" Christopher sat back in his chair. "Who said anything about you doing that? He's my son. Mine! Not yours."

"I am aware," Gil squeezed the words around his constricting heart. "Are you aware of where you are? Of where you'll be for who knows how long?"

"That doesn't change the fact he's mine."

"Of course not, but can't you see I'm his and your best option. I've got doctors in place and a support system in Butterfly Harbor. He's safe and happy, and Christopher, depending on where you serve your sentence, I can help—"

Christopher shook his head. "No. No, this isn't what I want. This isn't what I want for Eli. He's my son."

Gil stood, hoping, praying he could somehow get through to his brother. "It's either me or the system, and I'm not letting Eli get placed in a world full of strangers. Is that what you want for him? Do you hate me so much you'd rather Eli go into foster care than have him find a home with me? If so, that doesn't make you a good father, Christopher." Gil felt sick and headed for the door. "But it definitely makes you our father's son."

SITUATED IN THE center of a tire swing, Eli settled in her lap, Leah shielded her eyes against the sunshine and watched Gil appear at the entrance to the playground.

"Hey, Eli. Guess who's coming?" She'd been hoping for the best where Gil's meeting with his brother was concerned. But given how he had his hands stuffed in his pockets and how his head was tilted down, his shoulders slumped, her hope faded. "Oh boy." She rested one hand on Eli's back and the other on his tummy. "Something tells me Gil's going to need some of your special charm."

"Bwwwhafa!" Eli grunted and leaned into her chest. His hands grabbed for her in a way that had her cheeks warming.

"Clearly I should have snagged one of your bottles, huh?" There was no ladylike way to disentangle herself from the suspended tire swing, so she waited and plastered on a bright smile as Gil approached.

"Just in time for lunch," Leah teased as Gil stepped into the sand-filled play area. He stood in front of them, his eyes blocked from her sight by the sunglasses he wore. "How bad?"

"About what I expected." Even before he held out his hands, Eli was reaching for him. The second he had Eli, however, his entire demeanor changed. "I think we're going to have to come at things in a different way." He pressed his lips against Eli's temple. "I don't think he gets it. I'm still the enemy even though I'm trying to do what's best for his son."

"Not surprising, I suppose." Leah maneuvered to her feet. "If you honestly thought one conversation was going to end the years of hurt and resentment, you're more of an optimist than I gave you credit for. I need to get his bottle." She brushed off her backside and slogged back to the stroller. "Though you've done what my father always called planting the seed. Now you need to give it some time to germinate, then grow. We'll make sure Eli's taken care of, Gil." She smiled at him when he joined her. "And as a reward for your bravery, I'm not going to ask you for the details. Yet," she added when his eyebrows arched. She popped the lid off the bottle and passed it to Gil. "We'll need to discuss it, of course, professionally speaking, but take some time and decompress a bit, okay? Oh! Before I forget. Halloween's next week. Have you given any thought to what Eli's costume might be?"

"He could go as a baby." Gil chuckled as Eli grabbed for the bottle and stuffed it into his mouth. "No good?"

"You should take full advantage of the

chance you get to express your own intentions where costuming is concerned. Don't you remember last year, when Luke and Holly dressed the twins up like Raggedy Ann and Andy?"

"I do, actually."

"Well, I saw a cute children's clothing shop about a block back, and they had some really darling infant costumes. Let's go take a look before we find someplace for lunch."

Gil caught her arm when she stooped over to close the diaper bag. "The costume hunt is fine, but if you don't mind, I'd rather head home? I just… I'd just like to go home."

"Okay." She hid her frown behind yet another too-bright smile. "Home it is."

"WHAT TIME DID you tell Mandy to be here?"

Gil tightened the lid on the jar of strained peaches—apparently a big hit where Eli was concerned—and stashed it in the fridge. In the days since meeting with Christopher, the pressure he'd hoped to leave in Durante had surged afresh knowing Thursday night dinner with the Cocoon Club loomed. "I asked her to be here at four so I could show her around and give her instructions." He retrieved a damp washcloth and proceeded to wipe Eli down from nose to sticky fingertips.

"Mandy's babysat every child born in Butterfly Harbor for the past five years," Leah announced from where she was seated at his kitchen table. "She's got more infant experience than you do."

"I know." Honestly, Mandy Evans was one of the few people in town he felt he could trust Eli with implicitly. The almost sixteen-year-old was exceedingly responsible. Holding down two part-time jobs, one of which was as an ocean tour and dive guide for Monty Bettencourt's Wind Walkers, while getting straight As in her honor roll high school classes made her yet another promising beacon for the future of Butterfly Harbor. Provided she stuck around. "The Cocoon Club's house is only a few blocks away if there's any issue."

Leah toasted him with a bottle of water. "For the record, I think you made the right decision between the two costumes for Eli's first Halloween."

"Said the woman who pushed for the poop-emoji costume." When had he become the kind of man who spent an hour debating infant clothing options? "Contrary to his current occupation as a diaper-filling machine, I agree. He'll make a much cuter marshmallow with those chubby cheeks of his. I was thinking of taking him up to Duskywing Farm for Calliope's Halloween party." Since the opportunity he'd been waiting for had presented itself, he asked, "Can I talk you into joining us?"

"That depends," Leah said warily. "Do I have to dress up?"

"Of course." Gil feigned his offense. Eli's head began to droop along with his eyes.

"He loved the playground today."

"I know I'd have preferred it to where I spent my time," Gil admitted. "Can Christopher stop me looking after Eli?" It seemed the only thing he and his brother had in common was their love for Eli. Gil understood Christopher's fears over losing his son, but the reality was Gil wasn't fighting to keep Eli to spite his brother; he was fighting to keep Eli out of a system that could prevent him or Christopher from ever having a relationship with the boy.

"Technically? Yes. That said, Christopher

isn't in a very strong position, considering where he's currently residing," Leah said. "It's doubtful a judge isn't going to award you temporary custody, especially with Sylvie missing."

The idea of losing the little boy, even after only knowing him a few weeks, was unfathomable. Everything had changed because of him. He looked at Leah. Everything.

"Let's deal with it as it comes," Leah suggested. "And know that I'm not going to let anything separate you two. If that means a court battle, so be it."

"I thought you didn't want to step foot back in a courtroom."

"I don't. One reason I don't want us to get ahead of ourselves." Leah glanced at her watch. "I have to get home and change for tonight."

"Can you give me ten minutes?" Gil asked. "I'd love to grab a quick shower."

"Yeah, sure. No naps allowed this time." She got to her feet and took the damp rag from him. "I'll finish cleaning up in here."

"Great, thanks." He hurried upstairs, showered, changed and was just combing his hair when he heard the doorbell ring.

He checked the bedside clock. "Ten minutes early. An additional bonus point for Mandy Evans."

He heard not two, but multiple, female voices along with Eli's excited squeals when he reached the first floor. In the space of a few minutes, his living room had been taken over by Eli's toys, Mandy Evans and two additional little girls.

"Hi, Gil." Mandy, Eli poised confidently on her hip, gave him a quick wave. "Hope you don't mind, but I brought backup. I'm thinking of expanding my babysitting services to training others."

"It was my idea," Charlie Bradley announced as she popped to her feet and approached him. The eleven-year-old was known for her colorful and often times mismatched outfits. Her current attire consisted of bright pink pants, a neon yellow T-shirt with rainbow butterflies, and her crooked ponytails were accented with sparkling butterfly clips. But it was that big-toothed smile that slid into the heart of every resident of Butterfly Harbor, Gil included. "Mom says I can babysit Lily after I get supervised experience."

"That's where I come in," Mandy offered.

"Right," Charlie confirmed. "Since Mandy is everyone's go-to sitter—"

Gil glanced at Leah, who was obviously trying not to laugh.

"—I suggested she start giving interested parties like me lessons. I'm her guinea pig." Charlie straightened to attention. "Well, me and Stella. For tonight anyway. We'll take real good care of Elijah. Promise."

Stella Jones, who was nearing thirteen, gave a shy wave. When she moved, the tiny bells and shells she wore in her long curly hair tinkled and chimed. "Calliope and Xander are going to need help when she has the baby," Stella said in reference to her much-older sister. "I don't want to be left out."

"In that case, thank you, all three of you," Gil said, "for coming over this evening. You leaving, Leah?"

"I'll meet you at five," Leah told him as she scooted past him. "Feel free to leave my cell number with them as a fail-safe, if you want."

He followed her to the door. "I'll pick you up."

"Gil," Leah's warning tone was back. "It's only a few blocks away and..."

"And what?" He leaned against the door frame. "You afraid it's going to look like a date?"

"Not afraid, exactly," Leah hedged. "But I'm not sure it's appropriate so close to the election. You remember the election, don't you? For the job you're trying to keep?"

"I remember. I also recall telling you I'm going to win. Whether we're dating or not. I'll pick you up in about forty-five minutes."

"Give a girl time to get dressed, at least. Make it fifty," she countered as her gaze lifted to somewhere over his shoulder. From behind him, Gil heard scampering and whispered voices. "And don't forget to pay all three of them."

"Way ahead of you," he murmured, then, because he'd been wanting to for what seemed like forever, he pressed his mouth to hers. "See you in a bit."

"Mmm." Her lips formed a straight line, either to stop from smiling or to keep hold of the electricity that fired between them. "I'm beginning to think you should come with a warning label." She touched his arm before heading down the stairs.

"My mom and dad say you two are dating," Charlie announced when he returned to the living room. "Are you? Ow! What?" She glared at Stella and rubbed her arm. "I'm only asking what everyone wants to know."

"It's none of anyone's business and it's rude," Stella told her. "Calliope says we should wait for people to talk about their lives when they're ready to. We shouldn't push." But there was no mistaking the interest in Stella's eyes.

"Maybe I should make this lesson number one, guys," Mandy suggested. "No interrogating your charges' parents."

Eli blew a big raspberry.

"Couldn't have said it better myself, Eli." Gil motioned to the stairs. "How about I show you his room to get started?"

CHAPTER THIRTEEN

TROUBLE. THAT'S WHAT SHE was in now.

Leah slipped on her gold hoop earrings. The earrings she wore to important meetings, favorite events and the occasional date. Considering tonight consisted of all three, she tried to tell herself it wasn't anything more than a group of friends having dinner.

"A group of friends who could very well be slinging their desserts at each other by the end of it," she reminded herself as she smoothed her hands down the sides of the simple black dress. "Good enough to eat breakfast at a jewelry store." Along with the simple dress came the simple flat shoes, despite her gnawing desire to slip into the rhinestone-accented, mile-high pumps that had been in her closet ever since she bought them. The second she stepped out in public with those beauties on her feet and Gil on her arm, there wouldn't be any doubt left in

Butterfly Harbor that her relationship with Mayor Hamilton had moved beyond professional and straight into personal.

As her thoughts shifted to the election, the knot of unease that had lodged in her chest weeks before tightened. The passive excitement she'd felt as a candidate had faded, replaced with her growing acceptance she had no business being in this race.

"That's your heart talking, not your head." She shook off the doubt. Her reticence and regret had nothing to do with her inability or qualifications to be mayor and everything to do with not wanting to hurt Gil. He needed this job, not only because his future with Eli may hang in the balance but because, well, what else did he have? "That's not your responsibility," she told her reflection. "He's not your responsibility." Except…

Except maybe, in some ways, he was.

"You need to get this under control." The order was as straight and simple as she could make it. "Emotions and connections make things too complicated for you. They always have. Keep things light. Keep things calm." She jumped when her doorbell rang. "Keep things together."

Fingers pressed against the pendant at her throat, she retrieved the evening bag she'd pulled out of the closet earlier and headed for the door. The second she opened it, she could feel her knees threatening to fold and the rest of her melting into a puddle at his feet.

She'd clearly not been paying attention at his house, either that or he'd changed, because the sight of Gil Hamilton in black trousers, a stark white button-down shirt and narrow black tie had her wishing they were staying in for the evening. "You ready for this?" She cleared her throat to stop herself from squeaking. "According to Ezzie, the club's been in rare form today."

"I'm not worried." He held out his hand, and when she took it, he helped her onto her front porch. She turned around and locked the door, trying to look anywhere but at him. It wasn't fair.

She'd convinced herself years ago that she was happy with her life. Happy being alone. Happy being on her own.

And yet here she was, walking down her curving stone path, her hand lightly clasped in Gil's, wondering if this was the

start of something utterly unexpected and—
"Complicated."

"What is?" Gil asked as he led her to his car.

"Huh?"

"You said it's complicated." He pulled open the door, stepped back for her to climb in.

"Life," she said quickly. "Life's complicated." And so, she thought as she watched him continue around the front of the car, was love.

GIL HAD NO problem admitting to himself that he wasn't particularly looking forward to the evening. Not because he was well past believing the Cocoon Club would welcome him with open arms but because he didn't want to share Leah with anyone.

Especially after seeing her in that dress. His blood pressure had skyrocketed into the stratosphere the second she'd opened the door. And that million-watt smile of hers? It just lightened up all the darker corners of his heart.

He'd much rather have driven to the Flutterby Inn and spent the evening across the table from her at the five-star restaurant, testing and tasting whatever culinary creations Chef Jason Corwin was concocting. Then again, if the evening with the club ended early, they could easily shift over to the inn and enjoy coffee and dessert.

"I'm thinking we should have a signal, like a code word," Gil said as he took a left onto Checkerspot Drive. This particular stretch of town boasted a mishmash of architectural styles that represented the diverse line of the town's infrastructure. The home-landscape rehabilitation program that Lori Knight voluntarily oversaw added that extra flair to every neighborhood, making properties look especially enticing. "What do you think?"

"A code word?" Leah asked.

"You know, for when—if—things go sideways."

"You mean an escape plan," Leah teased. "So if I were to work the word *rutabaga* into the conversation, you'd know I was ready to call it a night."

"*Rutabaga.* Sure." Gil grinned. "That'll work."

"I was kidding."

He shrugged. "Too late. It's already planted

in my subconscious." When they pulled up in front of the corner, two-story Victorian, the nerves he'd been trying to keep at bay resurfaced. "Do you think they'll try to take me down before or after dessert?"

"It won't be that bad."

"You say that as if you mean it."

"Look at it like this," Leah said as they both caught sight of Ezzie coming toward them. "They're already voting for me, so it's not like you have anything to lose."

"You do remember that they TP'd my car after our first debate, right?"

"Considering Oscar's started hoarding Silly String, you should count yourself lucky." She shoved out of the car before Gil had a chance to come around and assist. "Hi, Ezzie. Sorry if we're late."

"Oh, no, you're fine. You look beautiful as always." Ezzie Fairchild's smile didn't quite reach her eyes. The Bostonian transplant had a lot packed into her five-foot-nothing frame, most of which was a no-nonsense attitude that made her the perfect caretaker and social organizer for the Cocoon Club. To Gil, she'd come off more New Jersey than Boston, with enough affection and love to give than the entire Eastern seaboard. "I was about to call you both, actually." She reached out for Gil's hand as he approached. "I'm not sure this is a good idea."

"Oh? Why not?" Maybe he and Leah would be spending their evening at the Flutterby Inn after all.

"Is everyone all right?" Leah shot him a look that let him know he'd asked the wrong question.

"Physically, they're fine." Ezzie glanced over her shoulder just as five pairs of eyes suddenly disappeared from the front window. "It's Myra. She's been in a pickle about this for days. Now she's refusing to attend, and honestly, it's made the rest of them feel as if they shouldn't, either."

"We don't want to seem like we're pressuring them into doing something they aren't comfortable with," Leah said and looked at him. "Maybe we should go."

"I'm not ready to *rutabaga* things just yet." Tonight was no longer about an election or even about a past he couldn't change. This was about an elderly woman who was clearly in pain. "Where is she?"

"Myra?" Ezzie blinked in surprise. "She's in the backyard."

"Why don't you two go on inside?" He veered off to the right and the side gate. "Let me see to her."

"I'm not so sure—" Ezzie moved to follow, but Leah stopped her.

"Let him try, Ezzie," Leah said. "He's better at this kind of thing than people give him credit for." She gave him a nod of encouragement before linking her arm through Ezzie's.

When Gil reached the side gate, he rested his hand on the weathered wood, getting his thoughts in order before unlatching it and stepping through. It had been years since he'd been here; the last time had been shortly after the group of seniors had pooled their limited resources and bought the place as a group home. Over the years, various improvements had been made, and meticulous attention had been paid to the landscaping in particular. Lori had been brought in a few times, but Gil knew it was Myra and Harold who had given it such care. Fall flowers lined the walkway and dotted the beds, like perfectly painted perennials. Tiny twinkling lights were threaded through the eucalyptus and other trees that created a forest-like area behind and around the house. Picture-perfect, Gil thought.

The story was that Myra had the idea for the memorial garden, to commemorate those loved ones the club had lost over the years.

And there, at one of the simple benches, sat regal, stoic Myra Abernathe, cloaked in what Gil could only identify as grief.

She stiffened at his approach, and he could see her expression shift to determination as she refused to look directly at him. Undeterred, Gil sat on the bench across from her. "Ezzie tells me you aren't up for socializing this evening."

"No, I'm not." Myra's orange hair seemed almost muted today. She wore a simple blue-flowered dress with a lace collar. "I know Ezzie and Leah had their hearts in the right place, but—"

"But other hearts can't be healed." Gil nodded, dropped his chin and thought of Myra's late husband Frank Abernathe. Memories surfaced and provided the words he hadn't been certain he'd find. "Did Frank ever tell you the story of when he and my grandfather taught me how to ride a bike?"

Myra's eyes shifted and her brow furrowed. "Not sure he ever did." Her hands twisted together.

"It was right after my mother left. My grandfather was trying to keep my mind off of things, and I had seen this rusted, dented bike in the window of the thrift shop weeks before. This was before Irving Drummond took it over and renamed it On a Wing, so you can imagine the state it was in. But the bike had new tires and a good chain and was just begging someone to ride it. I was saving up my allowance as fast as I could. That bike was a beauty. Ugly as sin, but a beauty. I'd stop by that store on my way home from school every day and just stare at it, dreaming of when I could ride it down Monarch Lane. When I finally had enough money, I announced over breakfast one morning that I was going to buy my bike. I don't think my father even heard me. He was working some business deal and barely looked up from his papers, but Granddad, he heard me loud and clear.

"I was worried, you see, because I'd never

ridden a bike before. The idea was scary, but it was still something I wanted to do, so Granddad went with me, and I bought my bike. I'd never spent so much money before. Twelve dollars and fifty cents." He shook his head, reveling in the wonder and innocence of childhood. "We walked that bike all the way to Skipper Park and when we got there, Frank was there, tending the flowerbeds."

"He did that for forty-three years," Myra confirmed. "Man could make a weed into a rose just by looking at it."

What a loss, Gil thought. For Myra and Butterfly Harbor. "Granddad tried to help me with the bike, but after that long walk, he was tuckered out, as he said," Gil added with a chuckle. "I tried, I don't know how many times, to stay balanced and to get that bike to move, but gravity kept winning. Until Frank came over and asked if he could lend a hand." Gil swallowed hard, recalling the kindness in Frank Abernathe's face. "He said I'd be fine practice for his grandkids one day, seeing as he didn't have any yet. And so, for the next two hours, Frank pushed and guided and ran behind me until

I got my bearings. Until I was racing around the park like a champion cyclist."

"My Frank was a good man. A kind man," Myra whispered and dabbed at her eyes. "I'm not surprised he did that."

"I can remember him and my granddad jumping and laughing and cheering like a couple of kids when I sped past them. It's one of the best memories of my childhood." He hesitated, leaned over and gave Myrna's hand a quick squeeze. "Two weeks later I went out to the garage to get my bike to ride to school and it had been replaced by a shiny new one, with all the bells and whistles. My bike, the bike I'd saved so hard for, wasn't there. When I asked my father about it, he said that no son of his was going to ride around the town he ran in a rusted-out piece of junk. I had an image to uphold, he told me. A responsibility to the town and to him. And then he said he'd thrown my bike in the garbage and it was gone."

He didn't look at Myra. He didn't want to see any sympathy, or worse, pity.

"I hated that new bike," Gil whispered. "More than I had ever hated anything. I rode it once that day to school and when I got there, I threw it in the dumpster behind the gym. I've never ridden another bike to this day." He took a breath. "I've never told anyone that story before. Losing that bike is no comparison to what you lost, Myra. I know that. I thought maybe..." He reached over again and laid his hand over her clasped ones. "I thought maybe you'd like to know that one of my best childhood memories is of your Frank."

When he stood, she reversed their hold, so she clung to him. "Thank you." She tilted her chin up and tears glistened in her eyes. "Thank you, Gil. That was very kind of you."

He tried to smile. "I know I've been a disappointment to you and so many others. I've made mistakes, probably because I was trying too hard to distance myself from my father. Maybe what I should have done, maybe what I should do, is try to be more like the man who stopped working with his flowers so he could help a little boy learn to ride his bike."

Myra nodded and looked away. "I think Frank would like that." She sniffled and gripped his hand tighter. "I would like that."

"How about you come inside and we can

have dinner. All of us together." He stepped back, as if inviting her to follow his lead. "Leah got all dressed up for the occasion."

"Did you bring that baby of yours?"

"No," Gil told her as she rose and walked with him toward the back stairs. "He had a long day today. But I can bring him by another time if you'd like to see him. I'm thinking he could probably use a whole houseful of honorary grandparents seeing as I'm all alone."

"Maybe you're not as alone as you think," Myra said in that matter-of-fact tone of hers. "This doesn't mean I'm voting for you, mind you. I promised Leah—"

"I'm thinking about voting for her myself," Gil interjected. "She's just about perfect, isn't she?"

"For becoming mayor?" Myra asked. "Or for you?"

Gil smiled up at the twilight sky. "Maybe both."

"THAT EVENING WENT in a completely unexpected direction. Pleasant, civil throughout and highly enjoyable." Leah looked over at Gil. He'd been surprisingly relaxed once he'd escorted Myra Abernathe into the house for dinner. "Exactly what did you say to Myra, anyway?"

Gil pulled up in front of her house, turned the engine off and sat back in his seat. "Just some memories I'd forgotten about. Do you think Oscar's going to be all right?"

"I bet he's going to have a hangover in the morning and will regret trying to spike your iced tea with whiskey," Leah said. "Good thing Alice warned us, otherwise I'd have had to drive you home."

"That tea was ninety proof," Gil agreed. "This turned into a really nice night. Thank you for helping to arrange it."

"You're welcome." She gripped her purse in her hands. "Did you want to come in for coffee? Maybe set some ground rules for the upcoming debate?"

"I'd best get back. We're already later than I told Mandy we'd be. So, Halloween?" he asked when she opened the door. "Calliope's big bash up at Duskywing Farm. Are we on? She's got the kids' stuff starting at three."

The three of them? Leah thought. Like a family? Say no. Say no…you shouldn't…

"It sounds like fun. I'll drive this time and

pick you up around four? I love seeing all the kids in their costumes before they head into town for trick-or-treating."

"Sounds like a plan. Leah?" He caught her arm, leaned over and kissed her. Yet another one of those soul-brushing, pulse-kicking kisses of his. "I like where this is headed," he said as he pressed his forehead to hers. "You?"

She nodded because she didn't have any words.

"Good. I'll call you tomorrow. Good night, Leah." He brushed his mouth against hers again and she climbed out of the car. She wasn't surprised when he waited until she had opened her front door and turned on a light before he started the vehicle and drove away. Still on her front porch, she watched until his taillights disappeared. He'd waited because he was that kind of man. The kind of man she'd always believed didn't exist.

The kind of man she'd never expected to find in Butterfly Harbor.

CHAPTER FOURTEEN

"GIL, WOULD YOU please try to relax and enjoy Halloween? All the debate arrangements are finalized for tomorrow. The seating and podiums will be set up in plenty of time. All you have to do is show up, preferably prepared. Okay?"

With Helena's strained "okay," Gil realized he'd pushed a bit too far. "You're right. I'm sorry." He shoved his free hand into his hair and dropped his chin to his chest.

Standing in the middle of his kitchen, the table covered with cards outlining various debate tactics and town statistical information regarding goals he had accomplished, accompanied by a crying baby upstairs, it made absolutely no sense why he was stressing over literally the one thing that was firmly in hand.

"I'll try to put all the election stuff out of my head and focus on the Halloween party."

"There you go." Helena may as well have been patting his head. "We might see you there. My daughter and her two kids are driving up and should be arriving anytime now."

Gil frowned. "Then, what are you doing in the office?"

"I have this boss who keeps trying to micromanage things that aren't in his control," Helena said sweetly. "Happy Halloween, Gil."

She hung up on him.

"Well, that was kind of rude." He should know. *Rude* had seemed his middle name this past week. He even knew why he was as cranky as Eli with a wet diaper. He and Leah had been relegated to texting conversations as both their schedules had filled completely. She'd had to go out of town for a couple of days to settle one of her clients' estates and he'd been barraged by a new flood of applications for new positions he hoped to fill, including a town attorney.

Screams echoed down the stairs and straight into Gil's ears.

"I'm coming, little guy." Gil abandoned the mess in the kitchen. The second he stepped foot in the nursery, Eli's crying ceased. The little guy sat there, in his crib, his face wet with tears, and gave Gil the biggest, brightest smile possible. "You, young man, are a tease."

He'd just lifted Eli into his arms when the doorbell rang.

"When it rains, it pours. Come on. Let's see if maybe Leah's early. That would be a nice surprise, wouldn't it?" And because it would, he hurried downstairs. The smile faded from his lips, however, at the unfamiliar face. "Can I help you?"

"Mr. Hamilton?" The man blinking out from behind thick-rimmed glasses clutched a briefcase in one hand and offered his card with the other. "Neal Simmons from social services. I believe you've been expecting me."

"Um. I was expecting a call, actually." Gil mustered up his overtaxed charm. The man was about Gil's age, with streaks of silver in his thinning dark hair. He had the appearance of a man with far too much to do and little time to do it in. "We're about to get ready to go to a Halloween party. Can we maybe do this another time?"

"This won't take too long." Beneath the

politeness, Gil sensed irritation. "Emergency placement means we all have to adjust our schedules and timelines. If I may?" He gestured inside.

"Yeah, sure." Gil had no choice but to step back. "Come on in."

"This is Elijah, I take it?"

"Unless I have another baby hiding around here somewhere." Gil forced a laugh that he swallowed when Mr. Simmons arched a brow. "Sorry, nervous, I guess. Yes, this is Elijah. Eli." He jostled Eli in his arms only to receive a perturbed expression from both baby and government official. "Please." He motioned toward the living room that unfortunately contained the untidy remnants of Gil and Eli's afternoon play session.

"I understand there have been developments in Eli's case." Mr. Simmons sat in the middle of the couch and produced a tablet, which he tapped open. "There's a medical condition to take into consideration?"

"Yes. But it's being monitored and is under control." Gil would have sat in the chair across from Mr. Simmons, but Eli preferred to be walked around. "I've managed to get him covered under my medical insurance."

"Fast work. Good." Mr. Simmons nodded and tapped a stylus against his screen. "And we have confirmation that you are a blood relative?"

"Yes, I'm his uncle. His father is my half brother, Christopher Russo."

"Ah, yes, I'm seeing a notation here. His attorney contacted our office earlier this week."

"His attorney?" Gil swallowed hard. "I didn't think public defenders handled civil and family matters."

"Mr. Chandler simply requested his client be allowed to make a statement regarding the placement of his infant son."

"Eli," Gil said. "His name is Eli."

"Uh, right. Eli." Unfazed, Mr. Simmons continued, "According to the paperwork your attorney filed, you're petitioning the court for temporary custody of Eli?"

"Yes. Yes, I am."

"Although it may turn into potentially long-term custody if I'm reading this file correctly. So, how did you come to be in possession of the—of Eli." Mr. Simmons glanced up.

"I found him on my front porch early one morning a few weeks ago. Along with a note asking me to take care of him. Sheriff Saxon was able to run the fingerprints on the note and identified Sylvie Edison, who is married to my brother."

"And where is Ms. Edison now?"

"No idea. All of this has to be in your notes. Leah told me she updated—"

"Just confirming that what we have in our records is still accurate," Mr. Simmons assured him. "Your brother is currently being held in Durante at the county jail, correct?"

"Yes, he's awaiting trial. You aren't going to take Eli away from me, are you?" It was the only question he wanted an answer to. "There's no one else to take him. I'm his family." He cradled Eli's head and pressed his lips to the boy's temple. The idea that he wouldn't have this fella in his life anymore was unimaginable.

"We like to keep children, especially infants, with family members whenever possible. Your employment situation is stable?"

"Yes." For now. "No job is a hundred percent secure, though. I can assure you Eli is my priority. He has been since he arrived."

Mr. Simmons nodded. "Noted. If you don't mind, I'd like to take a look around the house?"

"Of course. It's a bit of a mess. Eli's room is upstairs."

Mr. Simmons's smile was quick and unsympathetic. "I won't be long."

And he wasn't. It was, however, the longest ten minutes Gil had ever spent in his life. Pacing the living room with an increasingly restless Eli in his arms only reminded Gil of what was at stake.

"I didn't notice any character references in your file, Mr. Hamilton." Mr. Simmons said upon returning to the living room.

"My attorney said those wouldn't be needed yet."

"Well, with the accelerated application, it would be best to get those submitted as soon as possible." He packed up his things and hefted his briefcase. "It could make a difference in my final recommendation. I'll make my report to my superiors. You can expect to hear from us in a few weeks. In the meantime, enjoy your Halloween."

"That's it?" Gil followed him to the door. "What does this mean? Can Eli stay with me?"

"For the time being. Please have your lawyer report any changes to your situation, and Eli's, too."

Gil stopped himself from following after the man as he walked down the steps. He hadn't taken Eli. That was a good thing. But that didn't mean he wouldn't come back at some point and do so.

"What a nightmare," Gil muttered. "Yikes. We need to get dressed for the party. You ready to try some candy, Eli?" He stepped back into the house and closed the door. "I'll be your taste tester this year, but I bet next Halloween you'll want to gobble it all up."

If there was a next Halloween for them.

"I CAN'T BELIEVE you talked me into this ridiculous costume." Leah retrieved her costume and Gil's from the trunk of her car. It took her a minute to distinguish the oversize foam chocolate bar from the graham cracker. "S'mores. Who thinks to dress up like a s'more for Halloween?"

Fun Halloween music danced into Leah's ears. In the near distance, she could see strings of orange-and-purple lights accenting the wooden fence line of Calliope Costas's Duskywing Farm.

"This is what happens when you can't make up your mind," Gil said as he accepted the giant brown foam squares that were held together by bands of elastic. "I gave you plenty of time to decide, then had to take matters into my own hands."

"Uh-huh." She should have gone with the judge's robe. It would have been far easier and a lot more comfortable. She eyed the almost black rectangles with the familiar candy logo held together in the same way as Gil's "crackers," before she dropped hers over her head and transformed from neck to knees into a giant chocolate bar. She tried to look down, but the costume blocked her sighting her sneakers.

"Now, that's cute." Gil's grin widened. "All you need is the marshmallow. Speaking of, grab him, will you? I have to tighten my crackers."

"The lengths I'll go to for you, little man." Leah unhooked Eli from his car seat. As had become her habit, she ran her palms around his face, checking for an elevated temperature or, in the case of his arms and chubby legs, any swelling. He grunted and gurgled, as if telling her to hurry it up. He wanted to party! "This is the cutest costume in history," she announced as she hauled Eli out of the back seat. The giant rolls of stuffed bright white fabric covered him perfectly, and the smaller matching rounds were held on his head with elastic. "This is definite blackmail material when he gets older," Leah told Gil.

They joined the crowd headed up the hill to the farm. The sun had started its descent and the last rays of the day caught against the black lanterns casting bat-and-ghost-inspired shadows along the ground.

"Hello, Ophelia." Leah stopped at the gate, where the sleek grey cat sat perched as the party's official greeter. Sensing a new friend, Ophelia stretched out her neck and sniffed Eli's padded arm. Eli squealed, startling the animal, who quickly turned her attention to Gil.

"Uh-oh." Gil cringed. "What's this about, Ophelia?" He gaped as the cat rubbed her head up against Gil's chest. "Ophelia usually can't stand me."

"Must be the sugary foam." Leah giggled as Ophelia did indeed seem enamored of Gil's costume. "Oh, here comes Holly and Luke. And look at the twins," she gushed. Gil turned and slipped an arm around her waist. "Two peas in a pod. Literally."

"Clever costume," Gil teased the sheriff. "It's like you've worn that sheriff's uniform before."

"He's on duty." Holly rolled her eyes as she set Zoe down on her feet but held on to her hand. "He was supposed to be the farmer."

"Couldn't be helped." Luke chuckled. "I promised Fletcher and Matt they could have the night off to take the kids trick-or-treating."

"Where's Simon?" Gil asked.

"Still getting his costume together. Paige and Charlie are going to pick him up on their way."

"Hey, how'd his science project turn out? Did he win?"

"Honorable mention." Luke beamed. "He created a comic book series that features a superhero who teaches science within the stories. He illustrated it and everything. His teacher asked if she could send it to an editor friend of hers in New York."

"Don't tell Hunter he might have competition for being the only published writer in town," Holly joked. "Shall we head in?"

Before moving to Butterfly Harbor, Leah hadn't paid Halloween much mind. Whereas Calliope and Xander had gone all out with the decorations, from handcrafted cheesecloth ghosts bouncing up and down to the neon-lit giant spiders lined up across the expanse of growing vegetables. Booths had been set up for games with prizes and bags of treats, including popcorn balls and homemade marshmallows, something Leah found particularly delightful given the marshmallow in her arms. Calliope and Xander hadn't gone the creepy, scary, ghoulish route so many took during the season. It felt more celebratory. Cute. Fun.

"I understand you had a visitor this afternoon," she overheard Luke say to Gil. "Everything go all right with social services?" the sheriff asked.

"I guess," Gil said. "I'm supposed to hear back in a few weeks."

"Social services came by the house?" Leah spun around. "Why didn't you tell me?"

"Because there's nothing to tell."

"Hey, Holly, why don't we—" Luke steered his wife and the twins away.

"Who came by? Oh, that's cool." She picked up a long stick with a strung-up fake bat that was meant to fly around when it was spun. She tried it out for Eli, who giggled and tried to grab it.

"Neal Simmons. He seemed nice enough."

Leah stared when he hesitated, mentally tapping her foot.

"He might have mentioned Christopher had his attorney request that he make a statement to the court about Eli's placement."

"I see." Leah heard the coolness in her own voice. "This is really something you should tell your attorney."

"And now I have. Honestly, Leah, there's nothing that can be done today or over the weekend and with the party and the debate tomorrow night..."

"All right." She nodded. "I'll give you that, but from now on, you have to tell me everything, okay? I need to be able to plan for any bumps in the road."

"Understood." Gil took Eli out of her arms. "Can we enjoy ourselves and worry about all this later?"

Not wanting to stall the fun any longer, she turned around and, after digging some cash out of her pocket, bought a hot apple cider from one of the booths. Bushels and barrels of apples were priced to sell, along with pumpkins of every size. As the sun continued to dip, the pretty effect of the twinkling lights increased as did the volume of the music and crowd noise.

The fact that it was Eli's first real public appearance appeared to be garnering the most attention. Frankie and Roman Salazar, he dressed as a 1920s gangster and Frankie as his moll, found him first, and while Frankie was gushing over Eli's marshmallow costume, Alethea Costas and Declan Cartwright arrived. They had people snapping pictures on their phones to capture the image of a space princess and her smuggler fiancé. Jason and Abby Corwin made an appearance, with Jason wearing one of his chef jackets and carrying a stockpot containing their son, David, who was dressed like a lobster. Abby was wearing a sunflower costume, her face the sweet center of the bloom.

Leah's head was spinning with all the costumes and festivities. She smiled seeing Charlie Bradley racing around and gathering up her friends—Stella Jones, Phoebe MacBride and Marley O'Neill.

"Love the costume," Mandy Evans said, wearing a pseudo mermaid outfit. Her boyfriend, Kyle, shrugged. "They're dressed like a sandwich. What's the deal?"

"Oh, come on," Charlie called him out. "It's my favorite dessert."

"A classic," Stella clarified.

"We're classic," Gil murmured from behind her as the crowd moved on. "In other words…we're old."

"Could be worse," Leah said. Eli slumped sleepily onto Gil's shoulder. "He doing okay?"

"He sleeps a lot," Gil said, clearly trying not to sound worried. "He fell asleep while I was giving him his bottle before you picked us up."

"Well, it's exhausting being the center of attention." She rubbed Eli's back. "The Cocoon Club is planning on making an appearance. We should stay long enough to see them."

"I'm under strict orders from Ezzie to present Eli for inspection," Gil confirmed. "But I think someone else is hoping to get her hands on him first. Hello, Calliope."

"Gil. Leah." Calliope Costas moved toward them like mist. She was dressed all in white and had threaded tiny white beads and shells through her long red hair. "How are you enjoying the party?"

"It's wonderful. Um." Leah stepped back to examine her friend. "What are you dressed as?"

"Isn't it obvious?" Xander, Calliope's husband, strolled up behind her and placed his hands gently on her very rounded stomach. "She's the moon."

"It was the least offensive round object I could think of," Calliope joked. "Hello, Eli. May I, Gil?" She held out her arms.

"Oh, sure. Yeah." Gil handed a sleepy Eli over. The baby promptly went wide-eyed as Calliope settled him in her arms and stroked a finger down his cheek. "What a blessing," she whispered. "A miracle worker you are, do you know that?" She swayed, smiling at Eli. "Would you mind if I held him for a while? Why don't you two go and enjoy yourselves? If this one dozes off, I can always put him in Stella's old bassinet."

"The nursery's nearly finished," Xander explained. "Just come inside when you're ready to take him back."

Leah and Gil watched them walk into the house. "Do you suppose they maybe wanted some practice?" Leah asked.

"Or, knowing Calliope, she wanted to give us alone time." He reached out his hand and took hers. "Alone at last."

"Alone?" She let him tug her close. "Half the town is here. I'm glad we had this planned, though. I didn't want the next time we saw each other to be on the debate stage tomorrow night."

"Don't remind me," he muttered as they moved off toward the herb garden maze. "Jo's old house looks good out here." He pointed to the tiny house lit up in the far corner of the property. "I wonder what changes Alethea's made to it."

"You're changing the subject," she accused gently.

"You're dressed like a giant chocolate bar and I'm a graham cracker. Now is not the time to discuss our political adversities."

"Especially when we don't have any marshmallow between us," Leah said, nodding. "You do know ignoring problems won't make them go away."

"Fair enough," he said.

"How are you at darts? I want to win one of those gallons of Calliope's apple cider." She toasted him with what was left of her drink.

"I'd have to win two because I need one myself. Shall we?" He tugged her into his arms and they walked toward the gaming booths together.

"HEY, XANDER. LEAH AND I are ready to head out." Gil popped his head inside the stone cottage a few hours later. The kitchen was half the space of the house and was filled with the scent of fall, cider and the flavors of the coming season. "I didn't realize it was so late. I hope he wasn't too much trouble."

"He slept most of the time." Xander smiled and hefted a mug to his lips. "Party's finally breaking up?"

"Yeah." Gil came inside. "Kids left a while ago to trick-or-treat and the adults have about had it. Did you catch Simon Saxon's costume?"

"He puts Hollywood robots to shame," Xander agreed. "What we would have given to have a costume like that growing up, huh? I heard the Cocoon Club arrived in style."

"I'm not sure I'll ever look at '80s television the same way," Gil agreed. "Myra's version of Krystle Carrington might just go down in Butterfly Harbor history. Leah's outside waiting, so I'm just going to—" He hesitated, uncertain whether to head down the hall.

"Go on in." Xander's eyes sharpened. "She's waiting for you."

"Calliope? Why?"

"I just know she is." Xander shrugged. "Second door on the left."

Gil felt ridiculous entering a room that had been transformed into a wonderland of a nursery when he was still dressed as giant graham cracker squares. But his unease faded as he focused on the dim glow.

There had never been anything typical or predictable about Calliope Costas. She was a free spirit in every sense of the word, and her baby's nursery was no exception. Forest murals had been painted on the walls. The branches of tall, overhanging trees arched up and over to cover most of the ceiling. Smatterings of butterflies of various species dotted the leaves and filled the spaces in between.

Tiny LED lights had been added, not only as twinkling accents within those trees but also to mimic the starry night accented with a glow-in-the-dark painted moon that provide a night-light effect.

Calliope, still in her ethereal white gown, sat in a rocking chair by the window, Eli in her arms, humming gently.

Without looking up, she rested her fingertips on Eli's chest, offered a smile. "What a gift he's been for you," she murmured.

Pride and gratitude surged through him.

Gil stood in the doorway, marveling at the smattering of woodland creatures dotting the forest. The natural wood furniture made it appear as if the nursery had been crafted inside a fairytale.

"I heard about his heart issue," she said. "What's his prognosis?"

"I guess we're in wait-and-see mode," Gil said. "I'm taking him back for more tests next week. Until then—"

Calliope nodded. "Until then, you'll do all you can. You've changed for him. You've changed everything." She raised her gaze. With the moonlight shining in through the nursery window, she looked even more ethereal than she tended to. "You'll be a good stand-in for his father, Gil. You already are. You can stop doubting yourself."

Gil straightened. "What makes you think—"

"We've known each other most of our lives, you and I," she said softly. "I've seen the good and the not so good in you. But I'll always have a soft spot in my heart for the boy who protected me from Clayton Elliot after he cut off those braids of mine in sixth grade."

"I don't like bullies. Despite being one myself at times, I suppose." He sighed at her nod of agreement. "I came close, didn't I? To becoming the person I swore I never would."

Calliope inclined her head. "You skirted the line, yes. But you also had the right people around you. People who wouldn't let you take that last step. I'd hand him to you, but I can't lift both of us out of this chair."

Gil took Eli out of Calliope's hold. Cradling Eli close, he held out his hand for Calliope to grab on to. "I will be so happy when I can stand up on my own again." She cradled her stomach in her hands. "I have something to give you. Wait here, please."

How a woman so fully pregnant moved so gracefully would, Gil supposed, remain a mystery. She glided out of the room, and while Gil marveled at the intricacy of the mural, he felt a calmness descend.

"I found this at the spring fair." Calliope had returned with a rustic frame in her hand.

Small twigs and branches decorated the sides and when she handed it to him, he read. "Beauty is not the end result but in the struggle to become."

"I wasn't sure who it was meant for until now," Calliope told him.

"It's lovely." Touched, Gil accepted it. "The first decoration for Eli's nursery."

"If that's where you choose to keep it," Calliope said. "But it's yours, Gil. When I think of these words now, I will think about you. And how you've finally found your wings."

"Will I be able to keep him?" It didn't make sense, he knew, to ask such a question of anyone, but Calliope was known for her intuition. "My brother—"

"Your brother gave you this gift," Calliope said quietly. "Intentional or not, because of him, you have Eli. If you lead with that, if you keep that thought in your heart, things will work out as they're meant to."

The sound of excited shouts and giggling children exploded into the night.

"I believe Stella and her friends are home. I told them they could have a sleepover." She covered a yawn. "I should have factored in the sugar quotient. My error entirely. They'll never get to sleep."

Gil carried Eli outside, cradling him against his shoulder. He stood there for a moment, watching Leah in conversation with Monty and Sienna Bettencourt, who had been latecomers to the party. Nonetheless, Monty had a gallon of apple cider clutched in each hand.

But it was Leah he couldn't stop looking at. Leah, who had donned a chocolate-bar costume for hours on end and whose laughter lightened his heart. She'd captured him, right down to his soul.

And yet…

Reality beckoned. The debate was tomorrow. His last shot at convincing the people of Butterfly Harbor that, despite his lineage, he was made for this job. More importantly, that he could and would do better. Leah would understand. He hoped. And maybe when all this was behind them, they could start over, start fresh.

As if sensing him, Leah turned, her smile widening, then softening as her gaze dropped to Eli. Monty and Sienna walked along the road, hand in hand.

"He slept through the whole thing, didn't he?" Leah asked.

"Pretty much," Gil said. "You ready to go?"

"I am." She hefted the big reusable bag that was filled with fall treats. "I grabbed the last of the caramel apples before they packed up the booth. My teeth might hate me, but my stomach won't."

The drive back to Gil's house was quick and quiet. When Leah parked the car, the late-night ocean breeze coasted through and had Gil shivering. "Well, I guess tomorrow's the big day."

"I guess so." She nodded, clearly feeling as uncomfortable as he did. "And then the election on Tuesday."

"Right." He took a deep breath. "I've decided to take your advice. At the debate, I'm going to tell the truth about where the funding for the sanctuary came from. And why I almost cut the town's emergency services. People have a right to know and I should have been honest about it from the start."

"Better late than never." Leah's flash of a smile had him cringing. "Thanks for letting me know so I can prepare a response."

Her reaction confused him. "You don't think I should come clean?"

"At the debate? The last minute of your campaign? I'm sure the citizenry will take that in good faith." She shook her head. "This isn't any of my business, Gil. You need to do what you think you need to do. It doesn't matter what I think."

"Maybe it shouldn't, but it does to me. I can do a better job as mayor than I've been doing, Leah. I see that now."

"I'm not backing down, Gil. I hope you

didn't think I was. In fact, I'm more determined than ever to win. I still believe Butterfly Harbor needs fresh eyes and a clean slate, especially now that I know exactly how dire the financial situation was and continues to be. Voters might not believe we can get a fresh start with a Hamilton in office. Even if that Hamilton is you." She shoved out of the car and opened the back door to unlock Eli's car seat.

"And what about Eli?" Gil kept his voice down so as not to wake the baby. "What happens with him if I lose the election? I need the job, Leah. You don't."

Leah stopped moving and slowly, very slowly, stood up straight and looked at him across the hood of her car. "Are you honestly trying to use him to guilt me into withdrawing from the race?"

Gil's hands went up as if to deflect her shooting words. "That isn't what I meant. Exactly," he added when he realized that actually it was. "If you back out and endorse me—"

"Stop!" The word felt like an arrow to his heart. "Just stop before you make me start thinking the man I..." Her eyes went wide and she swallowed as if she'd been about to blurt something. Something she didn't want to voice. Something that had his heart teetering on the edge of hope. "Stop before you make me think the man I've gotten to know these past few weeks is nothing more than a charade." She hoisted the car seat out, brought Eli around and set him on the trunk, then retrieved Gil's Halloween goodies and the framed saying Calliope had given him.

Leah took a moment to read it, but the smirk it evoked had dread clanging deep in Gil's belly. "Calliope's usually pretty good with her gifts," she said and dropped the frame into his bag. "Guess even she can have an off night. I'll see you at the debate, Gil." She paused long enough to kiss Eli's forehead and straighten his marshmallow cap. "Sleep tight, little man."

Gil picked up the car seat, his Halloween bag in the other hand, slung the diaper bag over his shoulder and stood stone still as she drove away. Why didn't she understand? He needed the stability of this job to bolster his case to keep Eli. He'd seen it in Neal Simmons's eyes. The money didn't matter; it was attitude and compassion the social worker had been looking for in his cursory examination of Gil's home and life.

Gil needed to do whatever was necessary to keep this little boy safe and happy. It was a promise he'd made to both Eli and to himself. If that meant exposing the last of his secrets to the entire town, so be it. It was for the greater good.

He walked up the path to the porch stairs, an odd emptiness settling over him. An emptiness he now realized could only be filled by Leah Ellis.

CHAPTER FIFTEEN

LEAH STARTLED AWAKE, her breath caught in her throat. She stared into the darkness for a long moment, dragging herself out of the dream that had her heart racing like one of Declan Cartwright's race cars. The lacy silver curtains at her bedroom window billowed against the cool fall breeze. She turned her head toward the bedside clock. Two a.m.

She shot out of bed and closed the window and stood there, hand against her chest, as she calmed down.

"What was that?" She muttered into the darkened room. Had she heard something? Grabbing her cell phone and her lightweight embroidered robe, she did a quick tour of the house, just to ease her mind. Nerves, she told herself as she doubled back to the kitchen and turned on the machine for coffee. Nerves that weren't going to let her get to sleep again, that was for sure.

"What a perfect day to be exhausted." Saturdays were meant for fun and distraction, not prepping for a debate that, should things go her way, could drop Gil and Eli into a mess no one could drag them out of.

While the coffee brewed, she treated herself to a couple of the Chrysalis Bakery apple pie bagels she kept for carb emergencies and popped them in the oven. The sooner she smelled apple and cinnamon, the better.

Her voice mails had piled up. She'd wanted to enjoy the party last night and her time with Gil and Eli, so she'd essentially gone dark, and she was about to pay for that now. Fortunately, the first few were from Callie, just updating her on her schedule for next week. A few were from potential clients she could reach out to on Monday, but it was the call from a friend in social services that nearly stopped her heart.

"Hey, Leah. This is Antony Toscano. Sorry to be calling so late, but I just got home from work. Since you're representing Gil Hamilton in his foster parent adoption petition, I thought you'd want to know that the baby's father has made a complaint with the court, protesting the placement. I know the situation's complicated, but you should expect to be contacted by my supervisor on Monday. I think the only reason I heard about this is because of Gil Hamilton's position as mayor. Not sure if that's helping or hurting him. Nothing else I can tell you, but you have my number just in case."

Leah felt awful. Gil's straightforward custody plea had just taken a serious dive off the rails. Christopher wanting to make a statement to the court was one thing, but if he was contesting the temporary placement…

Without bothering to get dressed, she went into the second bedroom that served as her home office and powered up her computer. "I made a promise," she told herself as she returned to the kitchen to wait for the coffee to finish brewing. "He's not going to lose that little boy," she vowed. "He's not." Except he could.

And that terrified Leah more than anything.

GIL WASN'T CERTAIN what woke him, but he found himself starting wide-eyed at the clock by his bed. Two a.m.

He groaned, rolled over onto his back and

threw his arm over his eyes. It had taken him more than an hour to finally get to sleep. Out of routine, he reached to the other side of the bed and pulled the baby monitor closer, waiting for the sound of Eli's soft snores to lull him back to sleep. He jostled the machine, frowning since he didn't hear anything.

"Stupid plastic piece of junk." He threw off the blankets and went to the nursery next door. The turtle night-light on one of the shelves allowed him to make his way around. Before he even reached the crib, he knew something was wrong. "Eli?" He pressed his hand against the baby's chest, which was moving up and down as if he were panting. His skin, even through the fabric of his pajamas, was cold.

Gil clicked on the lamp next to the changing table and saw the blue tinge around Eli's lips instantly. He raced back to his phone, dialing 9-1-1 as he returned to Eli's side. "Yes, this is Gil Hamilton." He recited his address. "I have a six-month-old baby boy in cardiac distress." It felt odd, as if he were speaking from outside his body. But while he knew he was doing the only thing he could, all he wanted was to hold Eli in his arms and fix him.

He forced himself to throw on clothes and shoes before he carefully carried Eli downstairs. He could feel Eli's tiny heart beating so fast, too fast, and he was sweating up a storm. It seemed an eternity before the sound of sirens echoed in the distance. "You're going to be okay, Eli. You're going to be okay," he whispered, holding him against his shoulder, swaying back and forth as he waited for the emergency vehicles to appear.

The sight of the medically equipped SUV from the Butterfly Harbor Fire Department, jokingly nicknamed Dwayne, gave Gil hope. Seconds later, an ambulance pulled in behind it. Gil yanked open the front door as co–fire chief Roman Salazar sprinted up the steps. His black hair glinted in the moonlight and melded with the black T-shirt and cargo pants he wore as his uniform.

"Gil? What happened?" Roman demanded. "Tell me what's going on."

"I went in to check on him and he wasn't breathing right. The doctor told me what to look out for. Roman, help him." He handed Eli over. "He can't breathe."

"I've got him." He turned just as the paramedics rolled a stretcher out of the back of the ambulance. "Frankie said Eli is Dr. Phillips's patient?"

"Yes. He's been diagnosed with VSD."

Roman nodded as he placed tiny Eli onto his back on the stretcher. "Grab what you need. You can ride with him." Roman's announcement seemed to catch the EMTs off guard as he checked Eli's oxygen level via his finger pulse. "My call," Roman said as he fitted a small plastic breathing mask over Eli's pale face. "Jasper?"

Jasper O'Neill, BHFD's latest fully certified firefighter at only nineteen, hurried over. "Yes, Chief?"

"Call ahead to Butterfly Harbor General. Tell them we have Elijah Hamilton coming in with symptoms of severe VSD. Have them contact Dr. Phillips. Oh, and..." Roman glanced at Gil for a fraction of a second before he looked to his young coworker. Long enough for Gil to identify concern in the experienced firefighter's expression. "Tell them the baby's O2 level is at ninety."

"Got it." Jasper disappeared back into the SUV.

"Ninety." Gil felt the warmth drain from his face. The doctor had told him anything below ninety-five was cause for alarm. Phone and keys in hand, he closed up the house. Roman helped the EMTs guide the stretcher onto the ambulance, then motioned for Gil to climb in.

"Floor it," Roman ordered the EMTs as Gil settled on the narrow padded bench and rested his hand over Eli's tiny one. "I'll be right behind you." He slammed the door shut and slapped the roof twice on the ambulance.

Then the sirens blared and they zoomed away.

"I HEAR YOU! I'm coming!" Leah removed the damp facecloth off her forehead and made for the front door. She'd spent the past four hours digging through precedent after precedent, compiling a list of rulings that would work in Gil's favor should he have to fight for temporary custody in court.

She was finally feeling better about the situation but wanted Callie to have a go with her own research. Sometimes her paralegal saw things in a way that escaped Leah's overly practical and analytical mind.

After her shower, she'd thrown on yoga

pants and a tunic sweater with a bumblebee pattern and was combing her fingers through her wet hair when she opened the front door. "Frankie? It's—"

"Something wrong with your phone?" Frankie jabbed a finger at the cell on the nearby dining room table. "Gil's been trying to call you since three this morning."

"What? No, it's fine. I was just..." She waved Frankie inside and grabbed her phone. It was dead. "The battery must have drained. I couldn't sleep so I was working..." She trailed off just as Frankie's words registered. "Why was Gil calling?"

"Get your shoes and your purse and your charger," Frankie ordered. "It's Eli. He's had another episode and he's at the hospital. I'll drive you."

"Oh, no. No." But she didn't have to be told twice. She ran through the house, collecting sandals along with her bag, phone, charger and keys. She waited until they were driving before she asked any of the millions of questions zipping through her mind. "What can you tell me?"

The fact that Frankie's hands were locked white-knuckle tight around the steering wheel should have told her everything. Frankie was unflappable. It was why she was so good at her job and why she'd earned the co-chief position last year. There wasn't a crisis the woman couldn't tackle head-on.

"When Roman got to Gil's place, Eli's O2 level was around ninety. Last I heard they have it up to ninety-five."

"Still not good." One of Leah's coping mechanisms when presented with a problem or new issue was to research the life out of it. She'd read multiple articles about VSD and babies with holes in their hearts. She'd been as optimistic as the doctors where Eli was concerned. "What's the plan of action?" Leah held on to the chicken bar and winced as Frankie took a sharp right turn.

"They're trying to get him stabilized. His numbers need to be better before they make a final decision, but it's looking like surgery. Possibly noninvasive. They'll just have to see."

"Gil must be losing his mind." She hadn't been there when he'd called. It didn't matter that her cell had died.

"He says he's fine, but there's nothing worse than being all alone when someone you love is in danger. He'll be glad to see you," Frankie said. "Even if he doesn't say so."

"Thank you for coming to get me," Leah told her. "I know you don't get my and Gil's relationship."

"I don't have to get it." Frankie shook her head. "I just see that it works. He's been different since the fire last Christmas, but he's really changed since Eli came into his life. And you." Frankie frowned, took the last turn onto the road where the hospital was located. "He must have changed for the good, since you fell for him."

"Fell for him." Leah forced a laugh. "Is that code—"

"You're in love with him. I assume that's not news to you," Frankie said. "I'm guessing you're not particularly happy about it."

"I don't like complicated. And love is always complicated."

"Don't I know it. Try being married to your work spouse. Roman and I finally found a rhythm, you know? Schedules, routines, quirks. We've been coasting along pretty good and now blam-o."

Leah twisted in her seat. "Blam-o?"

"I'm pregnant." Frankie put her foot on the gas.

"You're what?"

"Just far enough along that we have to worry about Ezzie figuring it out before we can spring it on her." Frankie shot her a look. "Don't you dare tell her you know. She will never let me forget it."

"Frankie, this is wonderful. Congratulations. But why are you telling me before Ezzie?"

"Because you're here and she's still asleep and I've been dying to tell someone." Frankie shrugged. "Roman and I are taking her to dinner at the Flutterby Inn after the debate. We'll tell her then. And brace ourselves for the rest of our lives."

"I'm so happy for you guys." Happy enough that she'd almost forgotten where she was headed. And what was waiting for her. Which was, of course, Frankie's plan.

But the second Leah stepped foot in the pediatric ICU waiting room, all the fear and concern rushed back over her, but it was swamped by a tidal wave of emotion so powerful that her legs wobbled. "Gil."

Seated in the corner of the waiting room, a

half-drunk cup of coffee on the low table beside him, he looked up and blinked. "Leah." The relief shining in his eyes had her rushing toward him. The second he stood up, she threw herself into his arms and held on tight.

"I called, but all I got was your voice mail," he whispered.

"My cell died. I'm so sorry. I would have been—"

"I know." He clung to her, his arms tight around her as if he were finally letting himself feel what he needed to. "I couldn't leave to come find you. I couldn't leave him alone."

"Of course you couldn't. I wouldn't have wanted you to." She stepped back, caught his face between her hands. A face reflecting fear, courage and his fierce, fierce love for Elijah. "Tell me what's happening? Can I see him?"

Gil shook his head. "They couldn't wait. There's a second hole. They've taken him in for surgery. It all happened so fast. I didn't get the chance..." He tried to steady his breath. "I didn't get the chance to tell him I love him."

"He knows." Leah brought his face close

to hers, forced him to look into her eyes. "I promise you he knows, Gil. And you'll get the chance to tell him. I just know it."

"YOU'RE SUPPOSED TO eat it, not stab it."

"I'm sorry?" Gil glanced up from where he'd plunged his fork into the now-cold three-egg-and-mushroom omelet. Alethea Costas had dropped off breakfast for them en route to setting up the food truck by the beach. He told himself the only reason the waiting room wasn't overflowing with town residents and friends was because most people slept in on Saturday. Now, over an hour later, they still sat alone in the waiting room, Leah beside him, her own food uneaten.

"You need to eat." She set her breakfast aside and rubbed his arm.

"I could say the same to you. Besides, there's nowhere for it to go." He closed the container and shoved it farther away on the coffee table. The walls were closing in. "I'm all knots inside. It's been hours." He looked for Paige Bradley, who, in between her nursing duties, was checking in on them.

"He's so small. How can it be taking so long?" He stood and began to pace, something he'd been doing a lot since early this morning. "If I'd only woken up sooner, if I'd stayed up, I'd have heard him struggling—"

"You need to stop circling around to this." Leah drew her legs in under her. "You're human. You sleep. Take comfort in the fact that something did wake you up in time to be able to get him help."

"You don't understand." Gil knew he was rambling, but he couldn't seem to stop himself. "If this turns out to be something he'll have to live with for the rest of his life, how do I ever sleep again? For that matter, how does any parent sleep ever?"

"You'll sleep again," Leah assured him. "And whatever arises with Eli's condition, you'll adjust and you'll manage. Worrying about something before it happens is only going to burn out your hamster wheel."

He stopped, blinked, then stared. "What hamster wheel?"

"You know, that thing spinning in your head." She twirled her finger next to her ear. "The thing you can't jump off. Stop giving it energy. Better yet, how about a distraction?"

"A what?" Gil turned to where Leah was looking.

"Hi, Ozzy." Leah offered a slow, sleepy smile.

"I'm going on shift in a couple of hours, but I heard about Eli." The police deputy turned firefighter explained. "Thought I'd stop in and see if there's any word? How is he?"

"We're waiting to find out." Leah stood and went over to Gil's side. The comfort he felt when he drew her close almost doused the fear burning inside of him. "What's that?" She rose up on her toes and elbowed Gil. "That's one of Gale's specialty boxes from Chrysalis Bakery, isn't it?"

"When I stress, I crave sugar," Ozzy said with a quick grin. "Old habits die hard. She put in your favorites. For both of you," he added as he set the box on the table. "Save them to celebrate good news. Oh, and I brought something else." He held up a zippered hardcover case. "Thought maybe a game of backgammon might take your mind off things, Gil."

"I don't—" Gil started.

"That's a great idea," Leah said. "I'll go refill our coffees. You want one, Oz?"

"Thanks, Leah." Ozzy nodded and busied himself setting up the travel game.

"I don't want to play games," Gil muttered to Leah.

"Your friend is trying to help you, Gil." She brushed her fingers across his lips. "Let him. It's better than just letting your thoughts—"

"Gil! Leah!" Paige rounded the corner at top speed, her neon-orange plastic clogs squeaking against the polished linoleum. "Dr. Phillips is going to be out in a little while, but he said I could tell you the procedure went well. They were able to close up both holes, and Eli's oxygen levels are already back in the normal range."

"He's going to be okay?" Gil couldn't quite let himself believe it. He'd heard the words but couldn't seem to process their meaning.

"That little boy is going to be wailing his lungs out and driving you mad in no time." There was no misinterpreting Paige's happiness. "You'll need follow-up appointments, of course, and lab work and… We'll get into it later, but this is the other side, Gil. This is good news."

"Then, why did it take hours?" Gil asked. "Did something go wrong?"

"Gil, stop looking for trouble," Leah urged. "He's okay."

But Paige appeared to understand. "They had to decide what would give them the best chance of success. It took time. They ended up going in through his femoral artery and..." She waved off the explanation. "You don't need to hear all that. The point is they didn't have to open his chest which means he should be able to go home in a couple of days. Gil, this is the best possible outcome." She grabbed his arms and squeezed. "You can start breathing again. I promise," she whispered, as if trying to bring him out of a trance. "He's going to be okay."

"I bet it'll take him a while to purge the fear," Leah said in Gil's defense. "Thank you, Paige. Thank you so much."

"When can I see him?" Gil managed to ask.

"It won't be long. They're getting him back into his room now. Soon," Paige assured him. "I promise. I'll let you know when you can."

"You see?" Leah said, sounding almost

giddy as Paige headed to the nurse's station. "He's going to be fine. Everything's going to be okay. Gil?" She circled around him and rested her hands on his shoulders. "You all right?"

"I'm all right." It was odd how everything else in his life had ceased to matter when he'd been faced with losing Eli. He'd spent the last few hours trying to prepare himself for the worst. Things could easily have gone a different direction. Everything else felt so ridiculously trivial now. "I'm all right, Leah. Thanks to you." He pulled her close and buried his face in her neck. "I don't think I could have found my way through this without you."

"Of course you could have," she teased him as she hugged him back. "You're a good parent, Gil. And good parents can get through anything." She leaned back but still held his hands. "Folks need to hear the news. We should start returning some calls and texts," she suggested.

"Already on it!" Ozzy announced from his seat. "I've texted Roman at the station and he's calling Ezzie right now. Word'll spread fast enough."

"Maybe now you can eat something, huh?" Leah suggested. "Should we see what's in the bakery box?"

"Sure." He couldn't stop watching her; couldn't stop looking at her. Couldn't stop his heart from filling up to the point of spilling over.

"Oh, wow. Sugar bombs." Leah dipped her hand into the box and pulled up a pastry concoction that had been sliced open and filled with sweet cream and what looked like a fresh apple compote. "This would be great to eat before the debate."

"You could save it," Gil suggested. Something told him a sugar-hyped Leah would be even more entertaining than he was already anticipating.

"You're not serious," Leah gaped and set the pastry back inside the box. "Gil, you can't be thinking about going through with the debate now. Not with what's happened this morning."

"We are going through with it." He caught her shoulders in his hands and tugged her close. There were moments of perfect clarity, and he was having one right now. No doubts. No hesitation. No regrets. His life would never be the same and he'd fight to keep it that way. Caring for Eli, loving Leah, making Butterfly Harbor a real home. He finally knew how to have it all. "You wanted me to find something to focus on. This is it. Until Elijah leaves the hospital… I need this."

"Gil?" Paige called to him from where Dr. Phillips had joined her.

"We'll talk about this later," Leah warned.

"There's nothing to talk about," Gil told her and pressed his lips to hers. "Ozzy, take Leah home, will you? I'll see you in the school gym at five o'clock as planned. It's okay," he assured her when her expression said she doubted his words. "Everything's going to be all right, remember? I'll see you tonight."

With that, he strode down the hall toward his future.

"THAT WAS ODD." Leah turned to Ozzy, her brow furrowed. "He's acting weird, right? I mean, with everything that's happened, I get it, but…"

"Definitely weird," Ozzy agreed.

Considering Leah's own stress-induced fog, she could only imagine how rough it was for Gil to pull out of his. Still, something wasn't right. That faraway look in his eyes wasn't something she was used to. She flopped onto the chair beside Ozzy. "This whole recall-election situation sucks."

"For a number of reasons," Ozzy agreed a second time. "Especially since you're done for."

"Done for?"

"Jo's phrase. It's what she says about people who take the fall."

"The fall." Leah attempted a laugh. "That's ri—" She cut herself off when Ozzy arched a brow. "Accurate," she corrected and scrunched her face. "Okay, it's accurate. I'm crazy about the guy, and darn it, it just makes everything so messy."

"That's how you know it's real. And that it'll stick," Ozzy said. "You were along for the ride with me and Jo. You saw how bumpy it got when she realized she loved me."

"I did." Leah nodded. "But you weren't about to give up on her."

"Because I knew I'd never find with anyone else what I've found with her. And I'd wager that you feel the same about Gil."

"I still don't understand how it's even possible." Leah argued. "I'm running against him for his job. The only job he's ever really had."

"That's not true," Ozzy countered. "He was a community- and business-relations specialist before his father died. He's got great negotiating skills. They just got a bit buried under all the rest of the stuff he's had to do as mayor. All the cleanup he had on his hands because of his father. Don't forget, you've only really ever seen him as mayor. Not how he was before."

"I guess." It was something to think about. Speaking of things to think about… "So if you and Jo have been discussing my relationship with Gil, I can assume the rest of the town has been as well."

Ozzy snorted. "There's a reason they moved the debate tonight to the school gym, Leah. Everyone's planning on being there to see what happens between the two of you."

"You can't be serious?" Somehow she and Gil had become Butterfly Harbor's major news? "I figured the Cocoon Club for sure, but—"

"Only people I know who aren't planning

on attending are me and Matt, because we're on call. But that gym is going to be standing room only." He patted her knee and stood up. "Just keep in mind most of them can't wait for you to take him down."

"Thanks," she muttered. New doubts circled her head like cartoon canaries. "For the record, that doesn't help at all."

"Hmm," Ozzy said. "I didn't think it would."

"SORRY I'M LATE." Mandy Evans rushed into Eli's hospital room, her overstuffed backpack looped over one shoulder. "Mom had to take her car in to Declan's garage and the work lasted longer than she thought." She lowered her voice and stepped closer to the ICU crib. "Oh my gosh. The poor little guy. How is he?"

"Better." How Gil had gotten used to all the cords and wires and IVs, he'd never understand. Hopefully Eli would never remember a single second of any of this. "Thanks for coming to stay with him on short notice. I didn't want to leave him alone. I know the nurses will be around and that he'll mostly sleep—"

"I'm happy to take Eli duty. Gives me

some quiet space to study. Mom and Dad spend all their time shopping for baby furniture and they don't always agree. Ha. Don't even get me started on nursery themes."

"I shouldn't be gone long," he told her. "If you get hungry and want a pizza, call Zane's. It's on me."

"I ate before I came." Mandy maneuvered around him and dropped into his vacated chair. "If Eli wakes up, I'll be here. Don't worry."

"Thanks."

"Good luck!" Mandy called after him. "At the debate," she added at his questioning look. "That is where you're going, right?"

"Right. Of course. The debate." He nodded, waved at her with his phone in hand and headed out.

The instant he made it outside, he bent over, braced his hands on his thighs and squeezed his eyes shut so hard he saw stars. It took a few minutes for the world to right itself, for his legs to feel strong enough to carry him back into town. But when he took his first step, and then the next and the next, something inside of him—everything inside of him—shifted.

That little boy had become a part of his heart—a part of his soul—the instant he'd picked up that basket off the front porch.

But it wasn't only Eli that Gil had on his mind. Calliope had been right when she'd said Eli was a gift. It was his arrival that had opened Gil's heart and allowed Leah to slip in. He hadn't been ready for her before Eli. He hadn't been worthy of her. He was a changed man.

And he didn't ever, ever want to go back to who he once was.

Being at the hospital all day should have exhausted him, but as he navigated through the streets of Butterfly Harbor, he found his excitement grow. Not for the debate or the election or his job. But for the life he had now decided he wanted.

He took his time, wandering in and around the streets he'd grown up on. He passed the old Victorian that BethAnn Bottomley had lived in with her husband. He stopped in front of his former high school principal Mrs. Hastings's house, long enough to see her hobble by with her walker and offer him one of her friendly waves.

Fletcher and Paige Bradley's home sat

across the street, with the Monarch stained-glass window over their front door. It was the house Charlie had fallen in love with as soon as they'd arrived in town, and now, Charlie and her parents and her new baby sister, Iris, called it home.

He strolled past Cat's Eye Books and Chrysalis Bakery, spotted Sebastian Evans picking up an afternoon treat for himself and Brooke. Kyle Knight and Jasper O'Neill popped out of On a Wing thrift store with an old set of hubcaps tucked under their arms.

As Gil reached Monarch Lane and the ocean stretched out around him, he caught sight of *Nana's Dream*, one of Monty Bettencourt's boats, bobbing offshore, Duchess flying overhead. With Holly's diner bustling with late afternoon guests and the Flutterby Inn sitting atop the cliff like a beautiful beacon of welcome, the residual doubt and desperation that had been lifelong companions faded.

Alethea honked her horn and waved as she drove past him in her popular food truck, Flutterby Wheels, and across the street, Deputy Matt Knight and Declan Cartwright walked and no doubt talked about Declan's upcoming final racing season before they ducked inside Butterfly Junction, Lori Knight's flower and plant shop. A few doors down, Sienna Bettencourt shook hands with one of the local realtors before hurrying inside the long, deserted storefront and removed the "For Sale" sign in the window. New beginnings, Gil thought.

New life.

These were his people. His friends.

His family.

Gil chuckled to himself and shook his head. Who else other than family would have tolerated the person he'd been while embracing the man he was striving to become? Who else other than family would have given him a home?

His love for Butterfly Harbor was absolute.

And he hoped, maybe one day, its love for him would be the same.

CHAPTER SIXTEEN

"HE'S LATE."

"He'll be here." Amid the din of the crowd filling the high school gym, Leah offered Harvey Mills a strained smile. The older gentleman was a Butterfly Harbor institution even outside his running of the local hardware store. "He might still be at the hospital. Let me try giving him another call."

It wasn't that the crowd was getting restless. If anything, the nearly filled-to-capacity gym was humming with the sound of friends reconnecting and suspicions and predictions taking voice.

Leah left her place at the table near her assigned podium and hurried out, offering a quick wave to the Cocoon Club as she passed. She pressed Gil's number on her phone just as she pushed on the door, only to nearly bash into him as she stepped outside.

"There you are." Leah breathed a sigh of relief. "Is everything okay? Eli?"

"He's fine."

That made what she saw even stranger. "You didn't change."

"My clothes?" Gil said. "No, I didn't. Sorry. I decided to walk here. I had some thinking to do."

"I talked to Paige a little while ago. She said Eli's already thriving. His numbers are nearly perfect."

"Dr. Phillips wants to keep him an extra day or two just to make sure they didn't miss anything. You look nice."

"Oh, thanks." She ran a hand down the collar of her navy blazer. "It's my good luck suit." She hadn't worn this suit since her last closing argument. She felt she needed that confidence now. "You ready for this?"

"I am. Wait." He caught her arm when she started past him. "I'm going to see Christopher tomorrow morning."

"Really?"

"Sheriff Brodie's granting me a favor. I'd like you to come with me."

"As your attorney?"

"And as my friend." His smile was quick. "And maybe something more."

"Okay." The butterflies had arrived to swarm her stomach. "We can talk about this after the debate."

"I'll pick you up at nine," he said before he moved in and tilted her chin up with his finger. He kissed her. A brief press of his lips against hers, so gentle, so perfect, she gasped. "You're going to do great."

"I'm definitely more distracted now that you did that," she teased. "There's a full house in there."

"Good. Then I'll only have to do this once." He slid his hand down her arm and weaved his fingers through hers. "Do you mind?"

"No." She smiled up at him. "I don't mind at all." She reached for the door and pulled it open and led him inside.

The audience grew silent as they entered, before erupting into applause. Harvey Mills, looking more relieved than anything, approached.

"You good now?" Leah asked and held up their linked hands.

"I'm good. Harvey, nice to see you again.

Sorry I've missed our weekly backgammon games lately."

"No apology necessary, Gil. I hear you've got your hands full these days. How's Eli?"

"On the road to a full recovery, thanks." Gil nodded. "If it's all right with the two of you, I'd like to go first with an opening statement?"

"That's fine with me," Leah said. Personally, the sooner they got this over with, the better. She still couldn't shake the feeling something was off with Gil, but she chalked that up to debate nerves. "I'll just head on over to my station."

More scattered applause as first Leah, then Gil took their places behind their podiums. Harvey, as moderator and debate organizer, wore his Sunday best suit along with a slightly crooked blue tie. He tapped on the microphone in front of him before picking it up.

The audio feedback had everyone wincing, then laughing as Harvey attempted to adjust the settings, then he finally moved between the podiums to address the room.

As Harvey gave the rundown on the debate rules, Leah folded her suddenly sweaty hands on top of her notes, glancing over at Gil, who was already looking at her. The smile he gave her melted away the vestiges of doubt and concern. Accepting that she loved Gil seemed as easy now as sliding into the ocean on a hot summer day. Why had she even attempted to fight it?

"Before I ask the first question of our candidates," Harvey said, "each has the opportunity to present an opening statement. Mayor Gil Hamilton, the floor is yours for two minutes."

Gil pulled his gaze from hers and shifted his attention to the applauding crowd. "Thank you, Harvey. And thanks to all of you for turning out this evening," Gil said. "I also want to thank those who reached out to me regarding Elijah's condition. I'm happy to report that he's doing wonderfully, and I should be able to bring him home soon." More applause, so Gil waited for it to die down before continuing. "The past year has been a challenging one," he began. "I've told myself that I've done my best when it comes to being your mayor. I've attempted to repair the damage caused by my father, and while I've made some inroads, I've come to realize there's no repairing the past. The only way to truly move on is with someone else in charge."

Leah's gasp was swallowed up by the one from the audience. "Gil?" She spoke, but he had no way of hearing her. She stepped out from behind her podium, ready to walk toward him, but he held up his hand, stopping her. "Don't do this," she mouthed.

"I'm very proud of most of the work I've done as your mayor," Gil continued, looking at her until the room went quiet again. "But it's time for me to take a step back and do what feels right in this moment. Last year, I almost made the fatal mistake of cutting the emergency services budget. The reasons behind the decision don't matter." His gaze flickered quickly to Leah. "But that error in judgment led me here. I love this town. I think now more than ever. I want this to be a wonderful place for Eli to grow up in. I want him to have the childhood I always wanted. Therefore, I am withdrawing my name as a mayoral candidate and completely and wholeheartedly endorsing Leah Ellis as the next mayor of Butterfly Harbor."

The confusion, applause and astonishment of the audience drew Leah toward him. She ignored his gesture to stay back, and she dodged Harvey's hand as he reached for her arm as she passed. She didn't stop until she reached the place she was meant to be. The place she wanted to be. Standing beside Gil.

"You don't have to do this," she whispered when his arm slid around her waist and he drew her close.

"Yes, I do," he murmured and brushed his lips against her temple. He squeezed her tight and then waved to quiet the crowd. "As Leah pointed out to me recently, Butterfly Harbor can't truly move forward as long as there's a Hamilton in office. So I'm asking you all to do me a favor. Please, when you all vote on Tuesday, vote for Leah. She may be a newcomer," he added with one of his cheeky smiles, which earned him some laughs in the crowd. "But when she puts her heart into something, she makes it count in the best way. She's taken on this town and she's taken on me. She is, quite simply..." Gil paused and looked over at her. "The most amazing woman, the most amazing person, I've ever known."

He flipped the switch to turn off his microphone.

"I didn't want you to do this." Leah turned and gripped his shoulders. "There's no reason—"

"There's every reason. I want a life with Eli in it in some way. I also want to be the father I always wished that I had. And I want a life with you, Leah." He touched her cheek. "I love you, Leah Ellis. Because I know that'll take getting used to, I can wait for however long it takes for you to give me an answer."

She tilted her head, blinked back tears. "I don't need to sleep on it, Gil."

"Take the time," he urged and lifted her hand to his lips for a quick kiss. "I need to get back to the hospital, but I'll call you tonight with the deal I'd like us to propose to Christopher."

"Okay." She was a little perplexed, but the increased noise in the gym prevented her from asking more questions.

Gil released her, stepped away and left the gym.

"If that isn't one of the strangest things to have happened in this town since—" Harvey looked torn between laughter and confusion. "Here I thought people were just making things up, but you and Gil—"

"Yes," Leah confirmed. "Me and Gil. Can I have that, please?" She motioned to the microphone Harvey was still holding. She tapped it hard, making sure the noise broke through everyone's excited conversation. "Could folks please settle down? I have a rebuttal."

"You're not a quitter, too, are you?" Someone in the crowd shouted.

"Is that what you heard?" Leah demanded as her temper surged. "Is that what you all came here to see tonight? Some kind of small-town battle royal that knocked our mayor flat? For the record, that man is not a quitter."

"He quit," another voice shouted. "That's kind of the definition."

Leah had had enough. The Cocoon Club had been bad, but she could understand their long-building resentment of Gil and the Hamiltons in general. However, as for the rest… "We're about to have a boon in Butterfly Harbor. A big financial boon thanks to the butterfly sanctuary. The sanctuary Gil promised to build. Every single person in this room is going to benefit from that boon and you'll have Gil Hamilton to thank for it."

The rolling eyes and dismissive shouts frayed her last nerve.

"Morland Hamilton left this town with nothing," Leah raised her voice and moved closer. "As bad as you all think it was, it was far worse. But Gil didn't want to let any of you down. So he mortgaged his home to get the money for the build. Because he knew how important the project could be for Butterfly Harbor. And as for the emergency services budget, he had to choose between that and keeping the schools open. He made the only choice he could at the time, and when he realized his mistake, he stopped taking a salary to fill the budget hole so the fire department could stay open." She saw her words breaking through and the suspicion and anger fade from people's faces. "You all have been so determined to paint him as his corrupt father, you never stopped to think of what his father's actions did to him. Did any of you ever think about the courage it took for him to stay? He could have left. He could have let this town go completely under, but he didn't. He stayed and he fought and he tried to fix what was broken, not only for this town but for all of you. That's not a quitter. That's a good man."

She made it a point to look each member of the Cocoon Club in the eye. Then she scanned the crowd, found Frankie and Roman, and Abby and Jason Corwin, along with Holly and Luke and Hunter MacBride and dozens of others who had thrived in Butterfly Harbor in large part thanks to Gil.

"You know what really hurts my heart," Leah said, softening her tone. "It's that he doesn't think he's done anything that matters. He believes every single one of you will never see him for who he's been trying to be. Which tells me he doesn't know what this town is really capable of. I've seen this town come together to make big things happen and to help those who needed it. Well, he needs us now."

"We can't vote for him anymore, Leah," Myra said. "He's withdrawn from the race. What could we possibly do for him now?"

There it was, Leah thought in relief. The opening she'd been waiting and hoping for. The offer she knew would come because

Butterfly Harbor always, *always* took care of its own.

"Well, Myra, since you asked, there are, in fact, a few things we can all do to show our appreciation for Gil Hamilton. Let me tell you where I believe we can start."

WHATEVER WEIGHT HAD been lifted off Gil's shoulders with his decision to withdraw from the mayoral race yesterday had since been replaced by the dread of what the next few minutes could bring.

He was back in the interview room at the Durante Sheriff's station, only this time he had a secret weapon with him. He had Leah.

"That's two nights in a row I haven't slept," she grumbled as she reorganized the file folders on the table in front of her. "I haven't been this sleep-deprived since law school."

"I appreciate your sacrifice," Gil told her.

"I can't believe we still aren't talking about what happened at the debate. You told me you loved me, Gil."

"Yes, I did." With his back to her, he was able to grin like a loon. One of the best moments of his life, and he'd pulled it off in front of the entire town.

"And you're not letting me respond."

"Not yet. Not until everything is lined up."

"You do realize that's something I would say," she said sourly. "I'm going to need a tankard of coffee for the drive back. And I want to stop at that waffle house I saw just off the freeway. I didn't eat breakfast before we left. You're buying. And I'm eating. Everything on the menu."

"Not a problem."

"Okay, this agreeable, carefree Gil is starting to weird me out. Could you please have a little more attitude, just for me, so I can stay balanced?"

"I have no doubt my attitude will shift with Christopher's arrival. Speaking of." He stood as he caught sight of Sheriff Brodie escorting Christopher. He quickly took a seat next to Leah.

"Are you sure you want me to be your representative for this meeting?" Leah asked him one more time.

"I'm sure."

"Good." She smiled and rested her hands on top of her files. "That means you leave the talking to me. To me, Gil," she warned in what Gil recognized as her courtroom voice. "Don't make me kick you under the table with these shoes."

"Shoes? More like lethal weapons." How did she even walk in such deadly pointed toes and stiletto heels?

"Don't you forget it." The door opened behind them and Leah rose. "Mr. Russo. Sheriff Brodie. I'm Leah Ellis. Good to meet you." She reached out her hand in greeting. "Thank you for agreeing to see us."

"I'd say it was my pleasure, but that wouldn't be particularly true. Gil." Sheriff Brodie guided Christopher to the seat across from Gil. "I'll stay within earshot in case you need anything." He gave Gil a gentle punch on the shoulder on his way out.

"How's Eli?" Christopher asked before he even sat down. "My lawyer said he had another heart episode."

Gil nodded. "They've fixed his heart. He had surgery early yesterday morning. Our friend Calliope is with him in the hospital today while I'm here. He's not alone," Gil added. "And he's going to be fine."

Some of the tension left Christopher's

face. "Thank you." He sat and visibly relaxed. "Thank you for telling me."

"You're his father," Gil said and glanced at Leah. "Nothing is ever going to change that."

"Shouldn't I have my lawyer here?" Christopher asked.

"Let's get to that in a minute," Leah suggested. "I'd like to have a conversation with you first, Mr. Russo. May I call you Christopher?"

Gil's brother shrugged. "I guess."

"Great. I understand you've requested to make a statement with the court concerning Gil's application to foster your son Elijah."

"He's my son," Christopher said in the same harsh tone as he had the last time Gil had sat here. "I should have a say in where he ends up, and he belongs with me."

Leah sat quietly for a long moment, and Gil almost started to think she'd lost her train of thought. But rather than speaking, she flipped open the top folder and pulled one sheet of paper free. "This is a list of the crimes you're suspected of committing in Arizona, Christopher. As you can see, they're quite extensive. Car theft, burglary, selling stolen items..." She turned the paper over and continued the litany of possible charges. "Each one of these alleged crimes carries substantial prison time."

"Jail. Jail time," Christopher corrected.

"Actually, no. Unfortunately, you already have a criminal record, so that ups the stakes for you as far as sentencing. But let's put that aside for now." She did just that and set the next sheet in front of him. "This is what you are being charged with here in the state of California. Arson and assault are at the top of the list. Even without any convictions in California, altogether, you're possibly looking at more than fifteen years of incarceration. That's if you have adequate representation."

"My lawyer's pretty good."

"I agree." Leah nodded. "But here's my point. Even with the best outcome, you're looking at spending a good portion of time away from Eli. It's the harsh truth." Gil noticed that she spoke with conviction, but also compassion and that her gaze never left Christopher's. "I'm sorry to have to mention it, but Eli's current hospital bill is also a harsh truth."

"Leah—" Gil didn't care how much things cost when it came to Eli's care.

"It should come down, of course, considering Gil has him on his insurance now, but there's no guarantee Eli won't present with other issues later in life. And yes, before you ask, I do have a point. Wanting to prevent Gil from temporarily adopting your son will only hurt one person in the long run, Christopher. It'll hurt Eli. He needs stability. He needs to know he's home. Permanently home, for now. I'm asking you to think about how much your hatred of Gil really matters to you."

Christopher was obviously thinking things over. His Adam's apple worked as his jaw tensed. He scanned the papers Leah had set in front of him. As desperate as Gil was to convince his brother to see what was best, he couldn't keep quiet.

"I love that little boy," he said, fully expecting to feel Leah's shoe making an indentation on his. "It took all of ten minutes for him to claim a place in my heart. I know you love him, too, Christopher. I know that. I see it. I feel it."

"I don't want to go back to prison," Christopher whispered. "I'm going to miss everything with him. Everything."

"Or maybe you won't." Leah brushed her hand over Gil's as she opened another folder and set a different piece of paper in front of Christopher. "I told you what you were facing with an adequate defense attorney. Here's what a stellar one can get you."

Gil's head snapped around. "Leah, what are—"

She shook her head almost imperceptibly. "In theory, a stellar defense attorney could easily argue that the police have nothing other than circumstantial evidence against you in Arizona. Such a lawyer might also be able to arrange for a deal. That if reliable information came their way, leading to the arrest and conviction of the people who planned and carried out those crimes, it would eliminate all charges against you. As far as the charges here, if you were to plead guilty to lesser crimes, agree to a reduced concurrent sentence, along with mandatory counseling and a minimum of three years of probation upon your release, that stellar defense attorney could make it that you're out well before Eli were to graduate from high school."

"But how would that work? He wouldn't even know—"

"You are his father, Christopher," Gil repeated and shifted his legs under him. "I have no intention of ever telling him differently."

"The attorney could also make certain you served your time in a facility within a reasonable driving distance from Butterfly Harbor."

"I could see him?" Christopher blinked as if coming out of a trance. "You'd let me see him?"

Gil nodded. "So that once you're out, you can be a part of his life. That's what you want, right?"

"I just have to let you foster him," Christopher said. "That's all I have to do?"

"No," Leah said. "You also have to make the decision to become the kind of man Eli can be proud of. Change isn't easy, Christopher. But I've recently been shown that, given the right incentive, it's entirely possible. I'd also like you to be aware of the community your son will be growing up in." She set the top file aside and pushed the thicker folder beneath it toward him. "I have more than one hundred testimonials of Butterfly Harbor residents, offering character references for Gil for his application to temporarily adopt Eli."

"You have—what?" Gil reached for the file before Christopher could take it.

"That's only a fraction of the people who will know and love your son, Christopher," Leah said as Gil scanned the letters.

Gil couldn't believe what he was reading. Letters of parental and personal endorsement from Luke and Holly, from Jason and Abby Corwin, fire chiefs Roman and Frankie Salazar. Ozzy and Jo, Declan Cartwright and Alethea, Calliope and Xander Jones, Kendall and Hunter McBride. Sebastian Evans and Brooke followed by Monty and Sienna Bettencourt. Deputy Matt Knight and his wife, Lori, along with Deputy Fletcher Bradley and Paige. "Charlie," Gil whispered. "Charlie Bradley wrote me a letter?"

"And Mandy Evans, Kyle Knight, Jasper O'Neill. There's also BethAnn Bottomley and a few others. The best ones are at the bottom."

Heart pounding, Gil flipped through until he found the one from Myra Abernathe.

"It isn't just Gil who would be adopting Eli," Leah told Christopher. "It's all of Butterfly Harbor. You spent your entire life wanting to belong somewhere, Christopher. For someone to claim you. Please don't rob Eli of that opportunity now."

Gil could barely see through the tears he blinked back. "You did this," he said to Leah. "Didn't you?"

She shrugged. "I might have made the suggestion. Why do you think I was up all night? I had emails coming at me for hours."

"This all hinges on me having that stellar attorney," Christopher said. "Do you have someone in mind?"

"I do, actually." She held out her hand. "Leah Ellis. Pleased to meet you."

"Leah," Gil whispered. "You swore you'd never practice criminal law again."

"I did say that," she said as Christopher shook her hand. "Some things are worth changing your mind about. Do we have an agreement, Christopher?" She asked as she pulled out the completed temporary custody order minus one signature.

"That depends," Christopher eyed her. "Are you going to be part of Eli's life, too?"

"That's a good question," Gil said. "Are you?"

"I hope so," Leah smiled at Gil. "I truly hope so."

"IT'S OFFICIAL." LEAH CLICKED off her cell as Gil returned from the kitchen. They'd settled onto his sofa after stopping by the school gym to cast their votes and picking up Eli at the hospital. It was going to take time to get the baby's sleep patterns back into some order, but his prognosis was excellent, and Dr. Phillips didn't anticipate any further issues. She was still willing to bet it would take a while for Gil to start sleeping through the night, too. "That was the town's head election officer. As of December first, I'm the mayor of Butterfly Harbor."

"I knew it." Gil set a fresh bowl of popcorn on the coffee table. "Let me guess. It was a landslide."

Leah shrugged even as a new flock of butterflies settled in her stomach. "I wouldn't say it was a landslide…"

He smirked, scooped up a handful of popcorn and dropped it into his mouth. "Yeah, it was a landslide. Congratulations."

"I guess."

"You're going to do a great job." He picked up the remote and unmuted the TV. "And hey, if you have any questions, you know where to find me."

"Yes." Inspired, she shifted in her seat, curled her legs under and tucked his hair behind his ear. "I do know where to find you. I've also been thinking about something Ozzy told me the other day."

"Oh?" He muted the TV again, grabbed the bowl.

"He said you were a community- and business-relations specialist before you became mayor. What exactly did that entail?"

"That's code for 'I got people in a room to work out deals of mutual benefit.' Why?" he continued to munch while Leah just watched him. "I can hear the wheels turning in your head. Spit it out."

"I'm considering, as my first official mayoral act, hiring a town manager, someone to take operational things off my plate. Having someone who already knows the ins and outs of this town would be of great benefit and could help get my first term off to a great start." She grinned, leaned over and blew gently into his ear. "Seeing as you're currently unemployed—"

"Not quite yet. I have a few weeks left in my current position."

"How about after that?"

"How about you discuss it with the town council before you go offering me a job officially."

"Maybe I've already got a pretty good idea what they'll say."

He paused with the popcorn halfway to his mouth, faced her, narrowed his gaze. "You're really serious."

"I am. It makes sense. I'm still considered an outsider by some. Despite dropping out, you still got a healthy share of votes, Gil. Plus I'll need help working out all those financial kinks in the town's books."

"Yeah, I'm going to recuse myself from that and recommend you hire an independent auditor."

"See?" She slapped his shoulder gently.

"You're already helping me make better decisions."

He looked at her for a long moment. "I'm going to want a little flexibility with my schedule. Eli's got to come first."

"Agreed." She nodded. "And I have no problem with you working from that office right in there."

"Yeah?" He grinned. "Good thing it's already set up, then. Speaking of this place, Kendall and Jo are coming by tomorrow to discuss ideas for reconfiguring the space. I made the appointment for before four," he added. "You don't want to miss your surprise celebration party at the diner."

"How did you know about that?" Leah asked. "I only heard about it like ten minutes ago."

"I have my sources."

They both looked at the baby monitor when Eli began to cry.

"Kid has a great sense of timing," Gil said with a grin. "You want to go or should I?"

"You go. I'll make room for him on the couch." She scooted over and patted the space between them.

"Deal." Gil shoved himself up and headed

for the staircase. Leah sat there, chewing on her thumbnail as she listened to Gil and Eli chatter back and forth. She hadn't thought her heart could feel so full. But it was full. Of Gil and Eli and the future she hoped they could have together.

Her phone call with the authorities in Arizona regarding Christopher's case had been productive. A detective was coming out next week to take Christopher's statement. In the meantime, she had an appointment with the district attorneys in Durante and Butterfly Harbor to work out a deal for the California charges. It gave everyone what they needed: some closure along with some hope. And maybe, the start of a relationship for the brothers to build on.

But mostly, it meant Eli's temporary adoption should proceed unheeded. And that was the best news of all. It would be nice, starting her new town job with some positive changes behind her.

"Someone's hungry, I think." Gil carried a wide-eyed Eli into the living room.

Eli had on the cutest little sloth-patterned pajamas, which made Leah's hands itch to get her hands on the baby.

"Why don't you take him while I get his bottle," he suggested.

"Like I'm going to say no to that." Gil set Eli into her arms before he disappeared into the kitchen. "You do realize you've given us both enough of a scare to last us a decade at least," she told Eli, who grinned up at her. "No more crises for you, okay? I don't think ol' Gil can take it. Ouch." She scooted Eli over and felt something square and hard tucked in his pajamas. "What on earth is that?" She unsnapped a couple of snaps. "Gil? The doctor didn't say anything about a medical monitor, did he?" She couldn't remember that ever being mentioned, and it was something she would have made a note of. "What is...?"

"Did you say something?" Gil stepped into the room with Eli's bottle, one of those endearingly charming smiles on his face. "What's that?"

Leah stared down at the small square box that Eli attempted to grab. "I think this is mine," she told the baby. "Right?"

"Well, I don't know." Gil returned to the sofa and sat down. He placed the bottle on the table, then plucked the box out of her hand. "It might just be. You remember that conversation we had in the car when I first visited Christopher?"

"Vaguely."

"I still have a question left to ask you." He cracked open the box. "I feel like my life started when you walked into it, Leah. Will you marry me? Will you marry us?"

"That's a pretty gutsy question." Leah swallowed the tears burning her throat. The ring was beautiful. A solitary diamond in an antique setting. Simple. Practical. Perfect. "Considering I haven't even had the chance to tell you that I love you yet."

"Yes, you have. You said it when you walked over to me in the gym at the debate. And you said it again when you offered to defend my brother in court. And you say it every time you look at me or at Eli."

"Heaven help me, I'm marrying a romantic." She laughed and wiped away the tear that escaped to roll down her cheek. "What do you think about that, Eli?"

"Mwwfrraaaaa!"

"Couldn't have said it better myself. Is that a yes, Madam Mayor?"

She nodded. "It is. And for the record,

I do love you." She watched him slip the ring onto her finger before she kissed him. "There is one teeny problem with us getting married."

"What's that?" He looked suddenly uncertain.

"It means Butterfly Harbor will have a Hamilton as a mayor after all. You okay with that?"

"If it's the right Hamilton?" He drew her close. "You bet I am."

EPILOGUE

Three weeks later

"HURRY UP, CHARLIE! They're going to cut the ribbon and you wanted to be first inside."

Charlie Bradley grabbed her fried cinnamon donut off the pickup counter of Flutterby Wheels and took off after Simon. Excitement carried her across the playground and garden area as if she were being tugged along by a balloon. Her feet barely touched the ground.

She'd been waiting for the butterfly sanctuary to open for years and years and…well, ever since she first moved here and heard about it. It seemed she wasn't the only one who was excited. Everywhere she looked familiar faces beamed as the entire town turned up to celebrate.

She bobbed and weaved her way through the crowd. "Sorry, Lori!" She yelled over her shoulder as she bumped into the Knight family. “Leo, come on!” She backtracked long enough to grab the younger boy’s hand. “I’ll watch over him,” she promised Lori and Matt, who waved them off happily. “You okay, Leo?”

“I couldn’t see back there. Thanks.” He blinked big dark eyes up at Charlie. “Where are we going?”

“Up front. Leah said she’d save us all a spot. Stella! Marley! Phoebe!” She was like a siren wailing through the crowd, gathering up her friends as they raced toward the entrance of the sanctuary.

She’d hoped and hoped for perfect weather and she’d gotten it! There wasn’t a cloud in the sky, and even the sun seemed to be shining brighter. The eucalyptus trees surrounding the spot swayed in the gentle breeze and she could see the tiny flitter of monarch butterfly wings dancing in the air. She could smell the hot oil from her donut and the salty sea from the ocean on the other side of the cliffs.

As Phoebe and Stella and Marley joined up with her and Leo, Charlie continued over to where Mandy Evans and her boyfriend, Kyle, stood with Simon right beside the new mayor and the old mayor. Adults are so funny, Charlie thought. Who would ever have guessed Leah and Gil would get married, but they had. And now they were both looking after Elijah and making another family in Butterfly Harbor.

"You almost missed it," Simon nudged her arm when she skidded to a stop in front of him. "You ready?" he asked.

"I've been ready for ages!" She bounced on her toes, scanning the crowd until she found her mom and dad and baby sister. Rising up, she waved and they waved back. "This is the best day ever!"

"It's about to get better." Mandy reached over and plucked the cardboard tray out of her hand.

"Hey!" Charlie frowned.

"Charlie?" Leah called out from where she and Gil stood a few feet away. Gil carried Eli in his arms, and the baby seemed determined to capture one of the butterflies flitting through the air. "Come here, please."

"Me?" Charlie stumbled forward and Simon followed. Her friends all smiled and waved her on as she went over to Leah. "Is something wrong?"

"Not at all. Come stand here, please." Leah pointed to the space in front of her, then she held up her hands to call for quiet.

The crowd—the town—right down to the Cocoon Club, who had been given folding chairs right in the front row, went silent. "I know we've been waiting a long time for this day and it's been a hard road to get here. We all know who we have to thank, and we'll be doing so over the next few days, but special mention to Jo Bertoletti and her crew for getting the build completed within time and under budget."

"Hear, hear," Gil seconded and earned a smattering of laughter.

"Gil once said to me that Butterfly Harbor is a town focused on and for the future. And I'm sure we can all agree this project has had one special cheerleader right from the start. Charlie Bradley, on behalf of the town of Butterfly Harbor, we'd like you to do the ribbon-cutting honors." Lean pulled a pair of scissors out of her suit pocket.

"You mean it?" Charlie could barely squeak out the words as she took hold of the scissors. The ribbon stretched out in front of them, a bright orange one with tiny fabric butterflies attached. "Oh, wow. Where are my…?" She found her parents again instantly, standing amid the most amazing people and friends in the world. "I hope someone's getting a picture of this, because this is the best day of my life!" she shouted as she slipped the scissors around the ribbon and cut.

Cheers erupted as the ribbon broke apart. Charlie felt Leah's hand on her shoulder, guiding her out of the way as Charlie's friends flooded into the sanctuary and education center.

"You did great, Charlie." Leah's smile was so nice.

"Thank you," she whispered to her and Gil. She pressed her hands against her cheeks. "Thank you so much."

"There's one more thing you should see." Leah waved over Charlie's parents and their closest friends—all two dozen of them, Charlie noticed, joined them. "This is our dedication wall," the mayor told the group. "We'll be engraving plaques over the years for display, but we thought this would be the perfect one to start with." She removed the cloth covering the first plaque.

"Oh." Charlie spun at her mother's gasp. "What's wrong?"

"Nothing," her mom whispered as Holly placed a comforting hand on her shoulder.

"Up you go, kiddo." Her dad lifted her so

she could easily read the words on the plaque. She ran her fingers over thc engraving.

"'Charlie Bradley, who exhibits the heart and soul of Butterfly Harbor. Always fly high.'" Charlie looked back at her dad. "Wow. That's... Wow."

"It really is." Her dad kissed her cheek and set her on the ground. Charlie continued to stare up at the plaque above the door of the sanctuary and up into the trees where a cascade of butterflies sped into the sky.

She smiled through the tears and reached up as a solitary butterfly landed on her finger, its wings pulsing against the breeze.

In that moment, Charlie Bradley knew that it wouldn't matter where life took her, who she met or what she did. This was where she would always belong.

Butterfly Harbor was, and always would be...home.

* * * * *

For more charming
Butterfly Harbor Stories from acclaimed
author Anna J. Stewart
and Harlequin Heartwarming,
visit www.Harlequin.com today!

COMING NEXT MONTH FROM

#423 THE COWBOY SEAL'S CHALLENGE

Big Sky Navy Heroes • by Julianna Morris

Navy SEAL Jordan Maxwell returns to Montana ready to take over the family ranch. Proving himself to his grandfather is one thing—proving himself to single mom and ranch manager Paige Bannerman is another story.

#424 HEALING THE RANCHER

The Mountain Monroes • by Melinda Curtis

City girl Kendall Monroe needs to cowboy it up to win a much-needed work contract. Rancher and single dad Finn McAfee is willing to teach her lessons of the land. But will lessons of the heart prevail?

#425 A FAMILY FOR KEEPS

by Janice Sims

Sebastian Contreras and Marley Syminette were inseparable growing up in their small fishing town. The tides of friendship changed to love, but neither could admit their true feelings—until a surprising offer changes everything...

#426 HIS HOMETOWN REDEMPTION

by LeAnne Bristow

Caden Murphy can't start over without making amends for the biggest mistake of his life. But Stacy Tedford doesn't need an apology—she needs help at her family's cabin rentals! Can this temporary handyman find a permanent home?
